ANCIENT GUARDIANS:

The Hawaiian Legend of SHARKTOOTH and HAWKEYE

KANANI HURLEY

outskirtspress

DENVER, COLORADO

Outskirts Press, Inc.
http://www.outskirtspress.com

ISBN: 978-1-4787-5924-9

Library of Congress Control Number: 2015907700

Outskirts Press and the "OP" logo are trademarks belonging to Outskirts Press, Inc.

PRINTED IN THE UNITED STATES OF AMERICA

Synopsis

Her world was about to change, but would she be able to pre-serve her innocence and gentle nature? There, under the cool mist surrounding Mount Wai‘ale‘ale on the island of Kaua‘i, a young Hawaiian girl would be propelled from her serene garden paradise into the dark world of the great manō (shark) and the lofty sky of the majestic pueo (owl). Though she was young, and her voice soft, Kawehi would rise to surpass the expectations of all around her. Her destiny would stand as testament that greatness is founded upon long suffering and conviction, that true power can never be attained by those who ruthlessly abandon their humanity in pursuit of dom-inance--and that sometimes, great legends blossom from small, in-nocent whisperings.

Dear Reader,

Like many cultures, Hawaiians have their proverbs--they're called olelo noeau. There's an olelo noeau that says, "I ka ʻōlelo nō ke ola, I ka ʻōlelo nō ka make." It speaks to the power of our words--there is life and death in what we say. This novel is my way of using my words to breathe life into parts of my memories that I cherish dearly.

First, my heritage. My story is fictional, and like all writers, I added some flourish to certain parts, but the roots of my story remain grounded in my Hawaiian culture. This tale I've woven incorporates many Hawaiian words, practices, and beliefs that are slowly fading. For example, in ancient times, Hawaiians would carve kiʻi, or images, into stones to document major events that occurred. Similarly, I also utilize kiʻi to mark the significant events in this story. As such, at the beginning of every chapter, you will notice different combinations of kiʻi.

Throughout this tale, you will also see repeated reference to two particular ancestral guardians that appear on kiʻi throughout Hawaiʻi: the manō (shark) and the pueo (owl). In Hawaiian culture, these protectors are collectively known as ʻaumākua. They represent the core themes of this story: strength and wisdom. From the beginning to the end of this tale, you will see that I use both the Hawaiian and English terms for these guardians interchangeably.

As you read on, you will also encounter a kahakō, or macron, above the letter "a" in several Hawaiian words. Besides signaling to you, the reader, that the pronunciation of the word incorporates a long vowel sound, the macron also alerts you to the fact that this is the plural form of the word. For example, ‘aumākua is the plural form of ‘aumakua; kāhuna is the plural form of kahuna.

And most importantly, I wanted my words and my story to touch your lives with at least a fraction of the wonder, amazement, and love that my baby brother Kahoku filled eighteen years of my life with--to revive his beautiful spirit, even if only for a little while. Aloha wau iā ‘oe e Kahoku--I love you, Kahoku.

'Aumākua & Ki'i (=image) Interpretation

Image (Ki'i)	English	Hawaiian	Meaning
	Canoe	Wa'a	Journey
	Canoe Paddler	Hoe wa'a	Traveler; tested with quick changes of the ocean, sky and emotional changes of loved ones
	Family	'Ohana	Solidarity
	Lizard	Mo'o	'Aumakua; guardian of a location; very cunning.
	Owl	Pueo	'Aumakua; symbol of knowledge and wisdom
	Shark	Manō	'Aumakua; symbol of power and strength
	Silver Hawk	'Io 'āhinahina	'Io is an 'aumakua; spirit escort, protector;
	Sorcerer Teacher	Kahuna	Many different specialties; some practiced sorcery
	To surf (Surfing)	He'e Nalu	Wave rider
	Turtle	Honu	'Aumakua; symbolizes humility, long suffering and perseverance
	Warrior	Koa	The warrior can be honorable or malevolent
	Whale	Koholā	Symbol of spiritual connection with deceased family

Book 1. The Dawning of a New Day

Chapter 1:

A GREAT LOSS

My brother Kahoku was so handsome--his eyes the color of caramel, and his skin golden from the sun. He was smiling and looking up at me from under the blissful, calm surface of the water. Kahoku was at home in the water, just like the fish he hunted. As he swam up closer to our canoe, towing the line strung up with the many fish he had speared, I could see something peeking out of his pocket. Within seconds, Kahoku broke the surface of the water and swung his catch over and into our canoe. After he had climbed into the canoe, Kahoku reached into his pocket and handed me an oyster.

"Go on, Wehi. Open up the oyster and see what's inside," he said, smiling.

"Wow, Uku, it's a beautiful pearl!" I shouted, as I showed the pearl to my dad, who smiled and looked over at my brother.

"I remember when Wehi was a toddler and she was just starting to talk. Your mother and I tried so hard to coax Wehi into saying "momma" or "dada". You can imagine our surprise when, after weeks of trying to coax your sister, Wehi instead blurted out "Uku". I will never forget the expression on your mother's face when that happened--she was so surprised." Dad started to chuckle as he placed Kahoku's spear gun under the noho (seat) of the canoe. "Well, it is time to return home. Mom is waiting. Let's see what you caught, Kahoku."

"Speared some uhu [parrot fish], tako [octopus], and papio [juvenile trevally]. I wanted to catch something that everyone would enjoy for dinner tonight," replied my brother as he handed both of his fish and the octopus over to my dad.

My dad's eyes opened wide and his smile grew from ear to ear. Kahoku knew that our dad loved papio, and that our mom and I loved uhu and tako. It was going to be a feast! I was so excited thinking about our mom's expression when we brought this catch home, but then, when I looked over at Kahoku, sitting with all of his fish in our canoe, my excitement started to fade. A strange feeling washed over me, almost as if something was telling me to take a mental picture of this moment with my brother because this would be the last time that I would share simple, happy days like this with him.

When we arrived home, Mom had already turned the oven on, and had gotten the frying pan on the stove. "Wehi," she called out.

"Yes," I answered.

"Please go wash up before dinner."

"Okay, Makuahine [Mom]," I replied, as I passed by Kahoku's room, on my way to the bathroom.

Just as I was about to close the bathroom door, I overheard Kahoku on the phone talking to his friend Mason. "Yeah, got some good eats, Brah! You guys want to come over?" I shook my head. There was something about Mason that bothered me. I really enjoyed the company of Kahoku's other friend, Jonathon, who was always very polite and respectful. But Mason, on the other hand, was just the opposite. Take his ugly truck for example. My dad took great pride in his yard and spent countless hours mowing, raking, and watering the grass. He had asked Mason several times to park in the driveway and not on the grass, but Mason continued to park his truck on the grass instead of the driveway. One day, I got so mad at Mason for not listening to my dad that I screamed at him from my bedroom window to park his pilau (stinky, dirty) truck in the drive-way. He scowled at me for a while before moving it off the grass.

"Okay, Mason. No worries. Tell the guys I'll see them tomor-row at school. No leftovers, though. Wehi will make sure of that!" Kahoku then glanced over in my direction and smiled at me. I gig-gled and ran into the shower before he could come over and tickle me. When I had finished showering and had put on my pajamas, I returned to the kitchen and helped my mom set the table.

"Kahoku, what are your plans tomorrow?" asked my dad as he cleaned and prepared the fish.

"I thought I would go surfing with Mason and Jonathon after school. Mason's dad bought him a new surfboard and he wants to break it in," answered Kahoku.

"Well," said Dad with a chuckle, "don't catch all the waves--and the girls."

"Makua kāne [Dad], you know that I am seeing Lindsey. By the way, I let Mason catch most of the waves. Jonathon already told me that Mason is still recovering from Lindsey asking me to the prom instead of him. I don't want to do anything more to bring him down. He's one of my best friends."

The sizzle of the papio on the cast iron skillet and the smell of hot, fresh rice permeated throughout our house. "First of all," said Mom as she waved her spatula in the air and put her left hand on her hip, "Lindsey and you grew up together. It was natural that you became friends and then more. Mason should not hold a grudge against you for that." Kahoku helped Mom "fluff" the rice and then walked over to the sink to mix the poi. As he passed by Mom on his way back to the table, he kissed her cheek and smiled.

"Don't worry, Mom. I got everything handled."

"Typical," I said, as Kahoku sat down next to me.

"Wehi, what do you mean by that comment?" asked my Dad.

"Well, I know my brother," I blurted out. "He never wants you or Mom to fuss over him. He is just like a cute, cuddly golden retriever who goes around and tries to make everyone feel happy, not sad," I said as I looked over at my dad and smiled.

"Nice try, Wehi," said my dad, "but don't think that you are getting any closer to making your mother and I buy you that golden retriever puppy that you saw at the pet store last week." Kahoku grabbed my hand from under the table and smiled over at me. He knew that I really wanted that puppy.

"Don't worry, Wehi," whispered Kahoku, "I will talk to dad about the puppy tomorrow, when I get home from surfing."

"Kahoku, are you going to be playing football this year?" asked my dad, as he started to mix chili pepper water with soy sauce, to pour over his pan fried papio and hot rice.

"I don't think that I have what it takes to play football," responded Kahoku.

"I know that you would excel in football, Son. You just have to put in the time."

"Well, I really think that I don't have the talent for football, Dad. Maybe I should just stick with the sports that I have grown up with-- like soccer and basketball."

"You are too humble, Son. But, I will support your decision," said my dad as he smiled at Kahoku.

I had grown up watching my brother Kahoku excel in a whole variety of sports, like body surfing, soccer, basketball, fishing, and skateboarding. Winning competitions that involved all of the above was easy for him, but he wasn't boastful about his accomplishments. On many occasions, Mom and Dad would have to go and accept his trophies for him, as he would conveniently "disappear" from the award ceremonies. As for myself, well, I liked to brag about my kaikunāne (brother) all the time! In my mind, there was nothing that my big brother Kahoku couldn't do. I was so proud of him.

"Wow, Mālie, you have outdone yourself tonight. Look at all of this 'ono [delicious] food!" said my dad, as he carefully grabbed the bowls of rice and poi from my mom and placed it in front of the salad bowl.

"Thank you, Sweetheart. Well, let's eat before this fish gets cold," responded my mom after she had set the pan fried papio in the middle of the table, right next to the oven baked uhu and tako poke.

As Dad made me a plate, he couldn't stop admiring the oyster that Kahoku gave me, which I had placed next to my glass of water. "By the way, Kahoku," he started, "I wanted to ask you earlier how you found that oyster? Not many of them around here anymore, so I was quite surprised when you brought it into the canoe and gave it to your sister."

"I don't know how that happened, Dad," Kahoku replied. "This is going to sound crazy, but I kept returning to this one particular spot, almost like I was drawn to it. When I went back to it before I returned to the canoe, I saw this huge tako [octopus] going into this deep cave below the reef. Luckily, I was able to spear it and grab one of its arms before it disappeared. It was a pretty big tako! Took me a while to bring its entire body out of the cave, but when I did, I noticed it was tightly holding this oyster. Figured Wehi would get a kick out of opening it up and seeing if it had a pearl inside," said Kahoku as he reached over and tickled me. "What are you going to do with your pearl, Wehi?" he asked.

"Hmmm. I think I will clean up the oyster shell after dinner and put the pearl back inside until I save enough money to take it to the jeweler and have them make a necklace for me." Kahoku smiled and gave me a big hug.

When we were done eating, Kahoku stood up and looked over at me, "let's help Mom clean up," he said.

"Okay, Uku," I answered.

After Kahoku and I had placed all the dishes in the sink and cleaned up the oyster shell, Dad and Kahoku walked over to the woodworking shop in the back-yard while Mom and I finished washing the dishes. After Mom and I had wiped the table, we went into her room to watch a hula competition on television. She was always excited to watch familiar hula dances and loved to dance along. Usually, I would dance along with her, but on this night, I felt that I needed to be near Kahoku. "Mom," I started. "Tomorrow is the first day of school and I have to get all my school supplies together. Would it be all right with you if I went to my room instead of watching the hula competition?"

"Okay, Wehi; but don't stay up too late. Kahoku is taking you to school tomorrow, so be up and ready to go by seven sharp."

"Aloha ahiahi [good night], Mom. I love you," I shouted as I hurried out of her room.

I ran past my room and into the family room, then through the French doors and into the back-yard. Then, I slowly crept up alongside the outside of my dad's wood shop, and sat down on the big, jagged lava rock right next to the shop's tiny window. Neither Kahoku nor my dad could see me, but I could see them and hear everything they were saying.

"How's school going, Kahoku?" asked Dad.

"Well, I am trying harder in math, but I decided not to stay in physics, so I will be taking human anatomy instead," answered Kahoku.

"Well, at least you are being up front and honest with me, Kahoku. Your physics teacher called me earlier. She mentioned that she was disappointed to hear that you were dropping the class. She was surprised because you scored high on the physics pretest."

"I know, Dad, but I want to also continue playing soccer. Physics would take so much of my time. You know me; I love to do so many things. I don't want to be tied up at home studying all the time."

"Kahoku, I just wanted to know how school is going because I care about you and about the choices you make. You have all that it takes to go very far and succeed in life. You can go to any college and get a great education. If you want more of a challenge, you could get your degree, then join the military and train to be a helicopter pilot. I know that you are interested in flying, just like your cousin Ben. Have you gone up with him in his helicopter?"

"Yes, Dad. We are spending more time together. I really enjoy flying."

"Well, Kahoku, I trust that you will make the right decisions. You are graduating this year so I don't have to lecture you anymore. I just wanted to tell you that I love…"

Suddenly, the door to the workshop swung open and there stood my tūtū kāne (grandpa), Pono. "When did you get here, Dad? I didn't hear your car pull up," asked my father.

"Hello Manu; I came to speak to Kahoku, if that is all right with you," responded Grandpa Pono.

"Okay, Dad. Kahoku and I were just finishing up in here. Don't keep him up too long, though--school tomorrow."

"Okay, Manu. Tell my beautiful daughter-in-law, Mālie, that I said aloha [hello], and tell my inquisitive little granddaughter that I will come by again sometime this week to visit with her."

My dad turned and walked out of the shop and into the house, but I could still not bring myself to leave. I wanted to be next to Kahoku, despite how uncomfortable I felt while sitting on the jagged lava rock.

"Kahoku, I wanted to come by and discuss your training. Besides your cousin Ben and the two of us, does your dad or anyone else know?" asked Grandpa Pono.

"No, Grandpa. Dad thinks that I am spending time with Ben because I want to be a helicopter pilot," answered Kahoku.

"Well, if you decide on becoming a helicopter pilot, then I will support you one hundred percent, Kahoku!"

"But Grandpa, I don't think that I would enjoy flying a helicopter after what I have experienced."

"I understand how you feel, Kahoku. But we cannot tell others about our gifts. You were given a great responsibility. Your training will become much more difficult in the year to come. Don't worry. I will be right by your side, I promise you, Kahoku. Now, get some rest and I will see you on Saturday," said Grandpa Pono as he turned to head out the door.

"Okay, Pops," replied Kahoku, as he smiled at Grandpa Pono. My grandfather paused for a while and chuckled, then turned around to face my brother.

"You are the only one who calls me that," said Grandpa Pono, who grabbed Kahoku and gave him a big hug. Then Kahoku walked Grandpa Pono over to the door and gave him a fist bump before Grandpa Pono left.

After Kahoku had finished locking up my dad's woodshop, he quickly glanced over in my direction, almost as if he could sense that I was hiding there, and before I could say anything, he ran up to me and scooped me into his arms. "Come on, Wehi, let's go inside and get ready for bed. How long were you listening to…oh, never mind. Just promise me that you will not tell anyone what you overheard, okay?"

"I won't tell, Uku, I promise." And with that, my big brother carried me into my room, tucked me into bed, and kissed me good night. But I still had that lingering feeling that something bad was going to happen to him. I had a very hard time falling asleep, even with a stomach full of fish and poi. Eventually, my restless mind started winding down and I closed my eyes and dozed off.

"Get up, Little Lady. Breakfast is waiting for you on the table and Kahoku is almost ready to go," said Mom.

"Oh Mom, please…I don't want to go to school today."

"Kawehi, you need to get up right now if you want to eat breakfast before your brother leaves." I knew that my mom was getting a little upset with me because she called me by my full name, so I pushed back the bed covers and looked at her.

"All right Mom, but I didn't really sleep well."

My mom gave me a puzzled look. "Get up and get ready please," she said firmly.

"Okay," I muttered. But when she turned around and started walking outside to water her garden like she did every morning, I grabbed my bed cover, pulled it back over my head, and dozed off for just a second more.

"Hey, Wehi," said Kahoku as he gently peeled down the covers, "we gotta go. Come on, let me help you choose your clothes; then you gotta run and wash your face and brush your teeth. Mom is going to be really mad when she comes back inside and sees that we haven't left for school yet."

All of a sudden, I could feel my heart starting to pound as I jumped out of bed and ran into the bathroom to brush my teeth. The last thing I wanted was for Mom to be upset at Kahoku because I slept in. I ran back to my bedroom, put on the outfit that Kahoku had picked out, then ran into the kitchen and grabbed a piece of toast and my backpack.

"Don't worry about breakfast; I will stop and get you something on the way to school, Wehi," said Kahoku.

"Okay, Uku," I stuttered, as I stood there in the kitchen, chewing on the soggy piece of breakfast toast. I had barely swallowed the piece of toast before I bolted out of the house and hopped into the passenger side of Kahoku's pickup truck.

After stopping to get me a breakfast sandwich, Kahoku drove me to my elementary school. As soon as we pulled into the parking lot, we were greeted by Kahoku's girlfriend, Lindsey. She was always very nice to me, and I enjoyed her company. "Well, Wehi, fourth grade already!" said Lindsey as she leaned into the truck's passenger side window and kissed my cheek.

"Wehi, don't forget your breakfast sandwich," said Kahoku as he tucked the sandwich he had bought me into my backpack. Then he hopped out and came around to the passenger's side of his truck. After he helped me step out of his truck, Kahoku grabbed several napkins from his glove compartment and handed them to me. "Here you go. Make sure that you wipe the crumbs off of your mouth when you finish eating your sandwich. I don't want you to give those pesky boys any reason to pick on you--especially since I will not be picking you up after school today."

"Okay, Uku," I replied.

"Do you want to walk with us to Wehi's classroom, Lindsey?" asked Kahoku.

"Sure. Let's get going before the bell rings. Looks like everyone is already inside and sitting at their desks," replied Lindsey, as she and Kahoku escorted me inside the classroom building and over to my classroom's doorway at the end of the hall.

"Hold on, Lindsey. I just have one more thing to do." Then, out of the blue, my big brother grabbed my hands and twirled me around in the hallway. He always loved to spin me around until I became so dizzy and begged him to stop.

"Let's do it again! Come on, Uku!" I shouted. But then the bell rang.

"We will do this again tonight, after dinner. I promise," said Kahoku, before pulling me in and giving me a big hug. "Behave now. Mom will pick you up after school. I love you, Wehi," said Kahoku as he and Lindsey turned and walked away from my classroom. I waived at them as they got into his truck and drove out of the parking lot. Even though I could no longer see my brother's truck, I continued to stand in front of my classroom's doorway. That same feeling of missing him came over me again, but this time it was stronger than before. I felt like I was paralyzed and couldn't move--I just stood there, like a sentry guarding a castle gate, until my teacher came over to escort me to my desk.

Despite my slow start, the school day went by really quickly, and before I knew it, the final bell rang and my mom had picked me up from school. "Mom, is Kahoku still going surfing with Mason and Jonathon today?" I asked, as I put on my seat belt.

"As far as I know. Is something bothering you, Wehi? You look a little worried."

"I'm okay, Mom. I just miss Kahoku. That's all."

"Well," said my mom as she pulled out of the parking lot, "if we hurry and get all of our errands done, we can stop and pick up a pizza for dinner and surprise Kahoku when he gets home tonight."

Meanwhile, Kahoku had already taken Lindsey home, stopped by the gas station for a supersized drink, and was driving over to Mason's house. As he pulled into Mason's driveway, Kahoku was greeted by a tall, red-headed, freckle-faced young man. "Sure took you long enough to get here, Kahoku," said the young man.

Kahoku smiled at him and shook his head. "Not even, Jonathon. It has only been thirty minutes since the last school bell rang. Where's Mason?"

"In the house, talking with his dad. Been waiting out here for him. You know how it is. I didn't want to be in the middle of that boxing tournament," quipped Jonathon.

Kahoku put his head down and let out a sigh, then looked up at Jonathon. "I hope they are not fighting again."

"Yeah. Mason's dad can be really mean at times. Remember when Mason came to soccer practice with his hand wrapped?"

"Yeah, man, I do. He never told us what happened. But I over-heard the soccer coaches talking about how Mason stopped a fight between his old man and his handicapped grandfather."

Just then, both friends stopped their conversation as Mason came running up to greet them. "Hey guys, sorry for the wait. I was just letting my old man know where we are going to be surfing--you know how he worries."

Both Kahoku and Jonathon looked at each other and shrugged their shoulders, then grabbed their coolers, towels, and boards. They had this routine down to a science, and before Mason could even start his truck, Kahoku had already jumped into the passenger's seat and Jonathon had hopped into the truck bed, where he sat alongside Kahoku's board and Mason's new surfboard.

As the boys pulled up to the beach, in front of the spot where they had all surfed together since elementary school, they noticed that the new boy at school, the one from Maui, had followed them there. This new boy had a habit of showing up wherever Kahoku and his friends went, since he had moved to Kaua'i two weeks ago. To top it off, the boys noticed that he had gone out and bought the same brand of surf shorts that Mason was wearing.

"Man, he is getting on my last nerve," said Mason, as he sat there next to Kahoku and glared at the new boy. "Look at him, Kahoku. He is always following us, and now he's even wearing the same shorts as me! That's it! I am going to let him have it!"

Kahoku turned to Mason and tried to calm him down. "Mason, just let him be." Kahoku then put his hand on Mason's shoulder. "Mason, are you sure you're up to surfing today?"

"I am fine, Kahoku. I just need to clock that twerp, and I will feel even better!" quipped Mason, as he continued to glare at the new kid and crack his knuckles.

A little trickle of blood started to run down from Mason's nose, but he didn't seem to notice it. His pupils were small, like the tip of a ballpoint pen. Kahoku knew this look all too well. "Mason, I think that we should surf another day. Why don't you and Jonathon spend the night at my house? We can come back tomorrow morning."

"Dude, why you always wanna spoil the fun?" responded Mason.

"I am just worried about you," said Kahoku. "The waves are *really* big today and you need to be on your game and alert out there, Mason!"

"Dude, don't tell me what I can or cannot do. Man, you always think that you know what's best. Never fails. You know what? I'll let you handle that new boy then. I'm going to surf!" exclaimed Mason, as he stared at Kahoku while the blood from his nose trickled down his mouth and dripped onto his arm.

"Mason, I got nothing but love for you. But you've got me worried--I have seen you like this before. You said you were done with the drugs, Mason."

Mason turned away from Kahoku, jumped out of the truck, and started running toward the water. Kahoku hopped out of the passenger's seat and stood on the sand watching Mason race toward the shoreline. Before diving in, Mason looked back at Kahoku and shouted, "You wanna stay by the truck while I get all the waves? Go right ahead, Kahoku. Fine by me!"

Before Kahoku could say anything else, Mason had already dove into the ocean. "Something doesn't seem right with him, Kahoku. Did you see that glazed look in his eyes? Is he doing drugs again?" asked Jonathon, who had jumped out of the truck bed and was standing next to Kahoku on the sand.

"Pretty sure. Told him that we can surf later, but you know he's not listening. We just gotta watch him so he doesn't get hurt," said Kahoku, who was visibly worried.

"Kahoku, it's big out there. Mason will get hurt if he's not thinking straight…"

But before Jonathon could even finish his sentence, Kahoku had already ran clear across the beach toward the shoreline and was diving into the water. Jonathon panicked as he chased after Kahoku. Half of Mason's new board had washed up onto the shore. Jonathon grabbed the board and then looked out into the angry ocean to see where his friends were, but it was difficult to see either of them amidst the enormous swells. All Jonathon could do was hope that both of his friends were all right.

Meanwhile, Kahoku struggled to stay afloat amidst the brutal and unforgiving waves. He had never swum in such conditions, but he was determined to find Mason and bring him back to shore. The water around him was very murky because of the constant pounding of the waves, but that didn't discourage him. Just as Kahoku was about to swim further out past the first buoy, he caught a glimpse of Mason's bright-yellow surf shorts. As Kahoku swam closer to Mason, he could see Mason's unconscious body swaying back and forth in perfect timing with the surge of the water. *You should have listened to me and just stayed on the beach, Aikane [friend]*, thought Kahoku, as he grabbed Mason and started towing Mason toward the shoreline. *All I have to do now is get Mason to shore. I can do this. We will be all right. Sure, there will be questions to answer, especially from Dad, but this time will be different. I won't make excuses for Mason's behavior. This time I am going to tell Dad that Mason needs help. I am no longer going to keep Mason's drug problem a secret*, thought Kahoku.

As Kahoku continued swimming toward the beach, he caught sight of the other half of Mason's board. Kahoku grabbed the board, placed Mason on top, and then started pulling the board to shore. The waves were unrelenting, but Kahoku was making progress--he could see Jonathon pacing up and down the beach.

"Almost there! Hold on, Mason! You're going to be all right!" shouted Kahoku, as he looked over at Mason's unconscious body.

Suddenly, Kahoku felt something tug on his leg. He tried to

shake it off, but whatever it was, it would not let go. Mustering up all the strength he had left, Kahoku pushed the board toward shore and hoped that the oncoming wave would take Mason back to the beach. Kahoku could feel his body being pulled farther and farther out to sea. He was too far from shore, and too weak from resisting the force that was pulling him under the water. There was no going back now. Unable to surface for air, Kahoku knew it was just a matter of time before his lungs could no longer provide him with the oxygen he needed. Memories of holding his little sister Wehi for the very first time eased his anxiety. *I am going to miss you, Wehi,* he thought, as his mind wandered off on memories of his little sister's smile and her silly laugh. Then, everything just faded away.

Back on the beach, Jonathon carefully pulled Mason off his board and placed him on his beach towel. A tourist had called 9-1-1, and the paramedics had just stepped onto the beach. Seeing that help had arrived, Jonathon ran up to Mason's truck and grabbed Kahoku's board. He then returned to the shore and started walking out into the water. "Kahoku! Kahoku!" he screamed, hoping that Kahoku would surface. Not wasting any more time, Jonathon jumped onto the board and had just started to paddle out when he felt someone grab the board from behind him.

"Water's too rough, Young Man," said a police officer who had just arrived. "Let the lifeguards go out and find your friend."

"You don't understand. Kahoku saved Mason's life and now he needs help. I can't just stay here when he is out there! He's my best friend, Officer! He's my best friend!"

On the opposite side of town, Wehi and her mom, Mālie, had just gotten all their errands done. They were just about to run inside the pizzeria and pick up a pizza for Kahoku when a police officer, who worked with Wehi's dad, Manu, pulled up alongside their car in the parking lot.

"Hello, Kawehi. Hello, Mālie."

"Hello, Officer Ron. Mom and I were just about to pick up a pizza for my brother, Kahoku. Did you come to pick up a pizza too?"

"Sorry Wehi, I did not come to pick up a pizza--not today."

"Hello, Ron. Is there anything wrong? Am I parked in a no parking zone?" asked my mom.

"No, Mālie. Uh, can you and Wehi follow me over to the hospital?"

"Ron, did something bad happen to Manu?" asked my mom, but Officer Ron did not answer. "Ron, can you just answer the question? Please Ron, can you look at me instead of looking down at your feet and tell me if Manu is hurt?" implored my mom. But Officer Ron did not look up at my mom--he just continued to stare down at his feet.

After a few moments had passed, Officer Ron asked again, "Mālie, can you follow me to the hospital?"

My mom looked over at me, started the car, and then followed Officer Ron to the hospital. Neither of us knew what to say. All we could do was keep pace with Officer Ron's police car as it continued to flash its lights and pass other vehicles on the road.

When Mom and I arrived at the emergency room we were met by my grandpa Pono, who was the attending physician that day. "Pono, is Manu okay? What happened?" asked my mom.

"Grandpa Pono, is my dad hurt?" I asked.

"Mālie, Wehi, you both need to be strong, very strong. Follow me," answered my grandfather.

"Grandpa Pono, is my daddy okay?" I asked again, as I grabbed hold of my grandfather's hand and walked with him down the long, sterile corridor, past the nurses station, to a room in the back, far away from all the other rooms.

"Manu," announced Grandpa Pono, "Mālie and Wehi are here." But my father did not look at us right away. He was standing next to a hospital bed and looking down at an envelope that he held in his hands.

"This is the only piece of my son that will leave this cold room with me today," whispered my dad as he placed a lock of my brother's hair into the envelope then looked over at us. My father's eyes were red and swollen from the many tears that he had cried. My mother furrowed her eyebrows and peered over at my father.

"Manu, why did you say what you did? What is going on? What happened to my son? My baby--he's still with us, isn't he Manu?" asked my mom as she grabbed my hand. My dad slowly shook his head from side to side. My mom started to collapse onto the floor, but my grandfather quickly caught her. As my Grandpa Pono cradled my mom in his arms, my mom let out a cry to the heavens above, a cry that will forever remain etched in my mind. "My son, my son. NO GOD, not my baby! Not Kahoku!" wailed my mother as she stood up and ran to the other side of my brother's hospital bed. All the nurses that were in the room attending to my brother stopped for a brief moment to wipe the tears that fell from their eyes.

My dad gently reached over, hugged my brother and kissed his forehead. "I love you very much, Son," he said, tenderly. Then, in a voice that I had never heard before, my father cried out, "Father-in-Heaven, if there is a chance that my son's body can be healed, and if his soul still lingers here with us, please grant us more time with him. If Heaven is in need of another soul, please take my life and spare my son. Please do not let my son die before me! Please take me instead!" My father continued to sob as he lifted my brother up to his chest and held him close to his heart.

As I listened to my parents and looked over at my brother, I could feel my heart break and my body grow weak--as if my life too, had ended at that moment. The thought that my brother had passed away was too much for my heart to handle. I couldn't accept the fact that my brother would never wake up, or that my brother would never smile at me again. *No! This is not happening--it is all a bad dream,* I thought, as my mind refused to believe that my brother Kahoku was dead. The room starting spinning around me, but I refused to sit down. All I wanted to do was run away from this dreadful reality. But there was no place that I could run away to. Every part of me became frozen and still. Though I was aware of the immense suffering that my mom, dad, and my grandfather were experiencing, I had somehow become disconnected and affectless. I just stood in the doorway as my family fell to pieces before my eyes.

After holding my brother close to him for several minutes, my dad gently placed Kahoku back on the hospital bed's pillow and turned around to check on me. "Wehi, come stand next to me. Come let Kahoku hear your voice one more time. Come tell your big brother that you will always love him and that you will always keep the memory of him alive in your pu'uwai [heart]." But despite my dad's plea, I remained still. I wanted to go over and stand next to my father, but my legs would not move.

"Manu," pleaded my mom, "let her be. This is too much for her to process. Maybe we should say goodbye to our son and…" My mom started to fall apart again. "I don't know what I am saying. How can I say goodbye to my son? Manu, help me, please! I don't know what I should do!" cried my mom.

"I can't help anyone, Mālie," sobbed my father. "I don't even know how to help myself right now. I don't have the strength to do or say anything that will help anyone. I feel paralyzed, Mālie. I feel paralyzed!" cried my dad as he collapsed into the chair next to the side of Kahoku's bed and buried his face in his hands.

My parents' escalating anguish soon melted away my frozen state of being and nudged me into action. I knew that I needed to comfort and help them through this, even though I was struggling to come to terms with my brother's passing. Although I was scared of seeing my big brother so helpless and still, I mustered up what little strength I had and slowly walked over to his bed. My dad grabbed my hand and kissed it, while my mom walked around Kahoku's bed, sat down next to me, and put her head onto my shoulder. As I stood between both of my parents, I could no longer avoid the inevitable and looked down at my handsome brother. I struggled to hold back the tears when I saw the water dripping down from Kahoku's nose and ears. Though I wanted to break down and cry, I did not want to cause my parents more pain. But my resolve to be strong for the both of them was slowly unraveling. Once again, I completely withdrew myself from everything happening around me. My dad looked over at me and started to whisper something to me, but I could not hear him. All I could hear was the sound of my heart breaking as I placed my hand over my big brother's heart and looked at his handsome face.

The light in Kahoku's beautiful caramel-colored eyes was gone, and I could no longer deny the obvious--my brother was dead! My big brother Kahoku was gone, and in his absence, my mind could not stop replaying the last moments that Kahoku and I shared together.

Soon after the memories began, dark voices within my grieving soul started screaming at me, reminding me of the many opportunities that I had to warn Kahoku. *I should have told him that something bad was going to happen!*

Finally, when my parents stood up and kissed my brother goodbye, I broke down. I turned around and faced my distraught grandfather, who had taken a seat next to the doorway of Kahoku's hospital room. "Grandpa Pono, isn't there something that you could do to bring Kahoku back to us? Please, Grandpa Pono, please!"

"I am sorry, Wehi, but there is nothing that I can do to bring Kahoku back," responded my grandfather, as he got up from his seat and rushed over to my side. The journey now ahead of my family was one that would not include my brother, and I did not know how we could go on without him.

The weeks leading to Kahoku's farewell seemed to flow into one miserable blur. Storm after storm battered my little green island, but I didn't care. I had been living without the sun since Kahoku passed away. I kept myself busy by looking through all the gifts and pictures that Kahoku had given me. When I had gathered up all my memorabilia of him, I decided to put them into Kahoku's room next to all of his trophies. Somehow, being in his room and looking at all of his pictures gave me a little sense of peace.

My parents, however, could find no solace. My dad just sat in his rocking chair and looked out toward the mountains for hours on end, and my mom never left her bedroom. Grandpa Pono took some time off from the hospital to help my mom and dad make all the funeral arrangements. Although he tried really hard to be strong for all of us, I knew that Grandpa Pono missed Kahoku very much. On more than one occasion, I heard Grandpa Pono sobbing as he sat outside on the porch, next to the fragrant puakenikeni tree that he and Kahoku had planted several years ago.

The night before Kahoku's funeral, I found myself remembering how much fun Kahoku and I had whenever our family went camping by the beach or pig hunting in the mountains. As the memories continued to play out in my mind, I started to lament over my new reality, so I picked up one of my brother's pictures and stared at his handsome face. *How can I go camping without you, Uku? How can I enjoy Thanksgiving and Christmas without you, Uku? How can I enjoy anything without you, Uku?* I held Kahoku's picture close to my heart as I slowly knelt down next to his bed and pressed my face against the soft Hawaiian quilt so that my parents wouldn't hear me cry.

The next day brought a sense of unwelcome finality to my family. This was the day that we would bury my brother. After my

Grandfather Pono had given Kahoku's eulogy, all of the people who had come to mourn my brother made their way up to his casket to say goodbye. When it was my turn to go up and kiss Kahoku goodbye, my knees buckled and I fell to the ground. My dad quickly walked over to me, picked me up, and then carried me over to Kahoku's casket. I slowly wiggled my way out of my dad's arms and stood beside the blue stainless steel box that held what was most precious to me. A big part of me wanted to turn around and run out of the room, but at the same time, I could not bring myself to leave my brother's side. This was the last time I would see him. I knew that once the casket was closed and sealed, I would never see Kahoku's handsome face again, except in my memories.

After the burial, everyone gathered at Wailua River State Park. My mom and I got into our wa'a (canoe), then my dad and Grandpa Pono paddled us out into the bay, where we were encircled by my brother's friends, who were on their surfboards. After all of the surfers had joined hands, my cousin Ben dropped thousands of red and white rose petals from his helicopter above. After the last rose petal fell onto the water, I lifted my heavy, puffy eyes and looked over at all the people who had come to share this moment with us. That is when I noticed a grey-haired, muscular Hawaiian man paddling his surfboard right next to our canoe. He was my mom's father, my Grandpa Ke Ali'i, whom I had not seen since I was two years old. He had come to give the pule (prayer) for my brother, Kahoku.

Chapter 2

GRANDPA KE ALI'I'S BEDTIME STORIES

When we arrived home after Kahoku's services, we were greet-ed by several of our family members and close friends, who had already brought over food and cleaned up our hale (house). After my parents, both my grandfathers, and I had thanked each one of them, they all left quietly.

"Let's go sit in the family room and have a little to eat. Okay Wehi?" suggested my grandfather Pono. But I didn't answer him. I just missed Kahoku so much that I didn't even feel hungry. In fact, maybe I just didn't care if I was hungry. All I really wanted was to be left alone, so I walked into Kahoku's room, and left the door slightly ajar just in case my parents called out for me. I felt a little mad at myself for ignoring my grandpa Pono, but at the same time, I just didn't have the strength to do much of anything.

"Wehi, can I get you something to eat?" asked Grandpa Pono, who along with Grandpa Ke Ali'i, stood in the hallway next to Kahoku's bedroom.

"No thank you, Grandpa Pono," I muttered, as I climbed onto Kahoku's bed.

"Our little Granddaughter has barely eaten since that day that our Grandson passed away," said Grandpa Pono.

"She just needs some space so she can process what has happened. It will take some time, but she'll be all right," said Grandpa Ke Ali'i.

"I wish that I could take away Wehi's pain. She has been a big part of my life, Ke Ali'i, ever since she was born," replied Grandpa Pono as he stood next to Kahoku's bedroom door and slowly pushed it back a little further so that he could see me.

"I know, Pono. You have been very lucky to visit with our grandchildren so often," said Grandpa Ke Ali'i.

"You could have had the same opportunity if you didn't travel so often, Ke Ali'i," quipped Grandpa Pono.

"There are a few of us, Pono, that do not have a choice, but let's not talk about that right now," responded Grandpa Ke Ali'i, who slowly made his way into Kahoku's room. "Can I come in, Wehi?" he asked, but I didn't answer. I just wanted to be alone. "I just want to make sure that you are okay; then I will leave you alone," he continued, as he walked over to me, then lowered himself into a chair next to the bed and placed his large hand over my two little hands. "I know that I haven't come to see you for a very long time, Kawehi, and I want to apologize for not visiting with you and Kahoku more often," said Grandpa Ke Ali'i as he gently wiped away my tears that were slowly making their way onto Kahoku's pillow. "I am here now to cry with you, to hold you when your thoughts bring you back to that horrible day when you lost your brother, and to help you through this unbearable time. I know that you have not seen me for eight years, but I have thought about you and your brother every day, my little granddaughter."

Grandpa Ke Ali'i started to look around Kahoku's room--over every trophy, every ribbon, every drawing and every picture. One picture, in particular, caught his attention. As he stood up and approached the picture on the wall, his eyes grew very wide. He quickly took the picture down, then turned around and saw me staring at him.

"Don't worry, Wehi. I don't mean any disrespect for your brother's keepsakes. You are very protective over him, aren't you?" Grandpa Ke Aliʻi was now sitting right beside me again, but I kept my eyes focused only on the picture he now held in his big hands. "You don't have to answer my question, Wehi. I can see it in your eyes. Indeed, you are your brother's guardian, Little One."

Grandpa Ke Aliʻi then placed the picture in his jacket pocket. "I know that you are tired, and I know that you are fighting your body's need to sleep. You probably relive the moment you lost Kahoku over and over again when you close your eyes, don't you?" Tears started to fall again as Grandpa Ke Aliʻi reached over and cradled me in his arms. "Let me try to help you calm your mind so that you can sleep, Kawehi. I will tell you a bedtime story that my grandfather told me. It is a family bedtime story--one that has been passed down for many generations. This story is called The Legend of Sharktooth and Hawkeye.

"Long ago, when our first ancestors started voyaging over the ocean, using the stars as their guide to find new lands to build new homes for their families, the kūpuna asked the keepers of things sacred, or the kāhuna, to give the Hawaiian people guardians that would protect them throughout their journey and guide them so that they might flourish in their new home. The kāhuna fasted and prayed for many days, and for their fortitude, they were granted three powerful, dominant ʻaumākua [ancestral guardians]. The first was the pueo [owl], who would guide the Hawaiian people throughout their journey and help keep the knowledge of their ancestors safe. The second was the manō [shark], who would protect the Hawaiian people as they traveled over the vast ocean. Finally, the third ʻaumakua, the ʻio ʻāhinahina [silver hawk] would serve as a symbol of hope and encouragement, during times of hardship and discord. Over time, our ancestors began to thrive in their new home and had no need for their ʻaumākua, so these guardians went back to their origin: the owl into the deepest cave in the highest forest, the shark into the deepest ocean trench surrounding the islands, and the hawk into the heavens, far beyond our reach."

"Will they ever come back to us, Grandpa Ke Aliʻi?" I asked. I started to sit up a bit, even smiled a little when he nodded yes. Being with him and hearing his story made me feel a little better, as it had taken my mind off of Kahoku's passing for just a little while. My mom brought in slices of fresh coconut and to her surprise I grabbed a slice and quickly ate it as I waited for Grandpa Ke Aliʻi to continue with his story.

"Thanks, Dad. I am glad to see Wehi eating something," said my mom, as she left Kahoku's room.

Grandpa Pono then walked into Kahoku's room. "Don't mind me. I just want to listen in on Grandpa Ke Aliʻi's bedtime story. Maybe it will help me sleep too."

"You can listen too, Grandpa Pono. I like this story," I said as I ate another slice of coconut. "Do you want a slice of coconut?"

Grandpa Pono smiled at me, gently grabbed a slice of coconut from my hand, then walked over and took a seat by the foot of Kahoku's bed, and both of us continued to listen to Grandpa Ke Aliʻi's story.

"As the years passed, our ancestors continued to flourish on this isolated group of islands in the Pacific Ocean. Our people enjoyed the lush green forest and bountiful ocean waters. We were safe in this home we had made. But when our islands were visited by big ships from many different lands, our way of life changed forever. During this uncertain time, it was rumored that two brothers, who were both warriors, went in search of the ʻaumākua once again. One swam down the deepest ocean trench to find the manō, and the other searched the deepest cave in the highest forest for the pueo. But, alas, there was no means to travel far into the heavens to search for the ʻio ʻāhinahina.

"The brother who swam into the deepest trench found the most brilliant shark tooth lying on the sandy bottom of the trench. Instinctively, he grabbed the tooth and swam to shore. The brother who had searched the highest mountain cave found an ʻaʻā [sharp jagged stone] that resembled a pueo [owl]. Amazed at the stone's resemblance to an owl, the young warrior placed it carefully in his kapa [cloth] and went to find his brother.

"After showing one another what they had discovered, the two brothers traveled to the hale [house] of the oldest, most powerful kahuna. The kahuna bestowed on each brother the gifts of the ʻaumakua each had found, and promised to give the gift of the ʻaumākua to other warriors who were deserving. But they all needed to promise to follow three important rules. First, they must keep their gifts a secret from all outsiders--only those who had an understanding of these gifts may know. Second, they must never use their gifts to hurt innocent people. Instead, they must use their gifts to protect people from harm. Third, they must be able to control the animal instinct of these guardians--they must be able to keep possession of their humanity at all times. If any of these rules were broken, these gifts would not be passed on through that family line, which meant that when the individual passed away, his keiki [children] and moʻopuna [grandchildren] would not be granted the right to possess such gifts."

"Grandpa Ke Aliʻi, do you believe in the ʻaumākua?" I asked. I was starting to have a hard time focusing on Grandpa Ke Aliʻi's face, so I rubbed my dry eyes and propped myself up on my pillows. I really wanted to listen to Grandpa Ke Aliʻi's bedtime story, but my heavy eyelids had plans of their own. Despite my best efforts to stay awake, I just couldn't keep my eyelids from closing. As I drifted off to sleep, my Grandpa Ke Aliʻi's deep voice slowly faded away.

Chapter 3.

FAMILY SECRETS,
FAMILY NIGHTMARES

"Pono, we need to talk in private, away from our family. This cannot wait," said Ke Aliʻi urgently.

"All right. Let us go into Manu's shop outside," responded Pono.

"No. What I need to share with you must be kept between us for now. We must be careful. Meet me at Kaimana beach at the foot of Mount Leahi [Diamond Head] around midnight tomorrow," said Ke Aliʻi firmly.

"Why can't we find somewhere here on Kauaʻi to talk?" asked a puzzled Pono.

"I have to show you something that I have not shared with any family members, including my daughter Mālie," answered Ke Aliʻi.

"All right, Ke Aliʻi. Midnight tomorrow. Let us now go and console Manu and Mālie. I don't know how to ease their pain, Ke Aliʻi. I cannot bring our grandson back, and I fear that his death will shatter this family." Pono and Ke Aliʻi then walked into the family room and sat next to Manu and Mālie, who were remembering times they shared with their son Kahoku.

Shortly after Pono and Ke Aliʻi sat down, the doorbell rang.

It was Manu's hānai (adopted) brother Martin, who had just come back from National Guard training. "Manu, is there anything that I can do for you or your family? I am so sorry that I wasn't here for you, Brother."

"Mālie and I are taking it day by day. I am especially concerned for Wehi. You know how close she was to her brother." Suddenly Manu remembered the pearl that Kahoku had given to Wehi. "Hey Marty, can you wait here just a few more minutes?" Manu ran and got the pearl from Wehi's bedroom, then returned to the front door where Martin was waiting. "Marty, do you think you could take this pearl to the jeweler and ask him to put it on a chain for Wehi?"

"Anything for you and your family, Manu. Let me know if I can do anything more." Martin gave Manu a big hug, then quietly left, and Manu returned to Mālie's side.

"He was truly a wonderful grandson and brother," said Pono. "We all had high hopes for him, for his future. I also have fond memories of when he was just starting to walk. That was around the time that I let him sit on my shoulders. He never wanted me to carry him in my arms again--he only wanted to sit on my shoulders."

Manu looked over at Pono. "Yes, he always loved to be high above the ground. He had no fear of heights whatsoever," said Manu tearfully.

"I remember how he wanted to dive right into the waves, at only two years old. He loved the water," said Ke Aliʻi.

"Sounds like my son," said Mālie. "He loved the water and loved to fish!"

"He loved flying with Ben," said Manu. "I think that he would have decided on becoming a pilot. Even though I am afraid of heights, I would have loved to fly with him. My son, my son. How proud I am to have had you in my life. I will miss your smile, your jokes, your love for life, your strength. MY SON! How could you leave us? How could you die before your father? I am supposed to leave this earth before you! I LOVE YOU, Kahoku, I LOVE YOU!" Manu was now sobbing uncontrollably as he collapsed into Mālie's arms.

Neither Ke Ali'i nor Pono could come up with any words that would comfort either Manu or Mālie--no one could. The only person who could make their pain go away was now far away from all of them. Far, far away--where no one could see, touch, or speak with him. Exhausted from crying, Manu and Mālie fell asleep cradling one another. It was mid-morning the next day when both Ke Ali'i and Pono left the house. Everyone else was still sleeping.

"I will be going now, Pono. I will meet you at midnight."

"All right, Ke Ali'i. I am just going to check in with the hospital and then I will make my way there."

Pono arrived at Mount Leahi first and as he waited for Ke Ali'i to arrive, he started to wonder what it was that Ke Ali'i needed to show him that was so important and why it could not wait until a later time. But, just as Pono started to run scenarios through his mind, he caught a glimpse of Ke Ali'i coming in from the waves. As Ke Ali'i finally made it up to the beach; his entire body was covered in shimmering beads of water, each catching the moonlight and making him appear almost ethereal.

"Hello, Pono," said Ke Ali'i. "I hope that your journey here was an easy one."

"Yes. Not much turbulence. What of your journey? How strong were the currents?" asked Pono.

"Nothing that I could not handle, Pono. Please follow me. There is only one hidden entrance, and it is through a lava tube under the water. I know you would prefer an entrance that does not entail getting wet and holding your breath," stated Ke Ali'i.

"Thank you, Ke Ali'i, for your thoughtfulness, but I have been known to swim from time to time." Pono hated the thought of swimming through a lava tube, but he would never admit that to Ke Ali'i.

"You are going to have to hold on to me. I will travel through the water as quickly as I can. The tunnel will be tight and you will not be able to breathe for at least four minutes," warned Ke Ali'i.

Pono rolled his eyes and shrugged his broad shoulders. He hated being underwater for long periods of time, but he had no other option.

"I hope that my skin and my formidable appearance will not discourage you," said Ke Ali'i.

"I will be fine," replied Pono. "Let's get this over with so that I may return to Kaua'i and to Wehi."

Pono let Ke Ali'i swim out first so that he could chase all other manō away from the area. When Ke Ali'i had swum out far enough, Pono started swimming toward him. Pono began to feel very uncomfortable in the cold ocean water, especially when he could no longer feel the reef under his feet.

A big grey figure then swam up right alongside him. Though he was too proud to admit it, Pono was extremely shaken by the enormous size and strength of Ke Ali'i, now in his 'aumakua form. Pono, however, was comforted in knowing that there were no other manō as big as Ke Ali'i in the ocean that night; otherwise Ke Ali'i would not have been able to swim up to Pono so quickly. Pono placed his two hands over Ke Ali'i's dorsal fin, and the two then descended into a cave that was situated under the reef. Most people would think that the cave was indeed shallow at first glance, but the sandy bottom gave way easily, exposing the opening of a deep and dark lava tube. As soon as Ke Ali'i arrived at the bottom, the lava tube leveled off, but the visibility was very poor. All Pono could do was keep his eyes closed and hold on to Ke Ali'i's huge dorsal fin. Pono could feel his heart beating faster and harder as four minutes of holding his breath had begun taking a toll on his body. Yet, despite how uncomfortable he felt, he knew that he needed to trust in Ke Aliʻi's ability to get him to their destination before he became unconscious.

Several minutes had passed since Ke Aliʻi and Pono had started their journey under the water. Pono could feel his lungs burn for oxygen as he struggled to remain calm, but just as he was about to pass out, Ke Aliʻi started ascending. Although Ke Aliʻi knew that Pono needed oxygen quickly, he also knew that he could not ascend too quickly, otherwise he could seriously compromise Pono's health. When they finally reached the surface, Pono was so grateful that he was able to swim with his head above the water and that there was an ample supply of oxygen flowing through the tube, that he didn't even notice how restricted and tiny the lava tube had become.

As Pono gave his body the time it needed to acclimate, Ke Aliʻi changed back into his human form and pulled himself up onto the jagged lava rocks that formed the floor of the lava tube.

"Whew!" gasped Pono, still catching his breath. "I thought I would never see your ugly mug again."

Ke Aliʻi smiled, then pulled Pono up. Both men now had to leave the water and walk sideways, through a very tight corridor of sharp lava rock. Then, for the final two-hundred feet of their journey, both Ke Aliʻi and Pono had to get down onto their hands and knees in order to proceed through the warm, humid lava tube. When they had reached the end of the lava tube, they could finally stand up and walk comfortably.

"What a relief," muttered Pono. "It is cooler now, and I can finally breathe a little easier."

"Most people could not hold their breath as long as you did, Pono; neither could they travel this far over the sharp lava rocks then tolerate the heat and stuffiness of the lava tube we came through," said Ke Aliʻi. "We are almost there."

As Pono and Ke Aliʻi came to the end of the lava tube, a small, four foot steel door became visible. "Are there menehunes [small, enchanted Hawaiian people] that live here?" chuckled Pono.

Ke Ali'i started laughing a little. "I am sure that if the menehunes did live here, they would've built a more decent doorway than this."

Both men chuckled for a little while before Ke Ali'i entered the code that unlocked the door.

Pono's mouth dropped when they entered the underground room. There were cameras and other surveillance devices everywhere, but what fascinated him more was the number of ki'i pōhaku (petroglyphs) that were all over the cave.

"There is another way in through the top of Mount Leahi crater, but you would need government clearance to use that entrance. There are other lava tubes that descend into the ocean from this point and join O'ahu to the other islands. But, there is no rest stop along the way to catch your breath. It's just a clear shot to Kaua'i, Moloka'i, Lāna'i, Maui, and the Big Island," said Ke Ali'i.

"Something tells me that you are going to stretch the limits of my understanding of what it is that you are involved in, Ke Ali'i."

"Pono, I wish I was the only one involved, but after I caught a glimpse of something troubling in Kahoku's room last night, I now realize that it involves our entire family."

"What are you talking about, Ke Ali'i?" asked a confused Pono.

"Let me show you something first, before I tell you what I know," answered Ke Ali'i.

Both Pono and Ke Ali'i walked further into the huge underground cave which had been totally reinforced on the inside with steel beams and concrete foundations. At the far end of the cave was a rocky area leading to a medium-sized salt water pool. "If I am coming back from the other islands using one of the lava tubes under the ocean, then I enter the cave through this pool," said Ke Ali'i, as he placed his hands in the water and washed off some of the debris that had settled in between his fingers while he was crawling through the lava tube.

"How long has this been here, Ke Ali'i?" asked Pono, who was still in awe of his surroundings.

"Both the lava tube and the cave we walked into have been around far longer than our ancestors. The government only rein-forced part of it forty years ago. There are many man-made under-ground tunnels and bunkers hidden under all of the islands, but this one is actually built into pre-existing lava tubes, which I believe was originally used by our Hawaiian ancestors as a meeting area."

"A meeting area?" asked a bewildered Pono.

"Yes, Pono. But not just any meeting area. This was the meeting area for all of the elders of the 'aumākua."

Ke Ali'i then showed Pono the petroglyphs of the pueo etched on the rock walls of the cave and the petroglyphs of the manō etched on the rocks surrounding the water tunnel. "I never thought that I would ever see this," said Pono. "How long have you known of this place?"

"I have been working here for the past forty years, Pono. I was tasked by the government to use this room to head up a special divi-sion to guard against illegal smuggling between the islands using these very lava tubes. Originally, our division was responsible for keeping all the tunnels with ocean access secure. Then, about twenty years ago, we were also tasked with special operations in the Pacific Ocean and this tunnel has become our safe house, if you will."

Pono started walking throughout the underground cave, stop-ping to look at every petroglyph. "Go on, Ke Ali'i. I am still listen-ing to you," said Pono, as he continued to admire all the manō and pueo petroglyphs on the rock walls.

"My team is comprised of men who are of Hawaiian or part-Ha-waiian descent. They all are aware of the sacredness of this place," said Ke Ali'i.

"How can they travel through the lava tubes? Even with oxygen tanks and small diving propulsion vehicles, most people would get claustrophobic, not to mention physically exhausted because of the many miles they would have to travel under such conditions," remarked Pono.

"You are correct, Pono. It would be very difficult for a man to travel through the under-water tunnels that connect our islands--even with the use of modern day equipment. Only as a manō can I, or any other member of my team, utilize these lava tubes," replied Ke Aliʻi.

"I knew it," said Pono. "I had been told by my uncle that this place existed, but after speaking with other ʻaumākua brothers who had not heard of such a place, I came to the conclusion that the whereabouts of this meeting area would be known only to our ancestors." Pono shook his head and looked away from Ke Aliʻi for a moment, then he composed himself and said, "I wish I could have, or we could have, shown this to our grandson, Kahoku. He would have loved to see this."

Ke Aliʻi walked toward Pono and nodded his head in agreement. "Pono, it pains me to tell you this, but I feel very strongly that our grandson, Kahoku, did not drown. I think that he was taken from us by one of our own."

"What are you saying, Ke Aliʻi?" Pono couldn't believe what he had just heard. "To take an innocent life is kapu [forbidden]. Any kanaka [Hawaiian] responsible for such actions forfeits the gift of the ʻaumakua for himself and his keiki," said Pono sternly.

"Yes, Pono, you and I both understand this," answered Ke Aliʻi, who was now pacing back and forth in front of Pono. "Therefore, I believe we are dealing with a man who has found a way around the ʻaumākua code. He has found a way to hold on to his ability to transform into a manō in spite of his murderous actions. He has corrupted his ʻaumakua spirit and is now an obsessed, apex predator."

Pono could not believe what he was hearing. He was always

cautioned by the kūpuna and his uncle to abide by the ʻaumākua code. But, at the same time, Pono was also aware that such an individual is not unique. There have always been men who choose power over humanity and family. There have always been men who use their gifts for personal gain. But how did this man do it? How did he elude the code?

"How did you come across this information, Ke Aliʻi?" asked Pono.

Ke Aliʻi took a few minutes to think about how he could tell Pono everything he knew without bringing up the death of Pono's father, Mr. Nahele, and Pono's wife, Aukele. But there was no way around it. He had to be as direct as he could. "Pono, do you remember when your son, Manu, was found hanging from a koa tree in Kōkeʻe?"

"Yes, I remember." Pono's eyes started to well up with tears. "The memory of that day pains me even now. I miss my father and my wife Aukele so very much."

Ke Aliʻi knew that these memories would bring pain to Pono, but he was out of options. So he took a deep breath and then continued on. "Pono," said Ke Aliʻi, "I need to tell you more about that terrible day. I do not believe that your father and Aukele just vanished accidentally. I think that they were the first innocent people to fall victim to this predator."

At that moment, Pono had to muster up all the inner strength he had so as not to direct the growing anger inside him toward Ke Aliʻi. He knew that both of them were emotionally exhausted and that Ke Aliʻi was not intentionally setting out to make him upset. But this was very hard to hear. Looking deep within himself, Pono felt that there was a sense of truth to what Ke Aliʻi was trying to tell him. He already knew that the circumstances surrounding Kahoku's death did not make sense. Kahoku was a very strong swimmer and understood the ocean currents. He could not have drowned!

Pono's racing mind immediately took him back to the day that Kahoku was brought into the emergency room. Why was only one side of Kahoku's surf shorts tattered? The lifeguard who accompanied Kahoku in the ambulance said that Kahoku had probably been pounded by a wave and that his shorts got caught on the reef. But how could this be true? There were no scratch marks on his legs, arms, or other parts of his body. If Kahoku had been caught on the reef, he would have sustained some lacerations--especially since the waves were unrelenting on that particular day.

Pono's expression turned very dark. His chest started to heave in and out at a very fast pace, each breath bringing him closer to becoming his 'aumakua--the pueo. Ke Ali'i placed his hand on Pono's shoulder. "Pono, we need to sort this out first. We both need to think things through and not be so eager to want to get revenge; otherwise, we are no better than the one we seek," said Ke Ali'i calmly.

Pono's breathing started to slow down, but it took several minutes before his mind stopped racing. Never before had he felt such rage! He didn't like how it made him feel…like he had no control over himself. Ke Ali'i was right. Such rage could only do more damage and would not bring back his father, Aukele, or Kahoku. In the end, it would only corrupt his 'aumakua--the pueo--and lead to more disappointment.

As he tried to calm down, Pono suddenly remembered the last training session he shared with Kahoku, in which he told his grandson to avoid certain feelings such as rage because it would lead only to self-destruction. *It is my turn to listen to my own advice*, thought Pono, as he sat down on a flat stone that had been carved into a makeshift stool. "How do you know that Aukele and my father were also taken from us by this individual--or should I say murderer?"

"Many years have passed since that horrible day," answered Ke Ali'i. "Much information has been lost to time and inefficient record-keeping. Most of what I have to tell you comes from memory, not from what was written down by the investigators. There was speculation that your father-in-law, Senator William Braga, and your father, Mr. Nahele, were the primary targets of this predator. You see, the senator, who was a senior legislator at the time, had received information that illegal activities were going on under the ocean, in these very lava tubes. So he spearheaded a committee whose main purpose was to find a way to secure funding that would eventually lead to the establishment of my special unit. I believe it was this very act that brought about that fateful day in Kōke‘e."

"How did my father-in-law get this information in the first place?" asked Pono.

"Apparently, a fisherman told your father-in-law of 'an amazing event' he had witnessed while diving for lobster off of Polihale beach on Kaua‘i. From his vantage point at the bottom of the ocean floor, he saw four tiger sharks swimming away from the island of Ni‘ihau and heading toward the submerged cliffs of the Na Pali, and each of them was tethered to a large, floatable barrel. The fisherman quickly swam back to his boat and steered it over to the location where he had last seen the sharks, but he could not see them anymore. Then a couple minutes later, as he was heading back to his fishing spot, the fisherman spotted a bigger shark pulling a larger plastic barrel and heading in the same direction as the other sharks.

"Now any other person might think this was extremely unbelievable, but this fisherman knew that there was reason for concern. He had been told from others who had fished in the same location that strange things were going on there. It was not by coincidence that he was fishing there that day: he was there to investigate these strange occurrences. The next day, after making sure that there were no tiger sharks in the area, the intrepid fisherman swam the exact path that the tiger sharks had taken and found the opening of a very large lava tube. It would later be determined that this lava tube connected the island of Kaua‘i to the very place that we are standing in," said Ke Ali'i.

"Who was the fisherman that followed the tiger sharks?" asked Pono.

"That intrepid fisherman was your father, Pono," replied Ke Ali'i. "Your father then reported this to Aukele's dad, Senator Braga. Because your father was a fellow Kauaian, and had served in both the military and the police department, Senator Braga took your father's report seriously and lobbied the legislature to allocate funding to help the military secure all underwater lava tubes between the Hawaiian Islands. No information regarding 'aumākua involvement was disseminated, only information relating to men smuggling illegal materials was made known to the appropriate authorities. Your father believed that it was his responsibility to find evidence against the misguided Hawaiians who had used their 'aumākua irresponsibly. He did not want someone other than himself to investigate these occurrences because he did not want the public to find out about the 'aumākua.

"With the senator's help, your father was able to apprehend most of the perpetrators. But after many months of searching, your father and the senator could not catch the leaders of this group. To make matters worse, all of the individuals that had been captured refused to name their leaders, and eventually, all of them died in prison. Your father had no other option but to go and speak with the oldest kahuna who lived in Kōke'e: he was your father's only recourse.

"Senator Braga told investigators that your father was supposed to go up to Kōke'e alone, but when Aukele overheard your dad tell the senator that he would be taking the day off to go and speak with the kahuna, she asked your father if he could take her and her two girlfriends with him so that they could help her pick the fragrant maile leaves that she needed in order to make your graduation lei. Your son, Manu, was just a young child at the time. Aukele probably heard that the footpath, which led up to the kahuna's cabin, had an abundance of maile leaves.

"They had gotten more than halfway up to the cabin when the trouble started. According to police reports, only three sets of tracks went on ahead, while one set of tracks did not continue with the group. Further along the path, the officers found no tracks leading up to the kahuna's cabin, or tracks leading back to your dad's vehicle, so they concluded that no one completed the hike. All four adults just vanished from the trail. Your son Manu was the only one that the officers located, but he was found dangling in one of the koa trees about one mile up from the trail. The backpack that Manu was found in had gotten stuck on one of the branches of the koa tree, but no one could figure out how Manu got up there in the first place. Many of the officers started to think that your father, Aukele, and her two friends were abducted by an individual who had a helicopter, but this lead, like all the rest, soon fizzled out. There was even some speculation that the old kahuna, whom your father was going to visit, had set up booby traps along the footpath to keep out unwanted visitors. But this idea was soon dismissed because no traps were found and, more importantly, no evidence of the kahuna was found. According to officers, the cabin had been uninhabited for some time," said Ke Ali'i.

"Yes. Those were very tough times for both Manu and me," said Pono, as his eyes started to tear up. "After weeks of investigation, no bodies were recovered, and evidence of foul play had been forever hidden by the forest. The investigators had no other option but to close the case with no conclusive answers. My father-in-law, Senator Braga, passed away soon after that. I knew that his passing was due to a broken heart, which I was suffering from as well, but I had a responsibility to Manu, who was having a really hard time adjusting to life without his mother."

"Pono, has Manu shared anything with you, any memories that have come back to him since that day his mother disappeared?"

"No, Ke Aliʻi. Manu has not shared any information with me. I believe his mind has blocked it out to protect him from further depression. He does, however, have a great fear of heights. As a boy growing up, he never liked to climb trees or go sightseeing in the helicopter with his cousin Ben. I knew early on that he would most likely never experience his gift of the pueo ʻaumakua. That is why I was so amazed when I witnessed the first transformation of our grandson, Kahoku."

"Our grandson was an ʻaumakua?" asked Ke Aliʻi.

Ponoʻs countenance started to come alive. "Our grandson was an ʻio [hawk] ʻaumakua!" exclaimed Pono. Ke Aliʻi stood silent for a long time in astonishment at what Pono just revealed. He knew that such an ʻaumakua was extremely rare--never seen or written about since the dawning of the ʻaumākua. To Ke Aliʻiʻs recollection, the silver hawk ascended into the heavens, leaving only the manō and the pueo as the dominant ʻaumākua.

"I heard whisperings that this ʻaumakua might return to our people, but I never thought that it would be in my lifetime," said Ke Aliʻi. The rising of the waves in the water tunnel made both Pono and Ke Aliʻi aware that the tide was changing and that the dawn was upon them.

"This has been a long night for the both of us, Pono. We have disclosed many of our family secrets," said Ke Aliʻi.

"I agree, Ke Aliʻi, but there are still more secrets to sort out, more nightmares to put to rest, and I still have many more questions regarding the untimely passing of my wife Aukele and my father, as well as our grandson," replied Pono.

"I know that your mind is flooded with questions, as is mine. I promise, Pono, that I will continue to search for the answers, as I will be focusing all my attention on finding the person who took the life of our grandson. Please do not tell Manu of this. Both he and Mālie need this time together to start the healing process."

"Ke Aliʻi, when did you realize that Kahoku was killed by an ʻaumakua?" asked Pono.

"Like you, I didn't believe our grandson drowned; he was too strong a swimmer. So when I saw this picture on his bedroom wall," said Ke Aliʻi, as he handed the photo over to Pono, "I knew that our grandson was targeted and killed by one of our brothers--an ʻaumakua."

Chapter 4:

NĀ IWI (BONES)

Now back home on Kauaʻi, Pono decided to return to the same spot in Kōkeʻe where his wife Aukele, her two friends, and his father had last been seen. "So long ago," whispered Pono helplessly. "I don't know if I can find the answers I need."

Pono closed his eyes and allowed his body and mind to join with his ʻaumakua--the pueo (owl). After his transformation was complete, Pono began his journey to Kōkeʻe. His great chest heaved in and out as his enormous wings lifted him up into the night sky. Using his sharp vision and acute sense of direction, Pono quickly came upon the location in Kōkeʻe that stirred every sense in his body. This was the place where he had lost so much--the place that still haunted him the most!

The air was very chilly, and a crescent moon hung low in the night sky. Pono circled over the spot where Aukele and his father had been taken, then flew further up the footpath to the koa tree on which Manu had been found. Slowly, Pono descended from the sky and landed on one of the Koa tree's huge branches.

Looking around for a minute or so, Pono became aware that there were no sounds in the forest, except for the wind and the subsequent rustling of the trees. *How odd,* he thought, *just a couple ridges over I saw wild pua'a [pigs] and deer running through the forest, but there are no animals here--just the trees.* Suddenly, a loud shriek cut through the chilly darkness and a pair of shadows danced across the mountain ridge. Pono quickly glided onto the forest floor and took shelter under a fallen Plum tree. The ominous shadows soon merged with their masters--two pueo 'aumākua, whose colossal wings stirred up the fallen leaves on the footpath below as they beat in unison.

As the two pueo 'aumākua hovered above him for several minutes, Pono noticed that one of them was clutching a goat in its talons. *Pueo 'aumākua should not be hunting,* he thought, as he remained very still and listened to the whooshing sound of their beating wings. *I do not know either one of them,* concluded Pono, as the pair of winged hunters flew away and he slowly came out of his hiding place and stretched his wings.

Standing on the forest floor enclosed by a thick canopy of trees was not easy for a massive owl like Pono, who easily reached a height of eight feet. To make matters worse, the tree canopy was extremely tight and Pono did not want to break any branches and alert the pair of pueo 'aumākua that he had just seen. *Well, there is no better place than this to start looking for answers,* he thought, as he quickly retreated back under the fallen Plum tree. A few minutes later, Pono emerged from his hiding place and stepped onto the footpath wearing his clothes and shoes that he had packed in his satchel, which he always carried with him. Moving as quickly and quietly as he could, Pono started walking back toward the kahuna's cabin--back to the spot where his dad and Aukele had vanished many years ago.

However, after walking just a few feet or so, Pono realized that he could go no further without stumbling over branches. The canopy, though less dense further down the footpath, was still thick enough to stop the moonlight from shining through. Before taking another step forward, Pono adjusted his vision and was now seeing through his ʻaumakua's maka (eyes). Only those with years of experience could master such a feat. But this ability to simultaneously use the gifts of the ʻaumākua, while still in human form, was not to be taken lightly. An enormous amount of physical and mental energy was required. Pono knew that he needed to quickly find what he was looking for; otherwise, he could collapse from exhaustion and never make it back home.

While walking down the footpath, Pono's mind flashed back to when he first met his wife, Aukele. He was only seventeen years old and had just gotten his driver's license. His father, Mr. Nahele, had Pono drive him over to Senator Braga's house for a meeting.

"Well son, don't be shy. Go on and knock on the door," said Mr. Nahele, as he grabbed his briefcase before joining Pono at the front door.

"Hello, Mr. Nahele," said Aukele, smiling.

"Aloha, Aukele. This is my son, Pono," responded Mr. Nahele.

"Hello, Pono. Come inside. Would you both like something to drink?"

"Thank you, Aukele, but Pono and I don't want to trouble you. I am just here to speak with your dad for a little while," answered Mr. Nahele.

"All right, Mr. Nahele. My dad is expecting you. He is waiting in his office. Would you like me to take you to him?"

"That's okay, Aukele. I know where your father's office is," responded Mr. Nahele, as he stepped inside.

Aukele looked over at Pono, who was still standing outside on the porch, fidgeting with his car keys. "Pono, would you like to walk over to the park and sit on the swings while our dads speak to each other?" she asked, as the sweet fragrance of the puakenikeni blossom that she wore in her hair that day, wafted out into the porch.

From that moment on, Pono and Aukele were never apart, despite the senator's initial disapproval. The senator wanted his daughter to marry into an upper-class family, but Pono's family, though very hard-working and honest, was not affluent by any means. James Nahele, Pono's father, was well known throughout Kauai's tiny community. He had recently retired from the police department and had previously served in the military when he was a young man.

As time passed, and Mr. Nahele and Senator Braga got to know each other better, Senator Braga eventually welcomed Pono into his family. Later, when Pono moved to Oʻahu for undergraduate school, Senator Braga gave him a job as one of his legislative aides. Despite his hectic undergraduate studies, Pono worked very hard for the senator. In fact, Pono made such a good impression that Senator Braga pleaded with him to consider running for office someday, but Pono had other plans. Although disappointed that Pono was not interested in politics, Senator Braga continued to support Pono throughout his studies.

A chilly breeze suddenly blew over the Kōkeʻe mountain trail and jolted Pono back into the present. "Those were good times," he whispered, as he continued on the footpath down to the kahuna's cabin. When Pono finally reached the kahuna's property, he looked up at the tumbledown, neglected, old cabin, and sighed. "I remember when this place used to look neat and tidy. It seems just like yesterday that I was here with my uncle. That old kahuna never invited me into his cabin. I can still see him standing by his front door, shaking his index finger at me, telling me to stay outside and rake his lawn." Pono chuckled to himself, then looked over at all the fallen tree limbs and old cans that now littered the front yard of the cabin. "Hmmm. Perhaps I was the last person to clean this yard," he whispered, as he cautiously walked toward the cabin and slowly climbed up the rickety porch steps, which were riddled with cobwebs.

When he arrived at the front door, Pono suddenly remembered

the last time that he and his uncle had come to visit the old kahuna. Instead of cleaning the yard that day, Pono decided to eavesdrop on the two old friends, who were sitting close to the open window. *That's it! The old kahuna told my uncle that he had the power to punish 'aumākua who broke the rules.* Pono gasped. "Why did I not remember this sooner?" he whispered, as he sat down on a small, old tree stump that was placed off to the side of the cabin's window. "I wonder if this is the reason that 'aumākua are not adhering to the code. Could it be that there are no other kāhuna that have the ability to enforce the 'aumākua code?"

Despite the many questions that he had, Pono realized that he could not waste more time, so he stood up, rubbed his shirt across the window of the cabin, and peered in. Miraculously, a reflective object lying under the rotted floor boards inside the cabin, caught one of the moonbeams. Not wanting to kick in the door and make a sound that would alert the other pueo 'aumākua to his whereabouts, Pono quickly started peeling off the cabin's old siding. Both the siding and the underlying plywood, which had been softened by the elements and years of neglect, crumbled immediately into tiny pieces.

Still very aware that the two pueo 'aumākua could return to the area, Pono quickly entered the cabin and rushed over to the location where he had caught a glimpse of the reflective object. The acrid, musty smell of the cabin was overwhelming. There were no words to describe the putrid scent of rotting wood and animal droppings on the floor. It was obvious that no one had been living in the cabin for many, many years.

Pono kneeled down and peered through the holes in the decaying wooden floor boards. His eyes soon came to rest upon a diamond ring that was anchored in the dirt. Pono grabbed his pocket knife from his satchel and started lifting away the rotted floor boards. But Pono soon lost all of his gumption when he saw the many iwi [bones] that were strewn across the cabin's crawl space. As Pono's trembling hands reached for the diamond ring, his vision started to diminish. "I just need a little more time. Ke Akua [God], please allow the strength of my 'aumakua to sustain me for a few more minutes," he whispered. But it was too late. Pono dropped the ring and fell helplessly to the floor.

Several hours passed before Pono was able to regain consciousness and sit up. He quickly reached down between the floor boards and picked up the diamond ring then dusted off the gold band and read the inscription. "My ku'uipo Aukele, I will treasure you forever." Pono's eyes welled up with tears, but he knew that this was not the place or time to mourn. Pono quickly started to gather up all the other bones, but soon came to an abrupt stop when he noticed two skulls, lying side by side. *I don't understand. There were four people who went missing that day--why are there only two skulls?* Pono respectfully placed the skulls and the rest of the bones into his satchel. "Ke Akua, please pardon me for taking these bones from their resting place," whispered Pono, as he gingerly walked out of the cabin.

When Pono finally stepped onto the cabin's porch, the moon had almost disappeared behind the mountains of Kōke'e, and the familiar chill in the air reminded him of the urgency of his situation. After walking down the porch stairs, Pono became very weak. *Not again,* he thought, as he struggled to walk over to the footpath. Then, everything faded away.

"Grandpa Pono. Grandpa Pono, wake up!"

"Wehi. How did I get here?" asked Pono, still in a stupor.

"Hello, Uncle," said a familiar voice.

"Ben," responded Pono, "how did you find me? How did I get here?"

"Dad, we found you late last night on the footpath in front of the old kahuna's cabin," interjected Manu.

"But Manu, how did you know I was there? I didn't tell you that I was going up to Kōkeʻe." Pono sat up and then quickly scanned the room. "Where is my satchel?" he asked.

"Grandpa Pono," interrupted Wehi, "I had a bad dream last night that you were hurt and alone."

Pono looked over at Wehi, who continued to tug at her boar's tooth necklace that Manu had given her after Kahoku's funeral. It had come from one of two boars that Manu and Kahoku had caught for a luau a little over a year ago. The day following Kahoku's funeral, Manu gathered the tusks, cleaned them, and placed the strands of hair that he had retrieved from Kahoku, on the night of his death, into each tusk. Manu then sealed the open end of the boar tusk with a tiny and skillfully crafted piece of koa wood, under which he had engraved Kahoku's initials.

"Dad, you were supposed to come over for dinner last night. I called you several times but I only got your voice mail. I called the hospital to see if you were there but no one had seen you. Later on in the evening, Wehi awoke from a nightmare, screaming. She told me that you were hurt and lying in the woods next to a very scary cabin in Kōkeʻe. I called Ben, and we used his helicopter to get out there and bring you home. Why did you go out to that place, Dad? Why did you go alone?" asked Manu.

"Ben," said Pono, "thank you for helping Manu find me. Manu, I promise I will tell you everything you want to know, but for now, I would like to go home and rest." Manu could tell that Pono was exhausted and wanted to be alone.

"Wehi, go find Grandpa Pono's satchel in the helicopter and bring it back here for him," said Manu.

A little while later, Wehi came back into the room and ran up to Pono. "Here is your satchel, Grandpa Pono."

"Thank you, Wehi. I will see you soon," said Pono as he gave

Wehi a big hug then stood up from the bed and placed his satchel over his shoulder.

"Okay, Grandpa Pono," answered Wehi, as she helped him put his shoes on. "I love you, Grandpa Pono."

"I love you too, Wehi," said Pono.

"Pono, please take this food home," said Mālie, as she ran into the room and handed him the leftovers from dinner. "You need to eat and get some rest."

"Thank you for the food, Mālie. Don't worry. I will be all right." Pono gave Mālie a hug and then walked outside the house and got into Manu's truck.

Back at the cabin, two figures stood above the splintered floor, which had previously hidden the graveyard of human bones. "Well, the puzzle will soon unravel. The son of Nahele has finally started on his journey for answers," said a massive, sharp-toothed man.

"Do you think that Pono is the last extractor of the 'aumākua?" asked his companion.

"Perhaps," answered the sharp-toothed man. "If he is, he has yet to discover this for himself. We would not be here if Pono knew who he truly was. We must get rid of him and all of his family just to be safe. Come, let us leave this place before the other pueo 'aumākua return."

The early morning darkness served as the perfect cover for their departure from the cabin, as one lifted the other into the dark sky and carried him toward the island of Niʻihau.

Chapter 5:

CHOKE RAIN DROPS

It had been two months since Wehi had seen or heard from her grandpa Pono. Wehi's father, Manu, told her that Grandpa Pono had been extremely busy at the hospital and was also assisting the medical examiner's office in a cold case. But Wehi believed that this was her grandfather's way of keeping busy and coping with Kahoku's passing.

Having now moved most of her things into Kahoku's room, Wehi wanted so desperately to show her grandpa Pono how she had set up Kahoku's trophies and pictures next to her surfing medals. As she started to daydream about how her grandfather would react after he had seen what she had accomplished, Wehi's mom, Mālie, called out to her from the kitchen.

"Wehi, time to get dressed. The bus is coming soon and you need to be on time. Today is the day when your class goes on an excursion to the salt ponds, remember?"

"But Mom, I thought it was cancelled because of the 'choke' rain drops that we had this past week."

For the first time in months, Mālie, started laughing. Wehi had not heard her laugh since before Kahoku had passed away.

Mālie stopped what she was doing in the kitchen and came over to Kahoku's room. "Choke rain drops? That's what Kahoku used to say every time we had a flood." Mālie paused for a moment, and then picked up a picture of Kahoku from his desk. "My son, you have left us so many wonderful memories," she said as she put Kahoku's picture back on his desk, then walked out of the room and back to the kitchen to finish preparing Wehi's lunch for the excursion. "Now remember, Wehi, please do not wander away from everyone like you have done on past excursions. Stay close to the group and listen to your teachers."

"Okay, Mom. The bus is here--I gotta go!" announced Wehi, as she ran out of Kahoku's room and picked up her backpack, which was sitting on the coffee table by the front door.

But before Wehi could get out of the house, Mālie met her excited daughter at the front door and gave her a big hug. "Wehi, make sure that you don't forget this peanut butter and guava jelly sandwich on the bus," said Mālie as she buttoned up Wehi's jacket.

"Don't worry, Mom. I won't forget my sandwich. I love you." Wehi gave Mālie a big hug, grabbed her lunch bag, and ran outside to catch her bus.

The bus was buzzing with excitement. Everyone in Wehi's class was excited to go on the excursion. It had been raining so hard for the past week and everyone was ready to get out and enjoy the sun! But when they arrived at the salt ponds, the ground was still very soggy. It was a miracle that the school bus did not get stuck in the mud. Most of the salt ponds were filled with rainwater, and the ocean next to the ponds looked like chocolate milk. There was also a lot of debris floating in the bay.

"Yuck," said one of Wehi's classmates. "The ocean looks totally gross. Look at all the 'ōpala [trash] that is floating in the water!"

"Yeah. I bet there are many manō [sharks] in the water too," replied Wehi.

"Okay, kids," said one of the teachers, "settle down. We will be going on a short tour before we break for lunch. Please pay attention to where you walk. The flood waters have brought down a lot of debris from the mountains."

For the next two hours, Wehi and her classmates explored the salt ponds and learned about the laborious process of making Hawaiian salt. Luckily, the hard-working family who managed the salt ponds had harvested a few salt beds before the heavy rains, so Wehi and her classmates were able to mix the harvested salt with medicinal clay called 'alae. "Okay, keiki [children]," instructed Wehi's teacher, Miss Pua, "please package your salt mixtures so that you can take them home and share it with your families. When you are done, please wash your hands and go over to the picnic table and eat your lunches."

Wehi packaged her Hawaiian salt then washed up and walked over to the picnic table. After taking out her peanut butter and guava jelly sandwich from her lunch bag, Wehi started quickly devouring it. When it came to peanut butter and guava jelly, Wehi just didn't know how to eat slowly. Something about that creamy, nutty taste of the peanut butter and the sweet, fruity flavor of the guava jelly, sent her taste buds into overdrive! "Wehi, you need to chew your food slowly or else you are going to choke," said Miss Pua as she walked past Wehi's table. Wehi nodded at Miss Pua and smiled. Her mouth was too full of sweet bread, guava jelly, and peanut butter, to say anything.

After scarfing down her sandwich, Wehi decided to walk to the other end of the salt ponds, where she had heard a kitten's cry earlier. She knew that she would be disobeying her mother by wandering away from her group, but when little, furry mammals--like kittens and puppies--were involved, Wehi just couldn't help herself. *I can use the excuse that the rubbish can closest to the picnic table was full, so I needed to walk over to the far end of the salt ponds to use the other rubbish can. Hopefully, Miss Pua will not notice that I am gone.* Wehi got up quickly and started walking. As she came closer to the rubbish can, Wehi heard the distant cry of the kitten and the rush of the swollen river that flowed behind the large ironwood trees. *I need to find that poor little kitten. What if it wandered over to the river?*

As Wehi walked behind the ironwood trees and ventured deeper into the wooded area, her heart started beating faster. The sound of the rushing river continued to grow louder, as did the cry of the kitten. "I hope that the kitten is all right," she whispered, as she came closer and closer to the raging river. Suddenly, Wehi felt a warm, tingling sensation on her neck. She quickly grabbed her boar's tooth necklace and noticed that the warmth was coming from the tooth.

"Wehi, get out of here!" shouted Kahoku. Wehi was shocked. She quickly glanced over her shoulder, hoping to see her big brother, but all she saw was cane grass and guava trees.

Frantically Wehi screamed out, "Kahoku! Kahoku, is that you! Are you here?"

Again she heard Kahoku's voice, "Wehi, get out of here!" Wehi quickly turned and started running out of the woods, all the while looking over her shoulder to see if Kahoku was following her. "I know I heard Kahoku's voice!" she said vehemently, as she finally caught a glimpse of the familiar ironwood trees that marked the border between the woods and the salt ponds.

But before reaching the first ironwood tree, Wehi turned around one last time and caught a glimpse of a very scary person chasing her. *He looks like he has a mouth full of daggers for teeth*, she thought as she started to run faster and faster, clenching the boar's tooth tighter and tighter. Before she knew what was happening, Wehi ran right into her teacher, Miss Pua.

"Wehi Nahele, where have you been? The entire class has been looking for you!"

"I'm sorry, Miss Pua, I was just...."

"Wehi, there is no excuse for what you have done. You know better than to wander away."

"But, but--I thought there was a little kitten…."

"No excuses, Wehi. I will be calling your parents today to let them know that you wandered off again. Now it's time to get on the bus so that we can all go home."

"Okay," said Wehi, as she took her lunch bag and her backpack from Miss Pua and started walking toward the bus.

Throughout the entire bus ride home, Wehi was miserable. Everyone kept looking over at her and whispering to each other. *Yup*, she thought, *I am officially that girl--the strange little girl who wandered away and made all the teachers very upset for the rest of the excursion. Why can't everyone just mind their own business?*

As the bus dropped off Wehi's classmates, one by one, Wehi sat patiently in her seat and thought about what happened to her at the salt ponds. "I know that I heard my brother's voice," she whispered, as she wrote Kahoku's name on the foggy bus window. "I don't care if I get in trouble. I heard Kahoku's voice. That's all that matters." Then, just as the rain started to fall, so too did Wehi's tears.

Chapter 6:

SHARPSHOOTER

The bus ride home took a little longer than it normally would be-cause driving conditions had deteriorated within the last thirty minutes. The entire island was now under a flash flood warning ac-cording to the school bus driver, Mele. The low-lying streams that originated from Mount Waiʻaleʻale were becoming swollen over with rainwater and would soon start rushing over the main road to Wehi's house. Wehi had been in flood conditions before, so she just sat patiently in her seat and looked forward to the Portuguese bean soup that her mother, Mālie, had been slow cooking since this morn-ing. *Hopefully*, thought Wehi, *Miss Pua will call later this evening, after dinner*, or *maybe Miss Pua will be so preoccupied with the flood, that she will forget about what happened today.*

"We finally made it! Okay, Wehi. Home safe and sound. Get something warm to eat," said Mele.

Wehi stood up from her seat and started walking toward the front door of the bus. "Thank you, Mele. Drive safely," replied Wehi, as she stepped out of the bus and onto her driveway.

"Wehi, your socks are all wet and your shoes are all muddy," said Mālie, as Wehi walked in the front door. "I thought that you would be on your way home before the flood started. Why did your group leave so late? Why are you so dirty? Here, let me help you take off your shoes and socks. I am so glad that you are home, Wehi."

Wehi didn't want to tell Mālie that it was her fault that her class had left the salt ponds late, so she changed the subject. "Mom, can I go and get cleaned up and have some of your Portuguese bean soup? I am so tired and I have been thinking about Kahoku all day."

"Okay Wehi. I will get you a bowl of Portuguese bean soup, and then you can watch some television, since tomorrow is Saturday. We will work on your homework tomorrow night."

"Thank you, Mom. Is Dad coming home soon?"

"Go wash up and we will have an early dinner," replied Mālie.

Wehi stood still for a moment. *Something is wrong*, she thought. *Mom always lets me know when dad will be home so that I can at least stay up to give him a kiss before I go to sleep.* Wehi then started to walk toward the bathroom, at the end of the hallway. *I will ask Mom about Dad again when we are sitting at the dinner table,* she thought.

As Wehi passed by Kahoku's room, memories of how they would spend rainy days together started filling her mind. *I miss you so much. I remember how you and Dad would always play football when it flooded outside. I can still hear your laughter and see your smiling face as you tried to get pass dad to score a touchdown. How I miss your laughter, Big Brother.*

"Wehi, don't forget to scrub your fingernails. They are very pi-lau [dirty]. Did you fall in the mud while you were on your class excursion today?" asked Mālie, but Wehi didn't answer her. Instead, Wehi walked into the bathroom and closed the door, hoping that Mālie wouldn't ask her again to explain why she was so filthy.

After Wehi finished her bath and had put on her pajamas, she walked into the kitchen and overheard Mālie talking on her cell phone to someone in the police department. *I knew it!* thought

Wehi. *Something is going on. Dad is still not home yet, and mom is speaking with someone in the police department. As soon as she gets off the phone, I am going to ask her where Dad is.* After a couple of minutes had passed, Mālie finished her call and walked over to the stove to stir her Portuguese bean soup. "Mom, where is Dad? When will he be home?" asked Wehi. But Mālie did not answer.

"Wehi, why don't you help me get the spoons, and I will get our soup."

"What are you trying to hide, Mom?" asked Wehi, as she grabbed two spoons then sat down at the table with Mālie.

"Finish your soup and then I will tell you where Dad is, okay? Don't worry, Wehi; he is all right, but he won't be home for a while."

Hearing that her father was all right gave Wehi back her appetite, so she ate all of her soup, then cleaned up the dishes and sat down in the family room with Mālie. "Wehi, your dad had to go and catch a bad guy up in Kalalau Valley," admitted Mālie.

"Couldn't the police get someone else to go? I have only one dad."

"Yes, Wehi, you have only one dad, and he loves you very much. Don't worry, Little One. I am sure that Kahoku is watching over him," said Mālie, as she smiled at Wehi. "Come sit closer to me and I will braid your hair."

"No, Mom. I am just going to fall asleep if you braid my hair and I want to wait up for Dad," objected Wehi. Mālie shook her head back and forth, then moved closer to her resolute daughter and slowly started to braid her hair anyway--despite Wehi's initial objection. Although Wehi was not happy with Mālie, she eventually surrendered to her mother's persistence.

The lulling sound of the rain hitting the window and the fresh scent of falling rain drops soon overcame Wehi's valiant effort to stay awake and she found herself struggling to keep her eyes open.

But just as Wehi was about to close her eyes, she heard a loud knock on the front door. "Stay here, Wehi, and I will go see who is at our door," said Mālie.

"Okay, Mom," responded Wehi. As Mālie slowly opened the door, the wind carried the rain all the way into the family room, and Wehi could feel how wet it was outside.

"Where is Manu?" asked Pono, and Wehi knew at that moment that it was going to be a long, terrible, stormy night.

"Hello, Pono. We haven't seen or heard from you for a long time. We missed you. Wehi is just about to fall asleep in the family room." And as soon as Mālie ended her sentence, all Wehi could hear was the rain pounding against the family room windows, because Mālie had closed the front door and walked outside, under the portico, to speak with Pono.

"Sorry, Mālie. I didn't know that Wehi was about to go to sleep. I am just worried about Manu. Is he one of the officers up in Kalalau Valley?" asked Pono.

"Yes, Pono, he is. The police department wanted their sharp-shooters at the scene. Apparently a young man was injured by someone with a machete. Several tourists in the area claimed that they thought the man with the machete was also holding a second man hostage, but they were not one hundred percent certain. That is all I know at this time, Pono. I am sorry that I do not know any more."

"No need to apologize, Mālie. Look at this horrible flood! You know how bad it gets up there when it floods. The quiet, slow-running streams become raging rivers, making it almost impossible to hike into or out of Kalalau Valley."

"I know, Pono. I am worried about Manu too, but I don't want to worry Wehi. She has already been through so much with Kahoku's passing."

"I understand your need to protect her, but I don't think that your daughter is ignorant, Mālie. She is more aware of what is happening around her than most people would be. Well, let her know that I stopped by. Tell her I will come to see her tomorrow. Tell her that I love her."

"Okay, Pono, I will. Why don't you come in and have some Portuguese bean soup?"

"I will stop by tomorrow, Mālie, when Manu is home. I promise. I have to go to the hospital now, as many people have been injured during the flood. Take care."

"All right, Pono. Be safe," said Mālie, as she opened the front door and walked back into the house.

"Mom, why didn't Grandpa Pono come in to see me?"

"I told him that you were almost asleep. He said that he would come by tomorrow to spend some time with you. How long have you been up?" asked Mālie, as she walked back over to the couch and sat down next to Wehi.

"Not too long," answered Wehi. Mālie then got out her knitting kit as Wehi sat quietly on the couch. *Grandpa Pono probably stopped by to see if Dad was one of the policemen that had been ordered to go to Kalalau Valley. I guess that all parents worry about their children, no matter how old they are,* thought Wehi.

As Wehi looked out from the family room window to see how many puddles of water had formed on the porch, she couldn't pass up the opportunity to press her nose onto the window pane so that she could feel how cold the rain had made it. Then, just as it had done in the wooded area earlier, the boar's tooth around Wehi's neck became very warm. Wehi quickly hopped off of the couch, ran into Kahoku's room and grabbed her favorite picture of him. "I wonder if I will hear Kahoku's voice again?" she whispered as she cozied up on Kahoku's bed.

"Wehi, are you going to sleep already?" asked Mālie, who shut off the television and brought her pillows and her knitting materials into Kahoku's room and cuddled up next to Wehi. "Move over, Little One. I will sleep in here with you tonight. I don't want you to worry about your dad--he is going to be all right." Mālie then gently took Kahoku's picture out of Wehi's hands and put it back on Kahoku's dresser. Although the boar's tooth still felt warm against Wehi's skin, the sound of Mālie humming as she continued knitting was just enough to get Wehi to fall asleep.

Farther north, and two valleys away from Wehi's warm, dry house, Manu and Martin found themselves crouched behind a fallen albizia tree. "Manu, there he is. The guy must have evil magic, because I saw him fall off the mountain a few minutes ago when we fired that warning shot! What is with this guy?" asked Martin, who was completely baffled by what he had seen.

"That guy is playing games with us. No one can fall down hundreds of feet and then reappear--no man can survive a fall like that in the first place. Come on, Marty. He is just an illusionist! He's just trying to get in your head," said Manu, who glanced over at the news reporter and his cameraman. "I will continue to keep an eye on him, but I need you to go and tell the news reporter that he and his cameraman better get in that helicopter and get out of the valley before the rain returns!" exclaimed Manu.

Martin wasted no time in delivering Manu's message to the news reporter and his cameraman, who both left without any protest. When Martin returned, Manu was still watching the suspect through the gun scope. "This guy is showing no signs of fear whatsoever! I mean look at him, pacing back and forth like a tiger in a cage all the while looking in our direction," said Manu.

"See! Evil magic! Better just take the shot, Manu!" said Martin urgently.

"No. Just cover me. I am going to try and talk some sense into this guy."

"Come on, Manu; don't be a hero. This guy has not cooperated with us since we got here six hours ago. He just walked right over that young guy he killed earlier! I think he did it just to spite us!"

"We don't know what happened here, Marty. Let me at least try to speak with him, okay?"

"Fine, have it your way. But if he raises one finger, I am pulling the trigger, Manu," said Martin.

The rain started to fall again as Manu drew his sidearm and approached the large man who stood so close to the edge of the mountain. With every step Manu took, the deranged man's smile grew wider and his eyes got brighter. *What is with this guy?* Manu thought, as he got closer and closer to the large man holding a machete. "Sir, I need you to put your weapon down and put your hands above your head and get on the ground, face down."

"Come and get me, cop. I am not afraid of you!" taunted the large man.

"Like I said, drop the weapon, place your hands above your head, and get on the ground, face down!" yelled Manu.

By now the rain was coming down so heavily that Martin could not see Manu at all. The large man delighted in the worsening downpour and started taunting Manu even more. "Your friend cannot help you now, cop. You are mine!"

"I said drop your weapon!" shouted Manu as he approached the large man. But before Manu could do or say anything more, the large man grabbed Manu by the arm and jumped off the mountain, taking Manu with him.

It happened so fast that Manu barely had time to regain his mental faculties, and before he knew it, he was free-falling to the ocean, hundreds of feet below. Flashes of Kahoku, Wehi, and Mālie shot through his overwhelmed mind. How could he die like this? His family would be devastated if he left them, especially since Kahoku had only passed away several months ago. *I cannot leave them*, thought Manu, as the air rushed over him and he continued to free-fall to the ocean below.

Then, all of a sudden, Manu felt a tug on his legs. Something or someone had grabbed hold of him as he was plummeting toward the ocean below, and saved his life! He was now being carried back to the top of the mountain, but Manu could not identify who or what was taking him back because of the thick cloud cover. After several heart-pounding minutes had passed, Manu's rescuer finally put him down--right next to the old shack, which stood beside the body of the young man.

Still shaken from his harrowing experience, Manu found it difficult to stand up, as both of his legs and hands couldn't stop trembling and his stomach felt as if it had come up into his mouth. *How am I still alive? How did I get back here? Could it be that Martin had somehow saved me? No. There is no way Martin could have saved me while I was in a free-fall. Okay*, thought Manu, *if a man could not save me, then perhaps the stories about the 'aumākua are true.*

As Manu finally found the strength to stand up and the courage to face whomever or whatever it was that saved his life, his anxiety was suddenly calmed by a pair of gentle eyes looking down at him. "Dad, what are you doing here? Did you see who or what saved me?" asked Manu.

Pono then placed his hands on Manu's shoulders, and without saying a word, transformed into a great pueo (owl). Manu fell to the ground in shock, his mind refusing to believe what he had just seen. *Is this real? Am I hallucinating?* wondered Manu, as his mind kept replaying the day's events that led to this moment. "I was trying to apprehend a large guy with a machete. He was standing close to the edge of the mountain. He refused to put down the machete then he grabbed me, and suddenly we were both falling toward the ocean below. Then something stopped my fall. You stopped my fall and saved my life! Why didn't you tell me that you were an 'aumakua?" asked Manu, as he watched Pono change back into the father he recognized.

"There is no time to discuss this now. Martin is worrying about you. You must go back to him and tell him that your suspect got away," said Pono.

"No, he didn't," said Manu. "He fell, just like me."

"He is an 'aumakua, Manu. He was sent to kill you. The police will not find his body. He is long gone from this place. He probably went back to those who wish to do us harm. There is no doubt in my mind that we will again encounter him and others like him in the near future. We will talk more about this and all other family secrets tomorrow. I must go now, before Martin sees me." Pono then changed back into a pueo, descended into the valley and disappeared beneath the shroud of mist.

"Are you okay, Manu? What happened? Where's the guy?!" yelled Martin as he ran over to Manu. Manu put his head down. He did not know what to tell Martin.

"Sorry, Marty. He struck me down, then ran. I doubt we will find him in this rain. He could be anywhere."

"Do you think he fell over?"

"No, Marty, I don't think he fell over. You can call for a search and rescue, but I am pretty sure that they will not find his body down there."

"Well," said Martin, "we should just wait the storm out in this shack. We can call for the copters in the morning, when the storm lets up, to take us and the body back to the station. The captain called earlier, when I couldn't see you, and said that it was too dangerous to send another copter in tonight. I briefed him on what was going on. Said you were trying to talk the guy into giving himself up, but that the rain was coming down pretty hard and I no longer could see what was going on. The captain asked me to call him back when I found you. I'll go find an area where I can get a signal. See you in the shack."

Manu took off his jacket and walked over to the body of the young man, which was lying face up alongside the old shack. He found a burner phone in the young man's jacket, and saw that his last call was to the island of Maui. "Why did you go hiking on your own? How am I going to explain this to your family? I am sorry that your life had to end so suddenly and so violently," said Manu, as he placed his jacket over the victim's head and chest, pulled him onto the rickety old porch, and then went inside the dilapidated shack and closed the door.

Manu's mind was still racing with thoughts of what had just happened. Deep down, Manu wished that his father had never revealed himself as an 'aumakua, because it made Manu feel like everything he had come to depend on, such as the trust he shared with his father and his training as a police officer, had somehow failed him. *Why couldn't I have figured this out before it got to this point?* Manu walked over and helped Martin bring in an old hibachi grill that had been left out on the rickety porch.

The rain started to pound the cabin's tin roof, and the temperature dropped very quickly. Manu huddled by the old hibachi grill that Martin had gotten to work with some old wood and his lighter. But despite how tired he was and how warm and comfortable the old hibachi grill had made the room feel, Manu could not fall asleep. The sound of the raindrops hitting the tin roof just aggravated him even more. *How could my father keep this secret from me? What did he mean when he said that there are others that wish to do us harm? Did they have something to do with my son's death?*

As the rain continued to beat down on the tiny, dilapidated shack, the only thing keeping Manu sane was his rage, which grew with every minute that passed. "Whatever evil magic they have, it will not matter. If they killed my son, I will destroy all of them," he whispered.

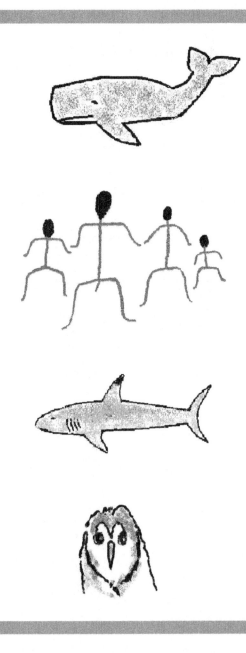

Chapter 7:

HO'OPONOPONO

Several hours later and back at home, Wehi had just opened her eyes when she remembered that her father, Manu, had not come home last night. "Mom, did Dad come home yet?" she asked, as she slowly got out of bed, but Mālie did not answer her. Wehi then rushed over to the bedroom window and saw something that put a great big smile on her face. There, in the driveway, was Manu's pickup truck. "Dad's home!" she yelled as she ran straight into the kitchen and looked out on to the front porch, where she saw Mālie dusting off and cleaning Manu's big muddy boots.

"Good morning, Wehi. Why are you up so early?" said a familiar voice. Wehi immediately turned around and saw her dad standing next to the kitchen table.

"Daddy! I am so glad that you are home!" shouted Wehi as she ran over to Manu and gave him a big hug. "Where were you? Mom and I were so worried! We waited for you all night!"

"Well, I am home now, and I am very hungry!" exclaimed Manu as he started chasing Wehi around the table.

"Good morning, Wehi," said Mālie as she walked into the kitchen. "Manu, I am so glad that you are home and that you are safe!

Wehi and I were very worried about you and so was your father, who stopped by last night. You probably should call him right now-- he was especially worried this time around, Manu. He looked a bit disheveled."

"Don't worry, Mālie. I'll call him after I take a shower. So, what's for breakfast?" asked Manu.

I can't believe it! Dad behaves just like me whenever I am trying to avoid an uncomfortable discussion: he changes the subject really quickly, thought Wehi, as she chuckled to herself.

Mālie rolled her eyes then walked over to the refrigerator. "You go take a shower, Manu. Wehi and I will fix you up something."

"Sounds good," said Manu as he walked down the hallway toward the bathroom. Soon after Manu shut the bathroom door, his cell phone, which was sitting on the kitchen table, started ringing.

"Wehi, can you please answer Daddy's kelepona [telephone]?"

"Okay, Mom," said Wehi, as she quickly ran over to the kitchen table and answered Manu's cell phone just in time. "Aloha kakahiaka [good morning]. Aloha, Grandpa Ke Aliʻi. Can you come over for breakfast? Okay, I will let Mom and Dad know. Hoʻoponopono? No, Grandpa Ke Aliʻi, I don't know what that is. Okay. I will see you soon." Wehi turned around to face Mālie, who had a very puzzled look on her face. "Mom, Grandpa Ke Aliʻi is coming to breakfast! He said that Grandpa Pono is picking him up from the airport and that they will be coming over soon!"

"Well, you better go and clean up the family room before they get here," said Mālie. "Did Grandpa Ke Aliʻi tell you why they are coming over?"

Wehi did not answer Mālie. She was already running through the family room like a tornado, picking up her blankets and hair bands so that the house would be more presentable for both of her grandfathers. Wehi was so excited that she was going to have breakfast with both of them. "Hmm. Mom, what does hoʻoponopono mean?"

asked Wehi, as she folded her blanket and then ran into her room to change her clothes.

Mālie didn't answer Wehi right away because she had gone into the back yard to pick some ripe papayas and bananas. When Mālie returned to the kitchen, she asked Wehi to go into the front yard to pick some torch ginger that grew right outside the kitchen window. After Wehi had finished picking the torch ginger, she came back into the kitchen, and waited patiently while Mālie placed the torch gingers in a vase. "The word Hoʻoponopono is used to describe an act of correction. When a family member asks for hoʻoponopono, it usually means that they want to apologize for something they did or did not do so that all family members can get along with one another. Is that the reason why both Grandpa Ke Aliʻi and Grandpa Pono are coming over?"

"That's what Grandpa Ke Aliʻi told me," replied Wehi.

"But I thought that we had already come together as a family and talked about all of our feelings after Kahoku's funeral. Is there something more we have to talk about?" asked Mālie.

"I don't know, Mom," replied Wehi.

"Manu, can you come here when you get out of the shower!" Mālie shouted, as she knew her voice needed to carry through the hallway and the bathroom door.

"Yes Mālie," replied Manu, as he opened the bathroom door. "I will be right there, sweetheart. I just have to put my dirty clothes in the laundry room first."

After a couple of seconds had passed, Manu joined Wehi and Mālie at the kitchen table. "Manu," started Mālie, "is there anything you want to tell me before both of our fathers arrive?"

"We'll talk about it as soon as they get here," answered Manu as he pulled his tee-shirt over his head. "Wehi, what are you and Mom cooking for breakfast?"

Mālie was visibly concerned, so Wehi turned up her enthusiasm.

"Well, Dad, I thought that maybe we could have some scrambled eggs and bacon with fresh fruit," she said, as she tried really hard to divert the tension between her parents. "Dad, would you like to play hide and seek with me?" she asked. "I will start counting, so you better find a good hiding spot!" shouted Wehi, as she ran into the family room.

Mālie looked over at Manu for a moment, then started preparing breakfast after Manu ran off to find a hiding spot. After an hour had passed, the entire house smelled of bacon and freshly baked guava scones. "Okay, you two. Do you think you could help me set the table before Grandpa Pono and Grandpa Ke Aliʻi get here?" asked Mālie.

"Oh, Mom. Can't we play just one more game of hide and seek?" pleaded Wehi.

"It's all right, Wehi. Mom has been in the kitchen doing everything by herself. The least we can do is help her set the table before both of your grandfathers arrive. We will play hide and seek later on."

"Okay Dad," said Wehi, as she walked over to the cabinets to get the plates and cups, but as she started setting the table, Wehi still couldn't help but wonder why her dad wanted to wait for both of her grandfathers to arrive before he told her mom the reason for this hoʻoponopono.

Suddenly, Wehi's mind flashed back to the previous day, when she ran into her teacher, Miss Pua, who went looking for her at the salt ponds. As Wehi continued setting the table, she became a little nervous. *What if the reason for this hoʻoponopono was to talk about the trouble I had gotten myself into at the salt ponds? Miss Pua had mentioned before that she volunteered on weekends at the emergency room where Grandpa Pono worked. What if she saw Grandpa Pono last night, when he was at the emergency room caring for people who got hurt in the flood, and told him what I had done?* thought

Wehi, as she ran back to the cabinet to grab the spoons and forks. Wehi started to perspire a little. *Uh-oh! Dad and Mom are going to be so mad at me,* she thought, as she placed the spoons and forks on the kitchen table and then rushed into the bathroom to splash some water on her face.

"Come on, Wehi, both Grandpa Ke Aliʻi and Grandpa Pono will be here soon!"

"Sorry, Mom. I just had to wash my hands," said Wehi as she quickly finished setting the table.

Wehi had just sat down next to Manu in the family room when she heard a deep, loud voice call out, "Where's my pretty girl?"

"Grandpa Ke Aliʻi!" yelled Wehi, as she ran over to the front door and gave him a big bear hug. "Thank you for my present! I love the pink dress you sent me. It's beautiful!"

"You sent our granddaughter a pink dress?" asked Pono. His puzzled look was enough to elicit a deep laugh from Ke Aliʻi.

"What is wrong with a pink dress for our young, beautiful grand-daughter?" asked Ke Aliʻi.

"Grandpa Pono," interjected Wehi, "I asked Grandpa Ke Aliʻi to get me a pink dress for Sunday school because I have outgrown all my other dresses."

Ke Aliʻi started to chuckle a little. "I bet Grandpa Pono didn't know that I have an impeccable taste in clothes," he said as he scooped Wehi up and gave her a big kiss.

"I see that you have been spending a lot more time with Wehi," said Pono. The look of validation in Pono's eyes made Ke Aliʻi smile.

"I have called and spoken with Wehi every weekend since Kahoku's funeral. I don't want to be as distant from her as I was with our grandson, Pono. I guess an old dog can learn new tricks after all," said Ke Aliʻi. Pono then gave Ke Aliʻi a firm pat on his shoulder.

"Well, when are we going to eat this big breakfast? Where is the bacon?" asked Pono.

"Okay everyone. Please come into the dining room so that we can kaukau [eat]," announced Mālie, who looked over at her father, Ke Aliʻi, and Pono. "It is really nice to have you both here. It has been a while. The last time we had both of you here together was when we said farewell to Kahoku," said Mālie, as she quickly wiped away the tears that started to run down her face.

"Ke Aliʻi, will you give the pule [prayer] for this ʻono [delicious] food?" asked Manu.

"I would love to," replied Ke Aliʻi.

After Ke Aliʻi finished the prayer, everyone filled their plates with the food set out before them and dug right in. Mālie had cut and plated fresh pineapples, bananas, and sweet papaya and also made crispy bacon, homemade guava scones with lilikoi (passion fruit) butter, and cheese omelets. The only thing that was missing was Kahoku's favorite dish--a macadamia nut-crusted opah (moonfish), which Mālie would make for breakfast every Sunday. But after Kahoku had passed away, this dish just never found its way back onto the table--it was another one of those things that just fade away after the passing of a loved one because it had become another painful reminder of someone who will never again have the opportunity to enjoy such an experience.

"Boy, I think that my canoe is going to sink on the way back to Oʻahu," said Ke Aliʻi who was rubbing his belly. "Look at my big ʻōpū [stomach]!"

"You didn't paddle your canoe here, Grandpa Ke Aliʻi. You came on an airplane."

"Okay, Wehi. You got me. But you know what? I probably should get a canoe and paddle it all the way back to Oʻahu so that I can work off all this good food that your mom prepared for us," replied Ke Aliʻi, as he continued to rub his stomach.

"Wehi, could you do a big favor for me?" asked Manu.

"Hmmm, okay, Dad. But only if you promise that we will finish our game of hide and seek later," said Wehi, mischievously.

"I promise, Wehi," said Manu. "Do you think you could clear the table and put all the food away?"

"Okay. Is the ho'oponopono going to start?" asked Wehi.

"Yes, Wehi. The adults are all going to be in the family room discussing a few things. When you finish cleaning up, you can go into our bedroom and watch television. Later on, we can go to the beach if you want to, or we can finish our game of hide and seek, okay?"

"Sure Dad," replied Wehi. "But shouldn't I be in the ho'oponopono meeting too?"

"Maybe the next time, Wehi," replied Manu.

"Manu, ho'oponopono is for the entire family. Don't you think that Wehi should be a part of what we are going to discuss?" asked Mālie.

"Not this time, Mālie. Wehi is too young for what we will be discussing," replied Manu, who then looked over at Wehi. "Go clean up the table, Wehi. We will be in the family room for a while," he said firmly.

Wehi cleaned up the table and washed the dishes, then went to watch television in her parents' room. Try as she may, Wehi just couldn't get comfortable. Her mind kept wondering if the adults were discussing what had happened to her at the salt ponds. *What if Miss Pua told Grandpa Pono something that wasn't true?* Wehi's palms started sweating. *Why did I go wandering off again? Why couldn't I just follow the rules in the first place?* "Okay Wehi," she whispered, "try and think of something positive."

As the ho'oponopono continued in the family room, Wehi found it increasingly difficult to stay in her parents' room, especially when she thought that the adults were discussing the incident at the salt ponds. After several hours had passed, Wehi's curiosity got the best of her, so she opened her parents' bedroom door and slowly crept through the hallway, then quickly ran into Kahoku's room, which was right next to the family room. Wehi then crouched behind Kahoku's trophy case and placed her left ear on the wall that separated Kahoku's room from the family room, all the while keeping her eyes focused on the door, just in case someone walked by.

The adults were listening to Mālie talk about how little time they had spent together as a family prior to Kahoku's death and that they all needed to try to spend more time together from now on. Wehi let out a sigh of relief. *Okay*, she thought, *they are not talking about me. Maybe I can creep back into Mom and Dad's room before someone comes in here and sees me.* But just as Wehi was about to take her ear off the wall, she heard Ke Aliʻi clear his throat.

"Mālie, thank you for reminding us about how we need to spend more time together. I think that we need to work harder at many things, but I also think that we need to be honest with each other. With that in mind, Pono and I need to tell you and Manu something very important."

"What is going on, Dad?" asked Mālie.

"Oh no," whispered Wehi. "Grandpa Ke Aliʻi and Grandpa Pono are going to tell mom and dad about what I did yesterday when I was at the salt ponds! Miss Pua probably told Grandpa Pono that I was the one responsible for my classmates not getting home earlier, and then Grandpa Pono called Grandpa Ke Aliʻi and told him. I better go back to Mom and Dad's bedroom before someone catches me eavesdropping--then I will really be in hot water!"

Wehi quickly ran out of Kahoku's room and got back onto her parents' bed. But as she tried to get comfortable, Wehi felt her boar's tooth necklace heat up against her neck and she wondered if she would hear Kahoku's voice again--just like she did yesterday when she was at the salt ponds. "Kahoku, are you here?" whispered Wehi. By now her concern had shifted away from the adults' conversation to her brother's whereabouts. Wehi got off the bed and looked under it, then walked over to the closets and slowly opened them, trying not to make any sound that might cause Mālie or Manu to come and check on her.

While in the closet, she heard Kahoku's voice again. "Wehi, everything is going to be okay, I promise you."

"Kahoku, where are you?" whispered Wehi, as she continued to search through her parents' room.

Again, Wehi heard Kahoku's voice tell her that everything would be okay, and although she could not find where her brother's voice was coming from, Wehi took comfort in knowing that somehow, someway, her big brother was right there in the room with her--and that was enough to make her feel at ease. Wehi climbed back onto her parents' bed and waited patiently for Kahoku's voice to speak to her again. But as the minutes passed, Wehi could feel her eyelids getting very heavy, despite the loud chatter of the mynah birds in the back yard.

As Wehi fell asleep in her parents' room, the adults continued on with the ho'oponopono. Realizing that what he was about to tell his daughter would upset her, Ke Ali'i walked over and sat next to Mālie on the couch. "Sweetheart, Pono and I did not want to have to tell you this so soon, but in light of what happened recently, we both feel that you need to know the truth about what happened to Kahoku."

"What are you talking about, Dad? Kahoku passed away while trying to save his friend's life," replied Mālie.

"Yes, sweetheart. Kahoku died while trying to save his friend but I don't think that he drowned," responded Ke Ali'i, as he grabbed Mālie's hands and held them for a moment while he collected his thoughts. "This is hard for all of us, Mālie, so just remember that we all love you very much, okay?"

Mālie continued to sit very still. "All right, Dad. What are you trying to tell me about my son?"

At that moment, Ke Aliʻi started to question his resolve to tell his daughter the truth. How could he tell Mālie that her son had been killed by an ʻaumakua? "Where do I start?" whispered Ke Aliʻi.

"Dad, what are you trying to say? Please, just tell me already. My heart cannot take this much longer," Mālie said tearfully.

"Your son, our grandson, was taken away from us by a heartless individual who is now trying to hurt all of us," responded Ke Aliʻi.

"How do you know that Kahoku was murdered? That makes no sense whatsoever! My son was not murdered. He died trying to save his friend. He drowned. Kahoku never hurt anyone. He did not have any enemies. My son was loved by everyone around him. Forgive me for saying this, Dad, but you were hardly around. How could you possibly know anything about this?"

"Mālie, please try to lower your voice. I don't want Wehi to hear about the horrible way in which Kahoku was taken from us," said Manu.

"And you," said Mālie as she looked over at Manu, "why aren't you surprised by all of this, Manu? Did you already know about this? How long have you been keeping this information from me?" Mālie put her head down in her hands, then looked back up at Manu and then over at her father, Ke Aliʻi. "This is ridiculous. How do you expect me to believe such rubbish?"

"Mālie, sweetheart," started Ke Aliʻi, "Pono and I have to tell you everything that we have hidden from both you and Manu for your entire lives. Hopefully, it will shed some light on why Kahoku was taken from all of us."

Mālie's hands started to shake. "You mean that you and Pono have something to do with what happened to my son?" Mālie sat up and started to walk toward the other side of the family room. Unable to control her grief, she started crying uncontrollably and couldn't stop pacing back and forth. After a few minutes had passed, Mālie finally stopped in the middle of the room, placed one hand on her hip and the other on the nape of her neck, and looked up at all of the men in her life, who were sitting across from her. "Who did this to my son? I want to know who did this to my son! Tell me who did this to my baby!"

Manu walked across the room to Mālie and then pulled her close to him and held her tightly in his arms. "Come and sit down with us," he said as he led her back to the couch where Pono and Ke Aliʻi were sitting.

"Mālie, do you remember when Manu and Ben found me up in Kōkeʻe couple months ago?" asked Pono.

"Of course I remember that. Wehi woke up in a cold sweat that evening. She ran into our room screaming that she had a bad dream and that you were in danger, all alone by an old house in the mountains. I never saw Wehi so frightened and disheveled. Manu tried calling you, but you never answered, so he called Ben and the two of them went up in the helicopter and found you exactly where Wehi said you would be."

"I was there because I needed to find answers surrounding the disappearances of my father and Manu's mother. Manu was too young to remember, but I remember that horrible day as if it was just yesterday. I pressed the authorities for answers, but all they told me was that Aukele, her two friends, and my father had disappeared up at Kōkeʻe." Pono paused for a moment and looked at Mālie, who glanced over at him with tears falling from her eyes.

"Many decades have passed and I still keep the memories of my father and Aukele alive in my heart and mind. I know that you can't hold or speak to memories, but that is how I survived all these years. Then, we lost Kahoku and I couldn't believe that another family member was taken from me--from all of us. I just couldn't make sense of it all until I spoke with Ke Aliʻi after Kahoku's funeral. That is when I knew that I needed to return to Kōkeʻe. I just wanted to see if I could find any more clues that would shed some light on what happened to those we lost. I should have informed you both before going up there alone," said Pono, apologetically.

Puzzled, Mālie turned to Ke Ali'i. "What is Pono talking about, Dad?"

"I didn't piece everything together until I saw an alarming picture hanging on Kahoku's bedroom wall. I spoke with Pono shortly after," responded Ke Ali'i.

"What picture are you speaking of, Dad? The only pictures in Kahoku's room are just photos of surfing tournaments or fishing expeditions that he went on with his friends."

"Mālie," said Ke Ali'i, "the truth of the matter is that even though authorities closed Pono's case years ago because they could not find any more evidence, I think that I have found a reason to continue investigating, and it is because of what happened to Kahoku and because of the picture that I found in his bedroom."

Mālie held up her hand and shook her head. "Again, Dad, what picture are you referring to?" asked Mālie. "The only pictures on Kahoku's wall are those of his friends and surfing tournaments," reiterated Mālie, who was visibly exhausted.

Ke Ali'i reached into his duffel bag, took the picture out, and showed it to Mālie. "I don't see anything out of the ordinary, Dad. It's just a picture taken from the deck of the fishing boat that Kahoku and his friends rented last summer. The only remarkable thing I see is the huge ahi that they are pulling up into the boat," said Mālie.

"If you look closely, you will see the fin of a shark in the background," said Ke Ali'i as he pointed to a black mark on the picture. "It looks like a thin black distortion because the camera is focused on the boys and the ahi that they are bringing up into the boat."

"I don't see a fin, Dad."

"Look closely, Mālie. The entire dorsal fin is colored black."

Mālie strained both of her tired, swollen eyes in order to see the fin that Ke Ali'i adamantly pointed to in the picture. "Okay, I see what you are talking about. But how does a shark fit in to all of this? There was no evidence that Kahoku had been attacked by a shark."

"Kahoku was not attacked by a shark--Kahoku was attacked by a man who is also a shark," stated Ke Ali'i.

Mālie felt the life drain out of her. She was physically and emotionally exhausted after crying so much, and now she was struggling mentally to grasp everything that Ke Ali'i was telling her. "I can't listen to this," said Mālie.

"Mālie, I need you to be strong. I know this is hard to believe, but you need to listen to everything that I am trying to tell you about how Kahoku died and how this is connected to the disappearances of both Pono's wife and his father. Mālie, you need to know who we are before you can start to understand why this is happening to our family," said Ke Ali'i.

"What do you mean, Dad? Are you trying to tell me that someone or some freak killed my son and is now trying to kill our entire family?"

"Yes," said Manu as he quickly interrupted and gently grabbed Mālie's shaking hands. "Something happened to me last night while I was in Kalalau Valley. Someone tried to kill...." Manu's voice started to fade away as Mālie started feeling more and more overwhelmed. The room was spinning, and Mālie felt as though the walls were closing in on her. She quickly took her hand away from Manu and tried to sit up, but couldn't catch her breath.

"Manu, Mālie is hyperventilating. Here, take this paper bag and give it to her," said Pono, as he handed Manu a paper bag that he had found in the kitchen. "Mālie, you need to breathe into the paper bag that Manu is giving you," instructed Pono. Manu knelt down alongside the couch on which Mālie was sitting and handed her the paper bag. "Slowly, Mālie. Try to calm yourself. Just focus on your breathing: one breath after another," advised Pono.

After a few minutes had passed, Mālie started to feel better and gave the paper bag back to Manu, but it was clear to everyone else in the room that she could not tolerate much more. As Pono and Ke Aliʻi stood up and started to walk to the door, Manu signaled over to them to sit back down. "Why don't the two of you stay here tonight?" he asked. "It has gotten late, and Mālie needs to rest, but we still need to finish this discussion. Let's all give ourselves a break and continue this in the morning."

It was now close to seven o'clock in the evening, and Manu knew that Ke Aliʻi was too worried about Mālie to travel back to Oʻahu. Furthermore, Manu knew that it was imperative to discuss everything before they separated again. He knew that they needed to come up with a plan to keep everyone safe, especially after what had happened to him while he was in Kalalau Valley. Ke Aliʻi and Pono looked at each other. "We will stay," said Ke Aliʻi, who along with Pono, walked back to the living room and sat down.

Wehi was sound asleep in her parents' room when Manu came in to check on her. As Manu approached the bed, he saw a tiny puakenikeni flower on Wehi's pillow. *Hmmm, how did this flower get here?* Manu leaned over and gave Wehi a kiss. But before leaving the room, Manu noticed that one of the windows was slightly open. *Strange. I don't remember opening that window this morning and I didn't hear Wehi open the window when we were talking in the family room,* he thought, as he walked over and closed the window before returning to Mālie, Pono and Ke Aliʻi.

"Mālie, did you open the bedroom window before breakfast?" asked Manu as he walked back into the family room.

Mālie was still recovering on the couch, but softly answered, "Yes, just a little so that the room wouldn't be so stuffy."

Manu let out a sigh of relief. *At least I can keep my family safe here at home. Wehi probably climbed out of the open window, picked the flower, climbed back in, and then placed it on her pillow and fell*

asleep, thought Manu, as he went into the kitchen and started preparing dinner for his family--nothing complicated, since breakfast
had been so extravagant. Everyone except Wehi and Mālie ate dinner. Manu's concern for Mālie grew when he noticed that she was
becoming increasingly withdrawn. "Mālie, do you want me to get
you anything?" But Mālie didn't answer him. "I am going to get the
children's rooms ready for your dad and my dad. I will come back
to check on you as soon as I am done," said Manu.

Manu then placed new linens on the beds and put new towels in
the bathroom before returning to the family room. "Okay, gentlemen, try and get some rest and we will continue our ho'oponopono
tomorrow morning. Don't worry about Mālie; I will stay with her for
a while," said Manu, who then went back into the kitchen, cleaned
up the dishes, and took out the trash. He was very tired, since he
had not gotten any sleep the previous night while he was in Kalalau
Valley. "Mālie, let's go to sleep," said Manu, as he returned to the
family room.

"I'm okay, Manu. I just want to sit out here for a little while,"
responded Mālie.

"Okay. I will leave the night light on for you in the hallway.
When you are ready, you can shut it off and come to bed. Good
night, Mālie," said Manu.

"Good night, Manu," answered Mālie.

"I love you, Mālie. We will get through this together, I promise,"
said Manu, who stood in the hallway looking at Mālie for a while
before walking into his room.

"How can they sleep when I cannot?" whispered Mālie. She
was still very frustrated and angry. *I need to get some fresh air*, she
thought as she walked over to the French doors. Her mind was racing. *How could someone kill my son? Why am I the last to know,
and why is everyone being so secretive?* Mālie's head was spinning
from all the new information she had learned, and she started to feel

like the walls were closing in on her again, so she opened the french doors quietly and started walking down the hill toward the beach.

When she arrived at the beach, the sound of the waves gently caressing the rocks on the shoreline immediately comforted her. As Mālie sat down on the sand and let the water wash over her toes, she remembered a moment she had shared with Kahoku. "The last time I was here at this beach you were here with me, my precious child," whispered Mālie as she gazed out on to the horizon and saw the moon's reflection on the smooth, glassy ocean surface. "I miss you so very much, my son." The calm breezes coming off of the ocean carried a familiar, soothing scent that immediately triggered more memories of walking on the beach, catching sand crabs, and building sandcastles with Kahoku.

"I remember bringing you to this beach every week when I was pregnant with Wehi. Manu was putting in overtime to make extra money to finish building our house so we seldom saw each other. But I never felt alone because you were always there, beside me--filling my life with laughter and so much love. Since you have passed away, my son, I try to fill my waking hours with happy thoughts of you, because when I am asleep, I re-live the day that you left us, over and over again, in my dreams. I would give anything to have the opportunity to hold you in my arms once more and tell you that I love you, my dear Kahoku."

Tears were now streaming down Mālie's face. Unable to contain her grief, Mālie pulled her knees up to her chest and wept for several minutes. "I am sorry that I couldn't be there when you needed me the most. I am sorry that I did not protect you! My dear Kahoku, help me understand why someone would take you from me?" cried Mālie, as her body temperature started to rise, and her skin started to feel very hot. She was now perspiring and feeling extremely uncomfortable. But Mālie could not stop thinking about the fact that her son had been murdered. "I can't bring myself to imagine how scared you must have been, at that moment, when you knew that you would not be coming home." Mālie's sadness slowly started slipping away as feelings of hatred and anger started to surface, and before she knew it, she could no longer deny her desire for vengeance as it coursed through her blood and started infecting all of her tissues with its deadly venom.

As she continued to sit on the sand, all Mālie could focus on was how the ocean seemed to crawl up to meet her. The cool feeling of the water beckoned her to come closer and dive in. Unable to control herself, and behaving as if she were in a stupor, Mālie quickly succumbed to the ocean's enticement and dove into the nearest wave, which shimmered like silver stars under the moonlight as it crested a few feet from where she had been sitting.

As soon as the cool water enveloped her body, Mālie immediately felt rejuvenated and her once-troubled mind was now focused and clear. All her worries seemed to leave her as she swam farther and farther out toward the one- mile buoy. Never before had she felt so free and powerful. She was finally at peace. *This is what I needed*, she thought, and before she knew it, she had passed the buoy and reached the tiny island, which was about a mile and a half from the beach. It was at that moment that Mālie realized she had not come up for air since diving into the ocean. *How is this possible? How could I have traveled all this way without surfacing for air?* But her body could not stop swimming. It was on auto pilot. *This is effortless!* thought Mālie, as she continued to swim past the island and farther out from shore.

Suddenly, without warning, Mālie became aware of a very big shape swimming above her. All of her senses were on overdrive. Immediately she knew that it was a tiger shark. Fear initially gripped her entire body, but then pure instinct kicked in. As Mālie ascended to the ocean's surface, the large tiger shark quickly swam away and eventually disappeared into the dark, cool water.

Now cruising along with the ocean currents, Mālie started becoming addicted to the silky feel of the salt water that gently glided along the contours of her body. The ocean environment had become intoxicating to her, and as she continued to swim, Mālie also started to feel more at home in the ocean, more so than she ever felt on land. But as Mālie continued to test out her new strength and speed, an insatiable hunger started to fester deep within.

Mālie had now traveled out about five miles from the beach before noticing that her ability to control her actions was slipping away. Fear started to take hold of her when she finally realized that she was on auto pilot and swimming out farther to hunt for food. What had started out as an exhilarating experience was now quickly deteriorating into a very scary reality and if she could not control her desire to hunt, Mālie would be lost forever to the ocean.

Back at home, Wehi suddenly woke up and grabbed her boar's tooth necklace. She was perspiring profusely and her pulse was racing.

"Dad, wake up! Mom is in trouble!"

Manu quickly jumped out of bed. "Wehi, your mom is in the family room. Don't worry. Settle down. We are all okay," said Manu, as he tried to calm Wehi down.

Both Pono and Ke Ali'i had now rushed into the room. "Mom is in trouble, Grandpa Ke Ali'i! We have to help her!" yelled Wehi.

Ke Ali'i ran into the family room, then checked the entire house and the yard before rushing back to Manu's room. "I can't find Mālie anywhere in the house or on the property, and all the cars are still parked in the driveway."

"She must have gone on foot, but where?" asked Pono.

"Kahoku and Mālie sometimes used the trail behind our house

to walk down to the beach. Maybe we should check the beach," said Manu.

"I will fly over the area," said Pono.

"Okay. Manu and I will take the car down to the beach. If we find Mālie, how will we let you know?" asked Ke Ali'i.

"Don't worry. I will circle back to check on you," said Pono as he quickly ran out of the house.

In the meantime, Manu, Ke Ali'i, and Wehi, got into the car and headed to the beach. After several minutes had passed, Pono joined them on the beach after circling over the area. "There is no one on the roads or around the beach area," reported Pono.

"The only other place we haven't checked is in the ocean," said Ke Ali'i.

"I will circle over the little island out there," said Pono. Manu quickly grabbed Wehi, pulled her over to where he was standing, and covered her eyes with his hands before both Pono and Ke Ali'i transformed into their 'aumākua.

"My wife is somewhere out there, yet all I can do is stay here on the beach. How will I live with myself if Mālie has been taken like Kahoku? How can I ever look at myself in the mirror knowing that I was not strong enough to protect my family?" Manu looked over at Wehi and started to weep.

"Don't worry, Dad," said Wehi, as she gave Manu a big hug. "Grandpa Pono and Grandpa Ke Ali'i will find Mom." Manu then wiped the tears from his eyes.

Meanwhile, unbeknownst to Manu and Wehi, who were back on the beach, Mālie was just about to fall victim to her voracious appetite. She had come upon a slow-swimming Hawaiian monk seal, who had been injured in discarded fishing nets. Mālie started picking up speed and quickly ascended from the ocean floor toward the surface where the seal was. She had lost all control over her 'aumakua and could no longer resist its desire to eat.

Just as her jaws opened to take that first bite, Mālie was hit fast and hard from the side, causing her to miss the seal. Although she was alarmed by the quickness and strength of the large figure that had rammed into her, Mālie's resolve to eat the seal prohibited her from leaving the area. As she started swimming back to the seal, which was now floundering at the surface, the large figure hit her again--but this time it was from below, flipping Mālie onto her belly and propelling her to the surface of the water. There Mālie floated for a couple of minutes, in a trance-like state. When she finally regained consciousness, she started struggling to swim.

What once felt so effortless and natural now felt taxing and uncomfortable. The water was not welcoming anymore. *Was it all just a bad dream? What am I doing all the way out here?* thought Mālie as she continued to tread water in the middle of the bay. But before panic could set in, Mālie felt big talons grab her arms and lift her gently from the water. As Pono carried Mālie over to Manu and Wehi, who were waiting for her on the beach, Mālie could feel her voracious appetite start to slip away, as the wind continued to gently blow through her long black hair and over her slender body.

"Mommy! I was so worried about you!" shouted Wehi, as she and Manu ran up to where Pono had gently placed Mālie. Wehi quickly covered Mālie with a towel that she kept in her surf bag in the trunk of the car. Both Ke Ali'i and Pono had now emerged from the shadows and rushed over to help Manu and Wehi tend to Mālie, who looked very weak and disheveled.

"Let's give Mālie a few minutes to get readjusted," said Pono.

"Is she going to be okay, Grandpa Pono?" asked Wehi.

"Yes, Wehi. I am going to be all right," answered Mālie, unexpectedly.

"Let's go home before someone sees us," said Manu as he lifted Mālie to her feet and helped her walk over to the car.

After Mālie sat down in the car, she pulled Wehi close to her. "I am sorry that I made you worry so much, Wehi."

"Mālie, why did you leave the house?" asked Manu.

"I don't remember everything, Manu. What was I doing out there in the ocean?" Mālie brushed her long wet hair back, then looked over at Ke Aliʻi. "All I remember is flying through the air and then seeing Manu and Wehi on the beach--but where is Ben and his helicopter?"

"Don't worry, Mālie. You will piece all of this together after you have rested and your mind comes to terms with who you are," answered Ke Aliʻi, as he kissed Mālie gently on the forehead before shutting her car door and getting into the passenger's seat. As soon as everyone was seated, Manu started the car.

"I thought I had lost you," said Manu as looked at Mālie through the rear view mirror. "Forgive me for not telling you the reason for this ho'oponopono, Mālie. I just found out about all of this last night during the standoff in Kalalau Valley. I lost control of the situation, and before I realized it, I was falling toward the rocks below. My last thought was that I would never see you or Wehi again and then, all of a sudden, my dad saved me. When we got up to the top, Dad informed me that our family is being hunted by these creatures."

"You mean one of my kind," whispered Mālie.

"What do you mean, one of your kind?" asked Manu.

"I mean a manō--a shark, like my father and myself. I am slowly starting to remember bits and pieces of what just happened to me," replied Mālie.

"There are many things that we need to say to each other," interrupted Ke Aliʻi, as Manu parked the car in the driveway. "Let us get out of this car and into the house before we continue. Come on, Wehi. Help me take your mom inside."

"Okay, Grandpa Ke Aliʻi," answered Wehi.

After they had all sat down in the family room, Pono addressed everyone. "We should thank Ke Akua [God] for bringing Mālie home safely. In light of what has just happened, both Ke Aliʻi and I realize that we should have been more forthright with all of you. Now that Mālie has experienced the strength and intensity of the ʻaumākua, it is of the utmost importance that we tell all of you about the rules that govern the ʻaumākua."

Then Ke Aliʻi spoke. "Whomever is responsible for taking Kahoku from all of us and trying to kill Manu last night will undoubtedly try again soon. I know that we all have thoughts of seeking vengeance for Kahoku, but we need to overcome these feelings. They will paralyze our minds and kill us slowly, from the inside out. Don't let this happen! Hold strong. I know this can be very difficult to do, as negative thoughts can easily creep up into your poʻo [head], but try to remember the love we share for one another. Justice will come, but it should not come at the expense of another's life."

"The code of the ʻaumākua is simple. We do not use our gifts to wantonly harm or kill. Instead, we use our gifts to protect those around us," began Pono.

Mālie started to fidget with her hands. Seeing how disheveled and lost she was, Ke Aliʻi walked over to her. "Mālie, have you heard what Pono and I have said?"

Mālie looked up at Ke Aliʻi. "Dad, I feel ashamed because I did let hate into my heart. I remember now how I ended up on the beach. After you told me how Kahoku was killed, I allowed negative thoughts to fill my mind. I became consumed by the need for vengeance."

Ke Aliʻi turned around and looked over at Pono, who looked very dismayed. "Please continue, Pono. Tell them everything about the code of the ʻaumākua. If we do not, we risk losing our children to the animal instincts of the ʻaumākua. We cannot let that happen!"

"Grandpa Ke Ali'i," interrupted Wehi, "can I please speak to everyone? I have something very important to say. I need to tell everyone what happened to me." Seeing how determined Wehi was to tell her story, and knowing that she was the one who alerted them to Mālie's disappearance, Ke Ali'i nodded in agreement then walked over and sat down by Pono.

"I have dreamed of my brother many times since his death. Sometimes we are just sitting down in his room and he is reading a story to me, or sometimes we are picking flowers in the yard, but tonight I dreamt that Kahoku took me by the hand and walked with me down to the beach. All of a sudden, the dream changed and I was seeing through the eyes of a very big shark that was hunting a seal. Then I heard Mom's thoughts, and I could feel that she was scared and did not want to kill the seal, but she could not stop hunting it. I got very upset because I tried to tell Mom to stop and come home. That is when I woke up and told Dad."

Wehi paused for a moment. *I wonder if I should also tell everyone about what happened to me when I was at the salt ponds?* But as Wehi looked over at Manu and saw how visibly upset he was, she decided not to say anything more. Instead, Wehi returned to her seat next to Mālie.

"What is everyone trying to say? Are you all telling me that Mālie is a manō 'aumakua? What is happening to everyone here? Are we all losing our minds? I must be having one bad dream after another. First, my father swoops in and stops me from falling into the ocean and then transforms from an owl to a man right in front of me. Then tonight, my father-in-law dives into the waves and becomes a shark--and now, you are all telling me that my wife is a shark as well? I must be going mad! You are all crazy, and I don't want my daughter to be subjected to any more this!"

"Manu," said Pono, "whether you choose to believe it or not, this is happening. The 'aumākua are real, and the sooner you accept this, the stronger our family will be. Your daughter already knows more than any of us. I am sorry for not telling you about the ʻaumākua sooner, but you showed no interest in learning more about our culture when you became a teenager. Your son Kahoku, however, loved to listen to my stories about the ʻaumākua and wanted to learn more about our ancestors and their beliefs. His search for knowledge soon culminated when he became an ʻio [hawk]. I was shocked when I witnessed his transformation, because the only two dominant ʻaumākua were the manō and the pueo. The only ʻio I had seen were the wild hawks that fly high over the valleys of the Big Island.

"You can imagine my surprise when I saw your son become an ʻio ʻaumakua. According to the ʻaumākua legend, the ʻio--specifically the ʻio ʻāhinahina [silver hawk]--served only as a beacon of hope and ascended into the heavens, unlike the pueo and manō ʻaumākua, who stayed behind to help all of the Hawaiian people.

"Initially, I did not know where to begin with Kahoku's training because he was an ʻio, not a pueo. But Kahoku didn't care; he just wanted me to train him in the same manner that I would train another pueo ʻaumakua. As time went on, I began to challenge Kahoku's abilities, and I soon realized that he had far exceeded any of my expectations. There was nothing that he could not do when he was an ʻio aumakua. Manu, your son excelled at every skill I taught him! Kahoku was so honored to have the gift of the ʻio that he wanted to learn more about his ʻaumakua, but I did not have all the answers.

"I struggled with the thought of taking Kahoku to the elders so that he could get the answers he needed, because I did not know if I could trust them. Instead, I just kept telling Kahoku that he needed to be patient and continue practicing because the answers he sought would come to him when the time was right. I should have just told Kahoku the truth! I should have just told him that I did not have all the answers he needed. Instead, I pretended that I knew everything.

My pride caused all of this to happen! I was supposed to protect him, but I failed."

"Why are you telling me this now, Dad?" asked Manu.

"I just want you to open your mind. I want you to see what is really happening around you," answered Pono.

"Why didn't you show me that you were an 'aumakua when I was a young boy? Why did you keep all of this a secret, Dad?" asked Manu.

"When I was a young boy, I accompanied my 'anakala [uncle] on many of his visits to Ni'ihau, where he enjoyed the company of the island's kūpuna, who, along with my uncle, told me many stories about the 'aumākua. Yet, in spite of the lessons they were trying to teach me, I chose not to pay attention. To me, the legends of the 'aumākua were just stories, just fairy tales. My uncle warned me to not limit my understanding of the world to what was only written down in science books. Maybe if I had been more humble and listened to what my uncle and the other kūpuna were trying to teach me, perhaps we would not be in this situation right now." Pono let out a deep sigh, then looked over at Manu.

"You see, just like you, Manu, I chose to focus only on what was deemed important and notable by society. I put all my energy into studying to become a medical doctor, and in the process, I forgot what I had learned as a young child from my uncle. After he retired from the military, my uncle dedicated the rest of his life to preserving the Hawaiian culture and the 'āina [land]. Because he did not have any children of his own, my uncle tried to teach me as much as he could about the 'aumākua whenever he and I would go up to clean Kōke'e Park or collect medicinal plants for his friend, a kahuna lā'au lapa'au [Hawaiian healer]. My uncle believed that one day I would inherit the gift of our family's 'aumakua--the pueo, so he put up with all my teenage tantrums. I wanted to talk about hot rods and rock and roll, but he would just snicker at me, grab my pepeiao [ear], and then lecture me about the importance of paying more attention to my Hawaiian heritage. I remember how frustrated he would get with both the local people and the malihini [visitors] whenever he would find 'ōpala [trash] dumped in the Kōke'e forest, as well as snakes and other non-native animals that were brought in to our islands by those who were indifferent to sustaining our native plants and wildlife. Although my uncle was at times very intimidating and overbearing, I realize now that all he was trying to do was to impart a greater sense of responsibility to me. My uncle believed that our lives were inextricably tied with our fragile 'āina and moana [ocean], and he wanted me to champion his cause when he was no longer here to do so.

"As I became an adult and made friends with many visitors from other states, I became disenchanted with my uncle's beliefs. Although he was very knowledgeable about our culture and our land, my uncle was apathetic toward Western ideas and would avoid teaching the malihini about our culture. My uncle's heart, for whatever reason, had become so hardened that he could not see that there were people from other walks of life who really wanted to preserve the Hawaiian culture and work with the Hawaiian people. Manu, I never saw my uncle again after I married your mom. He decided to go and live alone in the mountains, and he told my father not to search for him. My father tried to talk him out of leaving, but my uncle's strong will prevailed. All we could do was watch him walk away from us.

"I thought about my uncle, from time to time, but my life with your mom was full of love and laughter and very busy. Before I knew it, we were expecting you, Manu, and I felt like all the angels in Heaven were smiling down on us. The next four years went by really quickly and soon I was graduating from medical school. I had just picked up my cap and gown when I received a call from your mom's dad, Senator Braga. Your mom and her two friends, along with my father, had disappeared on a Kōkeʻe trail. You were with her that day, Manu, but miraculously, you had been found safe.

"The search went on for many months, but no one found any more clues about what had happened on that day. It was during this time that I found myself having very vivid dreams about searching for Aukele and my father from high above the forest canopy. But the end result was the always the same: I would wake up in a cold sweat on my porch floor. This dream occurred over and over again for a couple of weeks until one windy morning, when I awoke and found myself lying on a narrow ledge in the Kōkeʻe canyon. My first thoughts were *How did I get here? How am I going to get home?* The ledge that I had woken up on was too far down in the canyon to climb onto without any rappelling gear. I couldn't do anything, and there was no use in screaming for help, because no one would hear me. I had no other option but to wait for help, but who would even venture into that remote area? I waited for many hours, hoping to catch a glimpse of goat hunters or park rangers, but when the daylight diminished, I realized that no one would come to help me.

"As my fear grew, my heart rate increased, and I became nauseous. My skin felt as though it were peeling away from by body, and I felt a tingling throughout my legs and arms. The pain was so unbearable that it caused me to black out, but when I regained consciousness, I felt more powerful than I had ever felt before. I was no longer afraid. All of my senses were heightened and my fear of heights was nonexistent! I lifted myself high above the ledge, challenging the wind currents without hesitation or fear. What I was experiencing then has continued to amaze me to this very day. I was flying!

"But as I was on my way home, I started feeling extremely hungry, and my thoughts became focused on hunting. It was a miracle that at that moment I was able to remember one rule that my uncle and the other kūpuna had repeatedly told me regarding the 'aumākua--never give in to its most primal desire to kill for food. With whatever tiny bit of control I could muster up, I fought this overwhelming desire because I knew that if I failed, I would succumb to every other primal need and eventually lose control over the pueo 'aumakua." Pono paused for a moment to look at everyone. Manu, who was seated next to Mālie and Wehi, started shaking his head from side to side.

Ke Aliʻi then spoke out. "Manu, Mālie, please listen to what Pono is going to tell you. You need to know how important it is to control your 'aumakua."

"If you give in to the intense desire to kill and eat while you take the form of the animal that provides you with your power, you will eventually lose your humanity. Over time, just like a drug addict lives only for getting high, you live only to kill for survival, and when you reach this point, you no longer are human, just animal," concluded Pono.

Ke Aliʻi walked over to Mālie, who was staring at the floor. "I will never forget the moment that I first transformed into the manō 'aumakua," he said, as he gently reached over and grabbed both of his daughter's hands. "While away on a reconnaissance mission, my buddy and I got separated from our team. A storm had reached our location, and the waves that it generated started pounding our zodiac at an alarming rate. An exceptionally large wave flipped our zodiac over, but we were able to right the zodiac and everyone--except my buddy, managed to get back in. I searched for him by scanning the area around the zodiac, but I could not see him, so I dove into the ocean.

"The only way I could find my buddy was to let the ocean currents carry me in the same direction that they had carried him. I closed my eyes and calmed my thoughts. All I could hear was the beating of my heart. Shortly after that, I realized that I was swimming under the water at a very fast speed, without the need to surface for air.

"I couldn't believe the new abilities I had acquired, but I was too preoccupied with finding my buddy. Like a spider that feels every vibration on its web, I could feel the vibration of everything around me, and because of this new ability, I was able to locate my buddy. As I reached out to grab him, I realized that I did not have any arms to do so; that's when I knew what I had become and why I felt so at home under the water. I had heard my ill-tempered uncle boast about our family 'aumakua many times, but I never believed him. He was always drunk, and his visits would often culminate with him and my grandfather getting into some sort of physical altercation.

"But despite the disdain I have for my uncle, I am grateful that he did mention that our family 'aumakua was the shark; otherwise, I would have not been able to deal with the sudden change that I experienced while rescuing my buddy. As I lifted my buddy up to the surface of the ocean, I realized that the storm had passed, and that the rest of my team had already been rescued by a fishing vessel. Luckily, they had left the empty zodiac, and I was able to push my buddy into it. I then grabbed a hold of one of the ropes attached to the zodiac with my teeth and just started swimming toward the shallows of one of the islands in the region.

"At this point, my hunger was starting to completely overrun me. There were many other sharks and fish in the water, and as I was starting to lose control and give in to my hunger and hunt them, my buddy started moving around in the zodiac. I finally was able to take hold of myself. Shortly after, I returned to my human form.

"As I pulled my buddy onto the shore, I still could not come to terms with what I had just experienced. My mind was struggling to integrate the shark's senses and abilities into my human make up. Basically, I was having a hard time making sense of it all. I have since come to realize that I was experiencing the molehu [half-light] state, wherein your head feels like it is vibrating from the entire experience as an ʻaumakua. It took some time, but I became used to it," said Ke Aliʻi.

"Yes," concurred Pono, "it is the point of assimilation in which both your ʻaumakua form and your human form talk with one another to make sure that your conscience is clear and that you have not caused harm to innocent people. It occurs right at the same time that you become human again. My uncle used to say that molehu could be thought of in the same manner as the dichotomous sky above: when the night sky relinquishes its control to the first morning light--right at that moment before the sun takes over, the moon reports everything that occurred during the sun's absence. I have heard from experienced kūpuna that those who use their ʻaumākua to perform evil deeds no longer experience molehu because they no longer have a conscience. These are the very people that we are dealing with," said Pono, as he stared at Mālie and Manu.

Both Pono and Ke Aliʻi were so preoccupied with sharing as much information as they could that they did not notice how much time had passed. Soon the sun began to rise and the wild roosters started singing their morning songs. The breeze coming down from Mount Waiʻaleʻale cooled the entire house, and carried in the scent of plumeria, which freshened up the stuffiness of the family room. Mornings always made Wehi feel safe and rejuvenated, but this morning made her feel different. Her family was not safe, and Wehi knew that it would be a long time before they would feel that way again.

"From now on, we will all have to be more vigilant. Despite how difficult it is going to be, we will have to find a way to go on living our lives just as everybody else does," mentioned Ke Aliʻi, as he looked over at everyone in the room.

After a few minutes had passed, Pono walked into the kitchen and made hot chocolate for everyone. Shortly afterward, all the adults fell asleep in the family room, but Wehi was still pondering over what had just happened to her family. Unable to fall asleep, Wehi walked into Kahoku's room and grabbed a picture of him. "I miss you so much, Big Brother, but I am more aware than ever before that you are not too far away." A surge of courage came over Wehi as she made a promise to Kahoku to protect their family no matter what happened. "I am not going to let anything or anyone harm our family," she whispered, as she hugged Kahoku's picture.

The boar's tooth started feeling warm against Wehi's skin again, but her heart wasn't pounding like it had done in the past. "That's it," she whispered as she looked down at Kahoku's picture and then grabbed her necklace. "If my heart beats really fast when my necklace gets warm, then you are telling me that our family is in danger. If my necklace gets warm but my heart does not go crazy, then I know that you, big brother, are just here listening to me." Wehi smiled. She had come to understand the different signals that radiated from her boar's tooth necklace. Immediately, a feeling of warmth and comfort enveloped Wehi, and a sense of peace permeated through her soul, as she finally came to realize that she was not alone.

Chapter 8:

OLD RIVALS, NEW FEARS

The waves hitting the shores of Kē'ē beach on the island of Kaua'i let out a rhythmic beat that echoed far up into the high cliffs of the Nā Pali forest reserve. This area had long been revered as the place that the gods retreated to, since access into or out of Nā Pali was severely limited due to its prodigious, chiseled cliffs, which sharply rose over four-thousand feet above the ocean. It was here that Pono's nemesis, Kalei, found her perfect hiding place, although she preferred to call it "her sanctuary."

For almost forty years Kalei had lived here in seclusion from all other people, all of whom she found to be trivial, at best. Her mean-spirited temper and unceasing devotion to her mother, Kawahine, left Kalei devoid of personal relationships. Though she was quite attractive, Kalei's incessant need to bully all other 'aumākua who she worked with, gave rise to her reputation as a Hawaiian harpy. Sadly, a young visitor who was just about to meet Kalei for the first time, would soon realize just how true the rumors were.

The makani (wind) continued to stir up the ocean below the cliffs and was now launching a massive assault on the limited shrubs that surrounded Kalei's sea cave when two visitors trepidatiously made their way in.

"This goat you bring me, Kawika, is small and will feed only one of us," bellowed Kalei, who was still in the shadows at the far end of her sea cave.

"The hunt for wild pig will have to wait until tomorrow night," announced Kawika, as he warily walked into Kalei's sea cave with his younger friend. Kalei's big dark-brown eyes widened, as she scanned over her two visitors that had come to pay her homage.

"I know what we can do! Why don't the three of us participate in a little tournament? The winner will get to eat the entire goat by themselves--no need to share!" shouted Kalei, as she stepped out of the darkness. "However, I just want to let both of you know that this tournament will involve a little shedding of blood, maybe even clipping of wings, but I promise that I won't severely injure you," cackled Kalei, as she pursed her lips a bit, then slowly started approaching her two visitors that were holding the injured goat. "Are you afraid of me, young man?" Kalei had noticed that every time she took a step forward, her young visitor took several steps backward. "Perhaps you do not want to partake in this meager meal because you fear that you will sever your family ties with the 'aumākua. Don't believe everything you hear. Once the mighty kāhuna who enforce the code are all dead, the 'aumākua will no longer be held to such antiquated rules of conduct!"

"Please, Kalei, we have brought this goat for you in good faith and do not wish to fight you for it," responded Kawika.

"How dare you talk out of turn, Kawika! You have grown lazy and weak! This tournament may be exactly what you need!" Kalei was now running toward them, along a narrow ledge that circled the inside of her sea cave. In a matter of seconds, with a few feet left between her and her frightened guests, Kalei jumped off the ledge and free-fell a couple of feet, only to come back in pueo form. She now hovered in front of her two male guests. Her sheer size was intimidating, but more so was her resolve to take the goat forcibly away from Kawika. Panic set in, and Kawika lost his grip on the goat that he had brought to her. As it plummeted down to the water below, Kalei quickly snatched it up in her large, sharp talons.

"You are useless, Kawika!" she shouted, now back in her human form on the opposite side of the sea cave, where she stored most of her personal belongings. Under Kalei's callused feet lay a badly injured goat, whose blood slowly started to trickle down a tiny crevice and drip into the huge, green-colored pool of water that filled the sea cave beneath them.

As Kalei glared at her two visitors with her human eyes, the goat, despite being tired and very weak, tried to escape from beneath her feet. In what seemed to be a split second, Kalei's filthy, callused human feet became powerful sharp talons that quickly put an end to the goat's struggle and annoying bleating. "Your ability to transform quickly between human and pueo form is testament to your power," said Kawika, who was still visibly shaken by Kalei's quickness and strength.

"Don't try to weasel your way out of this, Kawika. You need to prove your worth to me. I will not have incompetent fools in my circle!" The giant waves crashing outside caused the water in the sea cave to rise and fall beneath Kalei and her guests.

"The storm is getting worse. Perhaps I should take our newest--and youngest--member home, if that is all right with you, Kalei?" asked Kawika, as he glanced over at Kalei then looked at his younger companion.

"No backbone whatsoever! You disgust me, Kawika!" yelled Kalei, who had just finished putting her clothes back on. "Have you heard any news of Pono?"

"Pono is still mourning over the death of his grandson. Perhaps this is not the right time to revisit your desire to seek revenge on

Pono for what his wife, Aukele, did to you so many years ago."

Kalei's eyes widened. "You are as stupid as you are ill-informed. I did not ask you to keep an eye on Pono because of the scar that Aukele placed on me!" Kalei's young visitor slowly started shuffling away from Kawika. "Where are you going?" asked Kalei, as she directed her gaze toward her young visitor.

"I just want to give you the room you need to discipline Kawika, if that is what you intend to do," said the young man, sheepishly.

Kalei let out a cynical laugh. "The storm outside has intensified. I would not be a gracious hostess if I just let you leave under these circumstances. Perhaps I should tell you about the incident that Kawika was referring to," said Kalei, as she walked toward the young man. "Better yet, would you like me to show you how Aukele placed this scar on me so many years ago?" The young man fell to his knees and quivered.

"In the short time that I have been here, I have deduced that you are very powerful, Kalei--both physically and mentally--and that you will not hesitate to hurt or maim anyone who challenges you, Great One. I can only surmise that you have no weaknesses and that you expect the same from all those who serve you. I will never again move without first hearing you tell me to do so."

"My, my. I will have to watch you more closely, young man. You see, I do not fall so easily for smooth talkers." Kalei grabbed the young man's mouth with her right hand and squeezed both of his lips together with her fingers until he winced from the pain. "Let this be a lesson for you, young man--do not try to flatter me again." Kalei looked over at Kawika before looking back at her young visitor. "You both will spend the entire evening in this cave and listen to my story. It will be a pleasant evening for me, but I am sure that it will be a long, grueling night for you both," said Kalei as she cackled loudly.

Both Aukele and Kalei's lineage could be traced back to very powerful kāhuna who were skilled in the Hawaiian magical arts. There were many different types of kāhuna that existed throughout Hawai'i. Most of them were highly proficient in different trades or crafts, like canoe-making, navigation, and agriculture. But a few, notably the kāhuna 'anā'anā, were well-versed in using prayer to bring sickness and death upon their enemies and were also known to send fireballs to destroy villages. These malevolent kāhuna were not social at all, and preferred to live in seclusion.

Another group of kāhuna focused on spiritual matters. The kāhuna nui was a small but elite group of individuals that had mastered more than one skill. They found fulfillment in teaching the Hawaiian people to respect the land and each other. Because they were also very intellectual, the kāhuna nui welcomed all opportunities to learn different art forms, and a few of them were rumored to have attained a connection with ancestral spirits.

But when a fierce mighty chief from the Big Island started to unify all of the kānaka maoli (native Hawaiians), all kāhuna started to worry about their future. Many of them, including the kāhuna nui and kāhuna 'anā'anā, fled to the island of Kaua'i--the last stronghold against unification.

Life on the island of Kaua'i was a welcome respite for the intellectual kāhuna nui, who found it easy to immerse themselves in the culture of the native people. They marveled at the skills of all of Kaua'i's kāhuna, but were especially drawn to Kaua'i's kāhuna lā'au lapa'au, who used their knowledge to heal sick people with indigenous plants and natural approaches. Life on Kaua'i, however, was not welcoming for the kāhuna 'anā'anā, who loathed the peaceful, easy-going nature of the island's inhabitants. Despite their fear of the mighty chief, most of them left Kaua'i and returned to their homes on the Big Island. But a small family of kāhuna 'anā'anā could not return to the Big Island because their father was very old and frail and would not survive the journey home. For his sake alone, his two daughters tried very hard to keep him comfortable as he lived out his last days on Kaua'i.

While trying to take care of an ailing father, one of the daughters of this powerful but elderly kahuna 'anā'anā met and fell in love with a young man--a kahuna lā'au lapa'au. As their love blossomed, so too did the young woman's desire to learn from the young man and his family, who had acquired many other valuable skills from the kāhuna nui that had also sought refuge on Kaua'i. Despite the ongoing war for unification, both lovers were able to find happiness, and continued to meld their skills together to protect Kaua'i's people.

The other daughter of the old, powerful kahuna 'anā'anā, was devastated by her sister's betrayal. After her father died, the spiteful sister tried to use her dark magic to kill the young kahuna lā'au lapa'au and all of his family. To her dismay, however, the young man's magic was too strong. Disappointed that she was not powerful enough to kill the young kahuna lā'au lapa'au, the spiteful sister returned to the Big Island. Her hatred toward the young man who stole her sister away from her would eventually be passed on to all of her descendants and would sadly find its way into the lives of two young women: Aukele and Kalei.

Aukele was a descendant of the sister who fell in love with the young kahuna from Kaua'i, and Kalei was a descendant of the sister who returned to the Big Island. Although neither Aukele nor Kalei knew that they were related, a strange twist of fate brought the two distant cousins together when Kalei's mother, Kawahine, moved to Kaua'i to work with a Hawaiian man named Makoa. This move came at a very awkward time for Kalei, who had just experienced her first transformation into a pueo ʻaumakua.

But despite Kalei's newly acquired power, Kalei was still a teenager. Although Kawahine had kept Kalei isolated for most of her life, she could no longer afford to do so because Kauaʻi's smaller community would take notice of Kalei's truancy. Though Kalei detested her mother's resolve to enroll her in school, Kawahine had no other option. Any hint of impropriety on her part would draw the attention of authorities and ultimately put an end to the illegal project that she was working on with Makoa.

On Kalei's first day of school, Aukele, who was the most amicable girl in Kalei's homeroom class, welcomed Kalei with open arms and introduced her to all of her friends. Kalei, however, was not used to being in a group--she wanted nothing to do with Aukele or anyone else. Years of living in seclusion with only her mom to interact with, had left Kalei devoid of any social skills.

However, after two years had passed, and Kalei developed into a young woman, her desire to be popular superseded her need for solitude. Kalei started paying more attention to the way she dressed, signed up for after school activities, and even made a few friends. During the start of her senior year in high school, Kalei decided to run for Homecoming Queen. But when Aukele's name was called, Kalei was immediately overcome with envy as she watched how all the young men whistled and fawned over Aukele. Not wanting to get up and join in the celebration, Kalei just sat in her seat and looked over at Aukele, who was smiling from ear to ear. *I hate you, Aukele,* thought Kalei. As she continued to glare at Aukele, Kalei felt her blood boil over with jealousy, all the while never noticing that her downward spiral into insanity had just begun.

As their senior year in high school progressed, Aukele was constantly reminded that Kalei did not like her. Day after day, slanderous catcalls aimed at Aukele echoed throughout the classroom, cafeteria and school halls. Then, one month before graduation,

Aukele overheard Kalei gossiping about her to another girl in the school bathroom. After Kalei's companion left the bathroom, Aukele emerged from her bathroom stall and walked over to the bathroom sink, where she was immediately confronted by Kalei. "My mother thinks that your father is full of himself, Aukele. In fact, your entire family is just a bunch of highfalutin locals who think that they can use their money to control every one around them."

Despite feeling hurt over Kalei's remarks, Aukele paid no attention to Kalei and started to comb her hair back into a ponytail. "Did you hear me, Rich Girl," seethed Kalei. Still, Aukele did not answer. Then, out of the blue, Kalei grabbed Aukele by her hair and started pulling her back into one of the bathroom stalls. Aukele, who was suddenly caught off guard by Kalei's aggression, spun around and inadvertently gouged the left side of Kalei's face with her comb. Kalei immediately let go of Aukele's hair and looked directly at her. "I'm not through with you yet. Just you wait, Aukele. I'll get you back for this!" Kalei then turned around and ran out of the bathroom. Though Kalei never physically confronted Aukele again, she still lurked behind the scenes; drumming up gossip about Aukele and her family.

After graduating from high school, Aukele went off to college, and shortly after, married Pono. Aukele and Pono then welcomed their son, Paul "Manu" Nahele into their family and settled into a small house by the university on the island of Oʻahu. Two years later, both Pono and Aukele decided that it would be best if Aukele moved back to Kauaʻi and got settled in before Pono graduated and returned to Kauaʻi to start his medical practice. When Aukele brought Manu home to Kauaʻi, it had already been several years since her high school graduation. The island was still very rural and Aukele loved that not much had changed. She and Manu quickly settled into a little cottage near her parents' home.

One day, while enjoying a stroll through her father's fruit farm,

Aukele, who had been under the impression that most of her high school classmates had left Kaua'i, was shocked to see Kalei working in one of her father's pineapple fields. Despite what had happened between them when they were in high school, Aukele was still very happy to see one of her classmates. "Hello, Kalei!" shouted Aukele, as she walked out into the pineapple field.

"Aloha, Aukele. It has been a long time since I last saw you. How have you been?" asked Kalei.

"I have been doing well, Kalei. It is nice to see you after all these years."

"It is nice to see you too, Aukele," said Kalei, as she walked over and gave Aukele a hug. "Look at me," said Kalei, pretending to wipe away tears that never fell onto her cheek, "I guess these past few years have made me into a big softie."

"Don't worry about it, Kalei. I am just so happy that we can finally talk to one another."

"Well, Aukele, I better get back to work."

"Okay Kalei. I am sure that I will see you again and that we will get to spend more time with each other." Aukele then turned around, walked out of the pineapple field, and continued her stroll through her father's fruit farm.

"You are so gullible, Aukele," whispered Kalei, as she picked up her spade and continued to poke holes into the black plastic mulch that was covering the pineapple field. "I can't wait to see your face when you realize that I was just putting on a charade. But for now, I just have to bide my time and pretend that I am your friend. When the right moment comes around, I will finally put an end to your father's investigation which almost cost my mother and I our freedom." Kalei stopped for a moment to wipe away the beads of sweat that were dripping down her forehead, adjusted her straw hat, and then continued poking holes into the black plastic mulch.

After she had placed fresh pineapple crowns into the holes that she had just made, Kalei walked over to the little country store, bought a cold drink, and phoned her mother, Kawahine. "Makuahine [mother], your plan is coming together nicely. I will soon be able to gather more information for you from the senator's unsuspecting daughter, Aukele. I am also keeping my eye on the girl that you had me pick up from Maui. I still don't know why you wanted me to bring her to Kaua'i, but she does whatever I tell her to do." Kalei hung up the phone after she had given her report to Kawahine. Since graduating from High School, Kalei had become Kawahine's right-hand assistant and thus was intimately involved in the illegal smuggling project that Kawahine and Makoa had started. But when an investigation was launched to capture all those involved in the smuggling operation, both Kawahine and Kalei quickly retreated to the summer home of Kawahine's late mother, Kekipi, on the Big Island. After some time had passed, Makoa informed Kawahine that Senator Braga was looking to hire several workers for his fruit farm. Kawahine immediately decided to send Kalei back to Kaua'i. But just as Kalei was about to leave, Kawahine asked her to first stop over on the island of Maui, and convince a young woman named Kēhau to go with her and work on Senator Braga's fruit farm.

After Kalei had successfully convinced Kēhau to move to Kaua'i, both women quickly started working for Senator Braga. During this time, the investigation into the illegal smuggling between the Hawaiian Islands, which had taken Mr. Nahele and Senator Braga several years to piece together, was slowly coming to a close. Most of the perpetrators had been apprehended. All that was left for Mr. Nahele and Senator Braga to do was identify and capture the leaders of the organization; then they could finally close the case. But all of the people that they had previously arrested refused to cooperate. Frustrated but still undeterred, Mr. Nahele decided to go and speak with the only other person that could help him: the oldest kahuna on Kaua'i, who lived alone in an isolated cabin up in Kōke'e.

In the midst of this investigation, an unsuspecting Aukele was planning a lūʻau (celebratory feast) for Pono, who was just about to graduate from medical school. A couple months had passed since she and Manu moved back to Kauaʻi and Aukele was looking forward to Pono's homecoming. Aukele was also looking forward to introducing Pono to Kalei, and to her new friend, Kēhau.

On a balmy evening in May, after putting Manu to sleep in his crib, Aukele sat at her kitchen table in her cottage, and started writing down every thing that she needed to do. She was just about to leave the kitchen and go to sleep when she heard someone walking up her front porch.

"Hello, Aukele," said Kēhau, as she knocked softly on Aukele's screen door.

"Aloha, Kēhau," replied Aukele. "How is Martin feeling tonight?"

"He is still under the weather," answered Kēhau as she stepped into Aukele's little cottage. "Marty is just getting over another cold. You know how toddlers are germ magnets. I just came by because I wanted to thank you for watching Marty for me. It has been very hard for me to find a sitter that can care for him," Kēhau then handed Aukele a tray full of warm brownies that she had just baked.

"Thank you for baking these brownies for Manu and me, but you didn't have to go through all that trouble. I enjoy watching Martin and Manu play together. I think that Manu believes that Martin is his little brother," mentioned Aukele.

"Well, I just wanted to show my Aloha to you and your son Manu, for helping take care of Marty when I have to go to work and harvest the pineapple and the lychee in your father's fields," replied Kēhau.

"Don't worry about it, Kēhau. I don't mind at all. Like I mentioned, Manu loves Martin's company. Plus, I enjoy watching the boys chase the chickens around the farm," replied Aukele, as she placed the tray of brownies on the table. "By the way, thank you for always bringing over fresh prawns for us. I love grilling and then eating them with some butter, but I think Manu prefers to keep them as pets. He just loves to play with them."

"You are welcome, Aukele. By the way, do you think that you could watch Marty for me tomorrow? I would like to go and catch some more prawns in your dad's stream that runs behind the pineapple and lychee fields."

"Oh, I am sorry, Kēhau. I am going to be in Kōkeʻe picking maile leaves for my husband's graduation lei."

All of a sudden, Kēhau turned around to see Kalei walking up Aukele's porch. "Aukele," interjected Kalei, "I just overheard that you are going to pick maile for your husband's graduation lei. I can go and help you." Kalei then glanced over at Kēhau, who was already walking down Aukele's porch. "Kēhau!" yelled Kalei, "Come back here. I have a question that I would like to ask you." Kalei chuckled softly to herself as she saw how Kēhau immediately stopped and put her head down before turning around and walking back to Aukele's screen door. "Can you come with us to Kōkeʻe tomorrow? We need your help to pick maile for the graduation lei that Aukele is making for her husband."

"I don't know if I can find a sitter for my son, Kalei."

"Don't worry, Kēhau. I will ask one of the other ladies to watch him," countered Kalei.

"Well, I don't know if Marty will be okay for most of the day with anyone else, Kalei, especially since he is not feeling well and…"

"Don't you see how important this is to our friend, Kēhau? Don't worry about your son. I am sure one of the ladies can watch after him," quipped Kalei.

"Kalei, thank you for your concern," interrupted Aukele, who could feel the tension between the two ladies. "But Kēhau should stay with her son."

"Don't worry, Aukele. You need two strong wāhine [women] to help you pick maile," said Kalei, whose gaze was firmly on Kēhau.

Fearing retaliation from Kalei, Kēhau quickly nodded in agreement. As Aukele closed her screen door and walked over to her telephone to call Mr. Nahele, Kalei took Kēhau firmly by the arm and led her into the pineapple fields. "You will do as I say," ordered Kalei, as she threw Kēhau onto the black plastic mulch that surrounded the newly planted pineapple. Kalei then composed herself and walked back to her cottage, but Kēhau couldn't move. All she could do was look up at the numerous stars plastered across the night sky.

"How I love the sweet smell of the freshly planted pineapple tops and the sound of the gurgling brook that runs behind the fields," whispered Kēhau. Tears started to roll down her cheeks as she picked herself up off the ground and headed back to her cottage and to her son, Martin.

As she opened her screen door, Kēhau wiped away her tears and placed a smile on her face for Martin. "Is everything all right Kēhau?" asked a co-worker who had come over to sit with Martin for a few minutes so that Kēhau could deliver the brownies to Aukele.

"Everything is fine. Thank you for taking care of Marty," replied Kēhau as she handed her co-worker her last small bag of prawns as compensation for watching Martin. As soon as her co-worker had walked away from her cottage, Kēhau lifted Martin up out of his playpen and gave him a big kiss. "Mommy loves you so much, Marty," she cooed as she cradled him in her arms.

In the meantime, Aukele had just finished speaking with her father-in-law, Mr. Nahele, over the phone. She had called to ask him if she could bring two of her friends with her tomorrow to Kōke'e to help her pick maile. Mr. Nahele, who was already going up to Kōke'e to speak with the old kahuna, saw no harm in letting Aukele's two friends tag along with Manu, Aukele, and himself.

After all, the drive to and from Kōke'e was very lengthy, and he could use some company. If they left early enough, they could all return home before it got dark.

The next morning found Aukele packing snacks for Manu and an extra set of hiking boots for herself--in case the footpath leading to the kahuna's house had become soft and muddy from Kōke'e's frequent rainfall. Just as Aukele placed her hiking gear onto her porch, she caught a glimpse of Mr. Nahele's truck parked at her father's home. "Manu," beamed Aukele as she turned around and faced her little son, "Papa Nahele will be here soon. Are you ready to go for a ride on Papa Nahele's truck?"

"Papa's coming!" cheered Manu as he ran around the small kitchen table. Minutes later, Mr. Nahele pulled up next to Aukele's cottage, and a very excited Manu ran out the porch door to greet his grandfather. "Papa, Papa, you're here! Let's go, Papa! Let's go!"

"Manu! How are you, my boy? You are getting so big!"

"Hello, Dad," said Aukele. "As you can see, Manu is very excited about going with you in your truck to Kōke'e."

Mr. Nahele chuckled. "He reminds me of Pono when he was this age. He always wanted to tag along. I wish I could bottle this moment in a glass jar and keep it with me forever. These are the moments that you remember. Shucks, no need to listen to me--I am just a sentimental old fool. Well, I stopped over at your dad's house and told him that you and your two friends would be going with me to Kōke'e. We better get going so we can be home before it gets dark." As Mr. Nahele picked up Manu and headed toward his truck, he saw Kalei and Kēhau walking up the road.

"Papa Nahele, these are the friends I told you about last night. They have been kind enough to volunteer to help me gather the maile leaves for Pono's graduation lei."

"Yes, I remember you telling me that they would be joining us," said Mr. Nahele. "Nice to meet both of you. Well, we better get going!"

Throughout the entire drive up the canyon, all the passengers, except Manu, remained quiet. "Grandpa, I love dis truck!" he shouted, as he maneuvered his little body closer to his grandfather. The truck let out a big "brummmm" as Mr. Nahele shifted into first gear so that the truck would have enough power to climb the steep and winding road up the Kōke'e canyon.

"Manu, this place is also known as the Little Grand Canyon of Kaua'i."

"Papa, what does canyon mean?" Mr. Nahele smiled, reached into the truck's glove box, and pulled out a Spam musubi for Manu to eat.

The drive to the top of Kōke'e would take an additional thirty minutes if the weather held out. Sometimes, however, the weather would change very quickly, and if it started raining, they would have to travel slower as the roads would become slippery. The lush ferns that grew alongside the road gave off a very fresh scent, and a cool mist started to descend upon them as the truck slowly but surely made its way up the canyon. Unsurprisingly, many rain drops started to hit the windshield of the truck, so Mr. Nahele thought it would be safer to stop at the next public rest area and walk the rest of the way.

"Ladies, from here on we will go on foot. The kahuna's house is about two miles from this rest area, and there are many maile leaves along the way."

Aukele got out of the passenger's seat, placed Manu in his baby backpack, and had Mr. Nahele secure it onto her back. A little more than halfway up the footpath to the kahuna's home, Aukele noticed that Kalei and Kēhau were walking very slowly behind her and Mr. Nahele. Aukele had already made many stops along the footpath to fill her bag with maile, but Kalei and Kēhau never seemed to catch up with her.

"I wonder what they are doing?" asked Mr. Nahele, who had been looking back as well. Aukele looked over at her father-in-law and shrugged her shoulders. As Aukele and Mr. Nahele continued to walk farther up the footpath, Kalei and Kēhau continued to fall behind, until they disappeared altogether.

"I guess your helpers just couldn't keep up with an old man and a woman carrying a toddler and a bag of maile," chuckled Mr. Nahele.

"Dad, something is not right here," said Aukele. "I feel as though something bad is about to happen."

"Don't worry. I can see the rooftop of the cabin. We are almost there. I won't take too much time with the kahuna, and then we will head back toward the truck with two bags of maile before your two pupule [crazy] friends come around," said Mr. Nahele. As he turned to continue up the footpath leading to the kahuna's cabin, a loud flutter of wings quickly silenced the beautiful songs of the indigenous forest birds--the 'apapane and 'elepaio.

"Run, Aukele! Run under the thick canopy of the forest! Get off the footpath!" shouted Mr. Nahele, but it was too late. An enormous pueo had already picked up Aukele and Manu and in a matter of seconds, one of the pueo's giant talons had pierced Aukele's right shoulder and ripped Manu's backpack harness. Mr. Nahele ran over to try and free Aukele and Manu from the grip of their captor, but despite his best efforts, he could not jump high enough to reach them. As the enormous pueo kept Mr. Nahele's attention by hovering over him, Kēhau approached him from behind and clobbered him over the head with a rock that she and Kalei had found on the footpath.

Kēhau then let out a heart-wrenching scream as she looked at the bloody rock in her hands. "Look at what you forced me to do, Kalei!" she shouted, as she threw the rock on the ground and looked over at the enormous pueo hovering above her. "I am sorry Aukele. I am so sorry," cried Kēhau as she fell to her knees. Kēhau's invisible shield of innocence that could have protected her from the wrath of the 'aumākua, had shattered and left her vulnerable. Without hesitation, Kalei descended upon Kēhau and used her sharp beak to pierce

Kēhau's heart. For the next few minutes, Kalei hovered over Kēhau, like a vulture over a carcass, to make sure that she was dead.

After Kalei had finally ascertained that Kēhau was no longer alive, Kalei started her ascent above the treetops, still clutching on to a wounded Aukele, who was still attached to the backpack that held her little son, Manu. But as fate would have it, the strap that had been frayed by Kalei's talons--which was also holding the backpack in place over Aukele's shoulders--snapped in half as they were passing over the tallest koa tree. Aukele knew that this was the only chance she would have to save her son. Despite her pain and awkward position, Aukele slid the backpack down her shoulder and placed it directly onto the top branch of the koa tree. *Goodbye, my son. I love you so much,* thought Aukele, as she continued to struggle so that Kalei would not notice that Manu was no longer traveling with them. But with each movement, Aukele's wound worsened and she started to lose a large amount of blood.

As the sun started to descend from the sky and the forest floor started to rustle with the sound of wild pigs foraging through leaves and turning over branches for food, shadows of two big pueo circled over the bodies of Mr. Nahele and Kēhau. They had both witnessed the gruesome tragedy that had recently taken place, from their vantage point in the sky above, but did not interfere. After Kalei had taken Aukele and Manu away, the two pueo continued to circle high above the cabin's rooftop for a while, making sure that there were no hikers or park rangers in the area. Finally satisfied that no one was around, both pueo swooped down in tandem, picked up the bodies of Kēhau and Mr. Nahele, and then started flying toward the island of Niʻihau.

When they arrived at their destination, the two pueo quickly transformed back into men, and were joined by Kalei, who had been waiting for them to arrive. "Why have you brought them here, Kalei?" shouted a gruff, loud voice that boomed over the sounds of the waves crashing into the rocks at the bottom of the damp, dark cave.

"I could not think of any other place where the authorities would not look," said Kalei, her voice a little less authoritative and more childlike. Kalei turned around to look at Aukele, whom she had positioned over a rock that was halfway submerged in the salt water. Aukele was bleeding profusely from the wound inflicted by Kalei's talons and had subsequently lost consciousness. The cold salt water had slowed Aukele's heart rate, but it had also carried her blood into the ocean surrounding the cave.

"She is a descendant of the kahuna'anā'anā and the kahuna lā'au lapa'au. So many generations have passed, but I can still taste her ancestry in her blood. Such is the power of the manō!" Kalei shivered as a very large, muscular man stepped out from the shadows of the partially submerged cave and started walking toward her. Just as Pono was able to change his form slightly and use only the eyes of his pueo 'aumakua when he needed to see in the dark, so too was this large man able to use the ability of the manō to "taste" the blood in the ocean and identify the ancestry of Aukele.

"I have brought the daughter of Senator Braga to you, Makoa," said Kalei as she remained very still.

Makoa did not respond. He just stood right in front of Kalei and continued to look down at her for several minutes before turning away and walking toward Kalei's two counterparts, who immediately fell to their knees. "Your followers are pathetic, Kalei," stated Makoa as he turned and walked away from them. "Manō would never be so submissive. Manō are the true warriors of the 'aumākua. Without the manō's strength our ancestors would never have been able to settle on these islands: they would have been lost to the ocean." Makoa then looked over at Aukele. "You will need to summon your mother here, Kalei, to heal the senator's daughter, or she will die."

"I have already sent for my mother. She should be here shortly," replied Kalei.

"What about these two here?" asked Makoa as he walked up to the bodies of Mr. Nahele and Kēhau, which had been placed side by side on a ledge above the water's reach.

"I had my followers move their bodies before someone found them," answered Kalei.

"Before the moon rises directly above us, have your followers bury these two bodies in the dry sand on the southernmost point of the island. When they have mummified, you will have to return their iwi to the ground on which they perished so that their spirits do not call the night marchers," bellowed Makoa.

"Kalei. Your mother, Kawahine, is here!" announced one of Kalei's followers, who quickly stood up and rushed outside the cave to greet Kawahine. As she entered the damp cave, Kawahine did not exchange any words with either Kalei or Makoa, but instead walked right past them and placed her hands on Aukele. Only then, when her hands touched Aukele, did Kawahine realize who Aukele was.

"Great is your power, descendant of our lost sister, but you are also the child of the haole lawmaker who hunts for us." Holding her right hand at eye level, a flash of light appeared within Kawahine's palm and took the form of a ball of bright red fire. "This fire is not one that will extinguish your life, but it will heal your wounds and hold your spirit to this body. It will also bind your spirit to the sorrow your heart feels. When you awaken, you will remember only that you were involved in a terrible boating accident and that your entire family perished," said Kawahine as she placed the fire into the gaping wound on Aukele's shoulder.

"She will sleep for several days as her body heals, and when she wakes, she will be in a state of despair," said Kawahine, as she pulled Aukele's wedding ring off of Aukele's finger, then looked over at Kalei and Makoa. "Within this time, you must find another man for her to start a new life with: a man who will only tell her what you have told him--no more and no less. This man must also promise to keep her hidden away so that no one will be able to identify her." Kawahine turned and walked away from Aukele and then grabbed Kalei by the shoulder. "Do not forget what we have learned today: Aukele comes from the same lineage as you, Kalei. She too has the power of our ancestors, just as you do. But, she also has the power of the kahuna lāʻau lapaʻau. Therefore, it is imperative that she never regain her memory of who she is. Many legends reference the great skills of the kāhuna of Kauaʻi. They have had many years to learn from other kāhuna who came here to escape the great unification," warned Kawahine.

"I will be leaving now, Kalei. Make sure that you and Makoa discard the remains of these two kānaka correctly, otherwise you will incur the wrath of the night marchers." Kawahine then walked over to the body of Kēhau, the young mother from Maui, and paused for a moment to stare at the fatal wound that Kalei had inflicted upon her. Before leaving, Kawahine turned around and gave Kalei a stern reminder. "Do not let your temper get the best of you. If you kill an innocent person, your ʻaumakua will be taken away from you. This time you were lucky that Aukele's power was strong enough to sustain her life until I got here. Don't think you will be so lucky next time."

As Kalei escorted her mom out of the damp cave, Makoa couldn't help but smile. *That arrogant Kawahine and her pathetic pueo followers found a way to punish Senator Braga and Mr. Nahele for their efforts in stopping our operation, and I didn't have to lift a single finger. But, more importantly, that witch Kawahine has given me a valuable piece of information that could forever change the code of the ʻaumākua. Kawahine is arrogant in her belief that she is smarter than I. Did she think that I would not find important pieces of information within her words of warning to Kalei? I now have all the information that I need to solidify myself as the dominant 'au-makua,* thought Makoa as he exited his cave.

A few minutes later, when Kalei returned to the damp cave, she noticed that Aukele's wounds were healing. Makoa soon returned with a young Hawaiian man. "Keala, you will take this woman as your own and make no mention of the manner in which I gave her to you. This woman will only remember that her family was killed in a boating accident. Eventually, she will comply with your advances," said Makoa. But just as Keala was about to walk toward Aukele, Makoa grabbed him by the arm and glared at him. "You must never talk about this to anyone!" ordered Makoa, as he slowly let go of Keala's arm.

Without further hesitation, Keala picked Aukele up and carried her out of the damp cave. "Makoa was right. You are very beautiful," said Keala, as he softly touched Aukele's face with his fingertips. "I will have no problem keeping this secret, because I want you all to myself. I will make you believe that I rescued you from the wreckage of the boating accident and that I went back to look for the rest of your family; however, despite all of my efforts, I could not find them," said Keala as he continued to stare down at an unconscious Aukele for a couple of minutes. As the moon started to climb higher in the night sky, Keala tightened his grip on Aukele, walked across the sandy beach, and disappeared into the night.

Back at Makoa's cave, Kalei had her followers transform back into their pueo 'aumākua and pick up the bodies of Mr. Nahele and Kēhau. As both followers hovered over Makoa's cave, Kalei reiterated Makoa's instructions. "You heard what you need to do. Hurry up and bury their bodies in the dry sand on the southernmost point of this island. Finish burying them before the moon rests directly overhead."

"Your mother better come through with all her promises," threatened Makoa. Kalei was in no position to argue with him; she was, after all, in a partially submerged cave that exited out into the vast Pacific Ocean. "Your mother, Kawahine, promised that if the manō and the pueo ʻaumākua cooperated, the trans-island underwater tunnel would make us wealthy beyond our imagination," pointed out Makoa.

"That goal was temporarily put on hold because of Senator Braga and Mr. Nahele's investigation. My mother and I have since rectified that, Makoa, and we just need to let some time pass before we can continue with the project," responded Kalei, who was unable to stare directly into the intimidating eyes of Makoa. "The promise is still being kept. We have cleaned up the mess and we are now back on track. Have you not seen the pueo effort in all of this thus far?" retorted Kalei.

"Don't talk down to me, Kalei. I have no respect for you just because the ancients believed the pueo ʻaumākua to be more intelligent than the manō ʻaumākua. Mark my words, this project will never come to fruition. The death of Mr. Nahele will only stop the authorities from discovering our identities. The senator will be sure to find a way to secure all the underwater lava tubes, thus putting an end to our operation. Don't be so smug in your alliances with the other pueo ʻaumākua, either. Anyone with experience in these matters know that alliances can and do change over time. What is mutually beneficial today may not be in an ever-changing tomorrow," scoffed Makoa.

Kalei stood silent for several minutes. She knew that Makoa was very intelligent. Having worked with him on the underwater lava tube project, Kalei realized that the belief of her grandmother, Kekipi, in which the pueo were superior to the manō, was misguided. The truth of the matter was that the manō were just as ingenious as the pueo, but the manō lacked a sense of cohesiveness. By their very nature, most manō were loners, so a man who had the gift of the manō ʻaumakua had to work twice as hard to not give in to its solitary nature.

Kalei also knew that Makoa, who was the descendant of the warrior who went in search for the manō ʻaumakua, was very clever. She had been told by Kawahine that Makoa was self-serving and very narcissistic and that he would be very difficult to work with. But after working with Makoa on the project, Kalei noticed that Makoa's views were similar to that of the pueo ʻaumākua. Makoa knew that by working together, a group could accomplish many goals and supersede any effort put forth by a single person. But that was where Makoa's similarity to the pueo ʻaumākua ended. Kalei knew that Makoa's allegiance to her group of pueo ʻaumākua as well as all other manō ʻaumākua was short-lived. As soon as he had gotten everything that he wanted, Makoa would revert back to his selfish ways.

Kalei however, still clung to and took some comfort in her belief that the pueo ʻaumākua did understand the importance of a long-lasting allegiance to each other, despite how dysfunctional some of her followers were. "I will be leaving now, Makoa."

As Makoa watched Kalei leave his cave, he could not stop thinking about his new plan--one that would change the fate of all ʻaumākua.

Two hours later, on the island of Maui, Kawahine had just returned home and was about to enjoy a glass of ʻōkolehao when she heard a knock at her door. "Has the sacrifice been made?" asked a middle-aged, tattooed Hawaiian man.

Chapter 9:

PROMISES, PROMISES

The night air was heavy with the fragrant scent of the white ginger that surrounded the upper perimeter of Kawahine's vast waiwai (property). As the moon came to rest directly above Kawahine's valley and the air began to buzz with the sound of crickets chirping, Kawahine reluctantly welcomed a guest into her cozy home. "E komo mai [welcome, come in], Kona. Come sit by the fireplace, and we will talk about our arrangement," she muttered.

The burly Hawaiian man strutted into Kawahine's home and sat down on a wooden chair by the fireplace. After Kawahine had settled comfortably into her worn-out rattan chair, Kona raised his greying eyebrows and stared directly at her, unruffled by the evil mana (power) she exuded. "This was not an arrangement; it was a promise. A promise solidified by human sacrifice, Kawahine."

Kawahine sat in silent contemplation for a few minutes. She was a very calculating person, thinking it best to listen to the entire conversation before interrupting or giving an opinion. Kawahine liked to study people and the manner in which they behaved around her. She knew that body language sometimes spoke louder than the words that came out of the waha (mouths) of people.

Kawahine's gaze now firmly rested on her familiar visitor, and both sat quietly, staring directly at each other for several minutes. Kawahine admired Kona's courage and his unwavering resolve to finalize the deal they had made, but she abhorred his male chauvinism.

"Kona, I remember the promise I made to you! Your descendants will wield the strength of the pueo 'aumākua, as agreed upon."

"When will my daughter, Kēhau, be coming home?!" demanded Kona, as his gaze shifted from Kawahine to the pocket knife he carried.

Kawahine sat up in her chair and took a sip of 'ōkolehao (Hawaiian moonshine) from her glass. She didn't flinch a bit when Kona placed his hands on his knife. "As you know, sometimes plans change and other options must be used to attain the goal," answered Kawahine, as she took another sip of 'ōkolehao.

"What do you mean? Where is my daughter, Kēhau?!" roared Kona, who was now starting to rise from his chair. His pulse started racing as he was slowly beginning to realize that the arrangement he had made with Kawahine was not working out in the manner in which he had planned.

"You agreed to offer up one of your family members as a sacrifice, Kona, and you agreed to do so without needing to know all the details. Suffice it to say that I needed to take care of a big problem, and that is why I sent my daughter Kalei to pick up Kēhau," said Kawahine, as she started chuckling over Kona's dismay.

"Kēhau's son was to be offered as the sacrifice, not my daughter!" cried Kona, as he fell back into his chair.

"Auwe [oh my]! You actually believed that I would use your grandson as the sacrifice and not your daughter, Kēhau?" retorted Kawahine, with a smug grin on her face. "You should have thought about that when we made our pact, but then again, you don't know the first thing about keeping promises, Kona. After all, you broke your promise to me the day I delivered your firstborn child...the day you abandoned me! You remember that, don't you?! My, my, my. I have never seen you so disheveled and lost, Kona. You were at one time a feared 'aumakua--but not anymore!" Kawahine was beside herself with emotion, filled with a sense of liberation from finally exacting revenge on Kona for jilting her all those years ago.

Kona lifted his gaze and stared at Kawahine as he started walking toward her with his knife in his hand, but Kawahine just looked over at him and took another sip of her 'ōkolehao. "I heard about the many accolades that you accumulated when you were a soldier, Kona, but I know that you attained such honors only because of your pueo 'aumakua, and now, without it, you are just an obstinate, weak fool. Your stupidity and arrogance ultimately led you back here to me to try and fix the disgrace you again brought upon yourself!" bellowed Kawahine, as she stood up from her chair. She was unwavered by Kona's rage. Kona continued advancing toward her until he saw a deep orange glow emanating from the fireball that she was fashioning within her right palm.

"Oh no. Where are my manners?" asked Kawahine, sarcastically. She chuckled as she saw how quickly Kona started to back away from her. "After all, I should thank you since you did help me get out of a very sticky situation, Kona. You see, I needed to find someone who would carry out a very deplorable act for me--but who would take such a great risk with their own life? Then, as luck would have it, you came to visit my mother, Kekipi, and I knew that I had found what I was looking for. You were so eager to regain the power of the pueo 'aumakua that you didn't even think about the consequences. If I had told my daughter, Kalei, to sacrifice your innocent grandson, she would end up in the same position as you--stripped of her pueo 'aumakua. Why would I want Kalei to do something that would take away her powerful gift? After all, I too benefit from Kalei's extraordinary talents. Instead, I ordered Kalei to make your daughter, Kēhau, kill the man who could have put an end to a very lucrative project that I was working on. It didn't take much for Kalei to make Kēhau comply--all Kalei had to do was threaten your grandson's well-being. Kēhau immediately went along with the plan and took the life of this man. In return, Kēhau's son, your grandson, was spared. However, after Kēhau took this innocent man's life, she became a liability. So Kalei, our daughter--your firstborn child--had to silence Kēhau. You see, Kēhau herself was the murderer of this innocent man, so Kalei's pueo 'aumakua remained intact."

Kona was speechless. In light of what Kawahine had just said, his anger against Kēhau's murderer, Kalei, had become muted. Kona did not know Kalei, nor did he know that she was his daughter. He had never imagined Kawahine would keep the child he fathered after he escaped from Kawahine while she was in labor. But before Kona's mind could make sense of what one sister had done to the other, Kawahine continued her verbal assault on him.

"My promise to you was already fulfilled, Kona--long before you came to seek counsel from my mother, Kekipi! I have already given you what you so badly desire! Your descendant, our daughter Kalei, already possesses the gift of the pueo 'aumakua!"

"How is this possible, Kawahine? The pueo 'aumakua was taken from me long ago. How can Kalei be my daughter if she has the gift of the pueo 'aumakua?" asked Kona, earnestly, as he stared directly into Kawahine's eyes then quickly darted his gaze to the ground so as not to incur any more of her vindictive wrath.

"Stupid fool. Haven't you ever wondered why I did not run away from you after I saw you attack the luna on the pineapple farm many years ago? Instead of screaming, I ran over and helped you escape, then hid you from the authorities for all those years. I was not afraid of you because I was familiar with the pueo 'aumākua long before meeting you, Kona. My father, who had died years before I met you, was a pueo 'aumakua," said Kawahine as she walked closer to Kona, all the while holding the orange fireball in her hand. "Kalei is your daughter, Kona, and just as you once did, she now possesses the power of the pueo 'aumakua--a gift from her grandfather."

Kona was in no position to fight with Kawahine. Not only had he grown weak without his pueo 'aumakua, but his heart, though blackened and hardened by the evil arts that he practiced, was broken over the daughter he lost. Feeling defeated, Kona turned away from Kawahine and walked out of her home, lamenting over the deal he struck with her--the deal that took Kēhau from him.

How could I have been tricked by Kawahine? thought Kona, as he steered his jalopy down the steep winding roads that bordered Kawahine's property. *Kawahine was supposed to use Martin as the sacrifice--not Kēhau.* Kona hit his palms up against the steering wheel then slammed on the worn-out brakes, enraged that he had been made a fool of. The jalopy started to fishtail for several seconds before hitting the side of the mountain and coming to a complete stop. *I had hoped that you would come back to me, Kēhau, so that I could teach you about our 'aumakua,* thought Kona, as he sat in quiet reflection over his relationship with his wayward daughter, Kēhau.

Despite his arrogance and his selfishness, Kona had become quite fond of Kēhau, who flattered him continuously by imploring him to regale her with stories of the valor of his pueo 'aumakua, which he used in the war. Out of all of the children that he had fathered with a younger, naïve woman he met after he had left Kawahine, Kona was sure that Kēhau was the one that would carry on his pueo 'aumakua legacy.

But as time passed and as Kēhau grew into a woman, Kona's influence over her started to wane. Kēhau became infatuated with illegal drugs and an ill-tempered man who was much older than she. When the older man's interest in her had diminished, Kēhau, who was seventeen years old and pregnant, turned to Kona for help. After all, Kona was her father. Surely he would get her out of the mess she had made. In time, Kēhau hoped, Kona would come to love her un-born son, whom she had already named after her older lover, Martin.

The day after a pregnant Kēhau moved back into Kona's house, Kona, who loathed the thought of caring for a grandson he didn't want, felt that he had no other option but to seek counsel with Kekipi, the most powerful of the kāhuna 'anā'anā. Though he had never met Kekipi in person, Kona knew of her vast power and knowledge.

Kona feared what Kekipi would do to him given his history with her daughter, Kawahine, but despite his fear, he realized that he couldn't waste any more time. Determined to regain the power of the pueo 'aumakua, Kona mustered up all the courage he had--and what little humility he could find--and went to speak with Kekipi. But by the time Kona arrived at Kekipi's compound, Kekipi was already on her deathbed. As Kona approached her bedside, he could feel how strong her evil power was, despite her frail physical appearance.

"What you are about to ask for comes with a high price. Only a few kāhuna, notably the oldest and most experienced kahuna who lives on Kaua'i, could potentially wield such power," said Kekipi as she looked up at Kona and then looked over at her daughter Kawahine, who was standing at her bedside as well. "I should thank you, Kona, for fueling my daughter's need to fervently study the dark arts," said Kekipi as she looked back at Kona. "Since you left her many years ago, Kawahine has excelled at learning everything she needs to in order for her to take my place," muttered Kekipi, as her breathing became more labored and her face became pallid.

"What is the name of this kahuna that I must speak with? I cannot waste more time. Tell me, old woman, so that I can go and speak with him!" shouted Kona. Kekipi was unimpressed by Kona's brouhaha, and she chuckled at his frustration. As Kona waited im-patiently for an answer, Kekipi motioned to Kawahine to prop her cachectic body up on pillows; then she took a sip of comfrey tea, all the while never releasing her gaze from Kona.

Though she wanted to punish Kona severely for his disrespect-
ful manners, Kekipi was very frail and weak, and her ability to deal
with such an insolent individual was quickly waning. As Kekipi
tried to sit up higher so that she could appear more intimidating,
her weak heart stopped, and she fell back onto the old quilted pillows. Kawahine rushed over to help Kekipi up, but it was too late.
Kekipi's raspy, eerie voice was silenced forever.

"Well, Kona, what will you do now?" asked Kawahine sar-
donically, as she placed her mother's guava wood cane alongside
Kekipi's body.

Kona did not know what to say. He had found himself a prisoner
to Kawahine again! But this time, Kawahine's choice of restraints
was withholding the information he so desperately wanted. "Do you
know the name of this kahuna on Kaua'i that I need to speak with?"
asked a pitiless Kona. Kawahine just continued to gaze at her mother's motionless body.

Sensing that Kawahine may not have the information he needed,
Kona became enraged. "You don't know the identity of this kahuna,
do you?! You are just toying with me!" he shouted, as he turned
around and started walking toward the door, all the while cursing
Kekipi for not giving him the information he so desperately desired.

"You're right. I don't know the name of the kahuna that my
mother spoke of, but I can provide you with what it is that you are
searching for. Don't wantonly dismiss my abilities, Kona! I have
lived with my mother for most of my life!" exclaimed Kawahine,
who was visibly upset at Kona's blatant disregard toward her. Kona
stopped and turned to face Kawahine.

"If you can promise me that my family will again wield the power of the pueo 'aumakua, what must I give in return?" asked Kona,
still reluctant to believe in Kawahine's abilities.

"You must offer up one of your family members as a sacrifice,
for what you desire is not easy to attain," responded Kawahine. Kona

thought about Kawahine's proposal for a while. He really had nothing to lose, except a little of his pride. When all was said and done, the anger that Kona projected on to Kēhau's unborn son, coupled with his desire to once again wield the power of the pueo 'aumakua, superseded his indignation.

"I promise to give you the sacrifice that you need," said a resolute Kona, as he slowly walked back toward Kawahine.

"Then I, Kawahine, daughter of Kekipi, do promise that upon such a sacrifice, your family will once again wield the power of the pueo 'aumakua." Both Kona and Kawahine then placed one of their index fingers over each of Kekipi's eyes and shut them in unison.

"When will this promise be fulfilled?" asked Kona.

Kawahine stood up slowly from her mother's bedside. She was relishing the thought of exacting revenge on Kona and had to restrain herself from smiling. "I will contact you when this sacrifice is needed. You will not be told any of the details. I expect you to comply immediately," answered Kawahine. Still feeling a little apprehensive about Kawahine's ability to follow through and deliver what she had promised, but knowing that he had no other options, Kona agreed, then left Kekipi's compound. His grandson, Martin, was born that very evening.

After Kona had left, Kawahine returned to her mother's bedside and sat beside her mother's body for a couple of hours before calling for assistance from Kekipi's power-hungry apprentices. They helped Kawahine wash Kekipi's body, then carefully wrapped Kekipi in kapa cloth. When they were done, Kekipi's body was placed into her family's ancestral gravesite by a select group of people who cared for her family's remains. As Kawahine mourned her mother, Kona kept his thoughts focused on regaining his pueo 'aumakua.

Though he was now a hollow, indignant man, Kona had grown up under the watchful eyes of a very moral and religious mother, who chose to live a simple life, despite her royal lineage. Every

Sunday, Kona's mother, who was a descendant of the island's last mō'ī (king), would take Kona to church. She was a single parent who found solace amongst the other churchgoers and encouraged her kolohe (troublemaker) son to join the priesthood when he graduated from high school. But Kona had other plans: he wanted to become the luna (boss) on the island's biggest pineapple farm. So, as soon as he graduated from high school, Kona started working as a pineapple picker for a wealthy family who owned the largest pineapple farm on the island.

Kona had been working on the pineapple farm for over ten years when his temper, and bad behavior, finally got the best of him. Other pickers started to complain about Kona's bad attitude and inability to work cohesively with the group, but when several pickers informed the luna that Kona was stealing parts from the farm's tractors and selling them, the luna--an older Portuguese man--who had already pardoned Kona's outbursts on multiple occasions, could no longer look the other way.

It was a cold, wet day and everyone on the pineapple farm was miserable--especially the Portuguese luna who detested having to fire any of his workers. The rain had made it almost impossible to pick any fruit, and all the pickers had gone through at least two sets of rubber boots. When the deluge had finally subsided, a young woman ran out from under the cover of the farm's potting shed and quickly made her way toward her Quonset hut. As she passed by one of the plantation's enormous tractors, she saw the luna of the plantation standing above Kona, who was tinkering with one of the farm's largest tractors that had recently been serviced by the resident mechanic. Just as the young woman was about to continue on her way over to her Quonset hut, she overheard an argument between the luna and Kona. When the young woman turned around to look back at the two men, she saw Kona suddenly transform into the pueo 'aumakua and slash the chest of the luna with his beak. But instead of screaming and running away, the young woman remained calm throughout the entire ordeal and waited patiently next to the tractor for Kona to transform back into a man. Kona, on the other hand, was far from calm--he was elated at what had just happened to him. After all, this was the first time in which he got to experience what he most desired: power. But Kona's feeling of power would be short-lived as he would soon fall victim to an even more powerful force.

Without hesitation, the young woman, who had witnessed Kona's transformation, led Kona deep into the rain forest, where she promised to keep him hidden far away from the police and the injured Portuguese luna. Trusting in the young woman's promises of protection, Kona followed her, but much to his chagrin, the forest soon became his prison. Kona was held captive for many years by the young woman who helped him disappear: Kawahine.

Kawahine kept Kona from using his pueo 'aumakua with evil spells that she had learned from her mother, Kekipi. But Kona never stopped searching for a way to escape. One night, Kona seduced Kawahine, who was so starved for affection that she let herself believe Kona's sudden interest in her was genuine. Just as Kona had planned, Kawahine conceived a child. All Kona had to do was wait. Then, after nine more months of captivity, Kona's chance at freedom presented itself when Kawahine went into labor and could no longer focus her spells on Kona.

Finally free from Kawahine's evil spells, Kona looked for opportunities that would allow him to utilize the power of his 'aumakua, and soon joined the military. While deployed overseas, Kona took great pleasure in using his pueo 'aumakua to infiltrate the camps of the enemies, under the cover of darkness, and steal many of their military secrets. As his rank and popularity quickly grew, so too did his arrogance and feelings of invincibility. On Kona's final night of deployment, a pregnant woman crossed his path during his transformation into the pueo 'aumakua. The woman, both startled and confused over what she had just witnessed, started screaming, and Kona quickly unleashed the same violence toward her that he had unleashed on the luna of the plantation several years before. But this time, the end result was very different. In a split second, the pregnant woman fell to the ground, silent and still.

When Kona returned home to Maui, he was faced with the reality that his gift had been taken from him and that he could no longer transform into the pueo ʻaumakua. He had no idea that killing an innocent person would cause him to lose his ʻaumakua, since he had never been taught about the ʻaumākua code. As the years went on, and his bitterness grew, Kona became obsessed with finding a way to wield the power of the pueo ʻaumakua once again, despite the odds that were stacked against him.

In his pursuit to restore his ʻaumakua legacy, Kona sought out and befriended many masters of the dark Hawaiian arts--the kāhuna ʻanāʻanā. Under their tutelage, Kona learned many things, but none of them could give him the information he needed to reinstate his pueo ʻaumakua. Instead, they advised Kona to go and speak with Kekipi, the oldest and most powerful kahuna ʻanāʻanā.

The next two years following the meeting that he had with Kekipi and Kawahine, proved to be very difficult for Kona, who had to put up with a grandson that cried often and needed all of Kēhau's attention. Kona was living like a hermit crab--attached to his bedroom, only venturing out to grab food from the kitchen or to use the restroom. Kona's preoccupation with the pueo ʻaumakua warped his mind so much that he projected all of his anger and bitterness upon his grandson. As his rage grew stronger and stronger, so too did his obsession over the promise that Kawahine had made to him. He would sacrifice everything to get his ʻaumakua back--including his grandson.

"Dad, your mind has drifted away again," said Kēhau, who had just walked into Kona's room to check on him. Ever since Martin was born, Kēhau noticed that her father seldom left his room and hardly spoke to her. "Are you thinking back on your days in the war? Maybe you can tell Marty about it when he grows up," implored Kēhau as she attempted to hand Martin over to Kona--hoping he would receive his grandson into his arms. But Kona did not flinch. He wanted nothing to do with Martin, and instead, turned away from both Kēhau and his grandson. Disappointed by Kona's indifference toward her son, Kēhau pulled Martin back in and squeezed him just a little tighter before walking out of Kona's room.

Finally, on a hot, sunny day, Kona's desire to rid himself of his young grandchild came to fruition. Kawahine had sent over a young girl to pick up Martin and Kēhau. "Hello, Kēhau. My name is Kalei, and I had been told by my mother that you were looking for work. I don't really know you, but my mom and your dad know each other. I am heading over to Kaua'i to work on Senator Braga's fruit farm, and I heard that the senator is looking for more workers. I also heard that the wages are pretty good." Kalei paused for a moment and looked over at Martin, and then looked back at Kēhau. "The senator also has a daughter who has a young son that your son could play with. She and I know each other from high school. The move will give you a chance to provide for your son and experience life on another island. Do you want to go with me?"

Kēhau looked over at Martin. She had painfully come to the realization that her father did not love Martin as she had hoped he would. "Yes Kalei, I will go with you to Kaua'i. Give me a couple minutes to go and get my things and I will meet you outside by your truck," replied Kēhau, who then walked into her room, gathered what little she had, picked up her son, and left her father's house.

Kona watched from his bedroom window as Kēhau walked toward the old yellow Datsun pickup truck that was waiting to take her and Martin to the airport. "The next time I see you, my daughter, you will no longer be burdened by your son, and I will finally be able to teach you about our family 'aumakua." After the old yellow Datsun truck had driven away, Kona shut the curtains in front of his bedroom window, stood up from his chair, and walked out of his bedroom. His days of living like a hermit crab in his own house were over, but years of unbearable anguish were already on the horizon.

Six months after Kēhau and Martin moved out, Kona would find himself regretting the promise he had made to Kawahine and he would spend the next forty years of his life searching for the power that he needed to exact the vengeance he so vehemently desired.

Chapter 10:

WAVE RIDER

"*He'e nalu*, or wave sliding, is a sport that originated here in Hawai'i. It is my favorite sport. I learned how to he'e nalu from my mother, who taught me as soon as I was able to stand on my two feet," said Wehi, as she looked out onto the familiar faces of her classmates.

"What do you know about the Hawaiian culture? You have red hair and light eyes. What kind of Hawaiian are you? The only Hawaiian you have is in your name!"

"Stop it, Keanu," said Miss Pua. "Wehi, please continue with your story."

Wehi could feel the tears starting to well up in her eyes. This was not the first time she had been harassed by Keanu. Ever since the second grade, he and his friends had picked on her because of her hapa haole (Hawaiian-Caucasian) looks. Back then, however, Kahoku was the one who would always rescue Wehi from the boys' verbal tauntings and sometimes, their physical abuse--like pulling her hair and kicking her in her buttocks ('ōkole). Kahoku's physical stature and speed frightened Keanu and his friends and every time they saw him coming, they would run away screaming at the top of their lungs. *I miss you, Kahoku. But I guess I have to be my own hero today*, thought Wehi, as she tried to compose herself.

Mustering up her resolve to finish her story, Wehi wiped the tears away and took a deep breath. As she stood alone in the middle of the classroom, a warm, tingling sensation started to radiate from her boar's tooth necklace. *Thank you for being here with me, Kahoku. I can do this*, thought Wehi, as she stood a little taller, knowing that her big brother was right next to her.

"Our Hawaiian culture is perpetuated and adored by many people across the world. For example, many people in other states and countries come to Hawai'i to participate in our hula and he'e nalu competitions. They come to celebrate and learn more about our way of life because they feel a connection to the Aloha spirit. I challenge all of you to look past outward appearances and see how all these people, who have no genetic ties to our islands, stand with us to honor our cultural heritage. To not embrace those who wish to help us perpetuate our culture is foolish and it will ultimately lead to the disappearance of such a special way of life that we who live here in Hawai'i treasure."

As she held the boar's tooth between her fingers, Wehi looked right at Keanu and his friends, who were sitting at the back of the classroom in a corner. "My name is Kawehi Kūlani Braga-Nahele. I am a little less than half Hawaiian, and I take hula lessons every Monday. I have learned how to ride the waves, or he'e nalu, from my mother, Mālie, who was taught by her father--my grandfather--Ke Ali'i. My other grandfather, Pono, helps heal those who are sick. Besides teaching many visiting professors about Hawaiian medicine, my grandpa Pono is also a doctor in our hospital's emergency room. In fact, many of you probably saw him last week at the surf contest. He was the doctor in the medical tent who helped Keanu when he sliced his foot on the reef after he fell off of his surfboard." The classroom immediately filled with laughter. Even

Keanu's friends couldn't help but laugh. They had all been at the surfing contest last week and witnessed how Keanu screamed like a little child when he was being taken to the medical tent.

"Okay, let's all settle down now," said Miss Pua. "Thank you for sharing with us, Wehi. We congratulate you on winning the surf competition last week. I know that your family is very proud of you." As Wehi sat down in her seat, Miss Pua stood up to address the class. "We all come with different perspectives, as we all were brought up with different beliefs, but I challenge all of you to look beyond what you see on the outside. You might find a very special individual who becomes a lifelong friend and teaches you more than any book could ever do. Live your life with aloha and do not judge others based on outward appearances. All of us need to step up and realize that we should be judged by how we treat each other, not by what we look like. Have a good weekend, haumana [students]!"

Keanu sat in his seat until everyone, except Wehi, had left the classroom. "Teacher's pet," he said as he stared at her for a while, then walked out to catch his bus home. Wehi just shrugged her shoulders. She had learned to live with Keanu's constant attempts to try to belittle her, but sometimes he still got the best of her.

"I am sorry that Keanu made you feel embarrassed," said Miss Pua.

"It's okay. I don't know why I let it bother me so much," answered Wehi.

"Well, it has been a very challenging time for you and your family. Let me gather my things, and I will wait with you until your dad arrives," said Miss Pua, who had been informed by Wehi's dad, Manu, that some of the men whom he had arrested in the past were now threatening Wehi and the rest of his family. Without hesitation, Miss Pua agreed to be there to greet Wehi when Manu dropped her off at school every morning and to stay with Wehi until Manu picked her up after school as well. Within this time, Wehi had grown very fond of Miss Pua.

"Hey there, my little he'e nalu princess!" shouted Manu from his pickup truck.

Miss Pua glanced at Manu and then looked over at Wehi. "Okay, Wehi. I will see you next week. Take care!"

"You too, Miss Pua," replied Wehi as she gave Miss Pua a big hug and then climbed into the passenger's seat next to Manu.

"Aloha, Pua. Have a nice, safe weekend. Thank you for waiting with Wehi!"

"No problem, Manu. Give my love to Mālie. Aloha!"

As Manu drove away from the school parking lot, he reached into a paper bag and pulled out a fish sandwich and fries for Wehi. "Wow, Dad! Thank you!" exclaimed Wehi.

"You are very welcome," chuckled Manu. "How about we go and sit on the beach where you won the surfing contest last week. You can finish your sandwich and watch the waves."

"Awesome, Dad! Let's go!" shouted Wehi, as she started to eat her fries. After parking the truck, Manu grabbed Kahoku's surfboard and sat down on the sand next to Wehi.

"Wow, Dad! Did you plan this?" asked Wehi as she unwrapped her fish sandwich.

"Well, it is a Friday, and I thought you might want to get a little surfing in before the start of the weekend. I can't let my little surfer girl miss out on all the waves!"

"Nice! But why didn't Mom come with you?"

"Well, Mom wasn't feeling well. I think that she's probably just a little tired. She did however, ask me to relay this message to you: go get 'em, girl!" Wehi started to laugh.

"It is good to see you laugh, Wehi," said Manu.

"I can't remember the last time I laughed this hard...it seems like forever," responded Wehi, as she finished her sandwich, then stretched out across the warm, shimmering sand, and made a sand angel. "We lucked out today because no one is here--the beach is TOTALLY ours, Dad!"

After playing in the sand for a couple of minutes, Wehi got up and dusted the sand off of her clothes, and then sat down on her favorite orange beach towel and reached over and gave Manu a big hug. "Thank you for bringing me to my favorite beach Dad. Thank you for spending the afternoon with me." Wehi paused for a moment and took a deep breath in. "I love how the warm sand smells like the coconut suntan oils used by sunbathers and how it mixes together with the salty smell of the ocean. It makes me feel so comfortable," she said, as she and Manu sat there together looking out onto the glistening, blue water. After a couple of minutes, Wehi glanced over at Kahoku's surfboard.

"Someone is aching to go in!" laughed Manu.

"This is a good day for surfing Dad. There is a light offshore breeze, and the waves look clean, not choppy."

"Wehi, I agree with whatever you just said." Manu started to chuckle.

"Mom taught me, Dad. Don't worry, I won't tell her that you didn't understand."

"Why, thank you, Wehi. But contrary to popular belief, your mom did teach me a little about surfing. In fact, we used to surf together when we were younger, but she always put me to shame." Manu got up and walked over to Kahoku's board. "I think that your big brother would want you to use his surfboard," he said, as he carefully carried it over to Wehi, then wiped away his tears and smiled. "Go get 'em, my little he'e nalu girl."

Wehi hugged Manu, then went to change into her surf clothes that he had brought from home. The sand had started to cool off as the sun slowly started to make its way toward Mount Wai'ale'ale. "Okay, Dad. I'll see you in a little bit. I am just going to paddle out a little and catch a couple waves. Can you hold on to my boar's tooth?

I don't want to lose it. When I come back, we can go get a take-out pizza for dinner and surprise Mom." Wehi handed Manu her boar's tooth necklace then finished waxing Kahoku's surfboard. It didn't matter that the surfboard was much bigger than she was; Wehi was just so excited to use it. *I can't believe that I get to ride Kahoku's surfboard*, she thought, as she picked it up and waded out into the ocean.

When she got onto Kahoku's board, Wehi felt exhilarated. The water was warm, and there was no strong current whatsoever so she was able to quickly paddle out and wait for the perfect set. While sitting on Kahoku's surfboard and waiting for the perfect wave, Wehi ran her fingers over Kahoku's picture, which Manu had placed on Kahoku's surfboard after his funeral. "I miss you plenty, big braddah," she whispered, after kissing his picture. Suddenly, Wehi felt the ocean start to pull her board back a little. *This is it!* she thought, as she immediately got into position and prepared to catch her first wave.

But before the wave arrived, Wehi felt something bump the underside of Kahoku's board. *Oh no! Please swim away, manō! Please swim away!* Wehi immediately got down on her hands and knees and then grabbed the sides of the surfboard. Just then, a big shark rammed its head up onto the back end of the board. Wehi's heart started beating uncontrollably. Fear gripped her entire body as she reluctantly turned her head and saw a pair of cold, black eyes staring back at her. The tiger shark's huge mouth, filled with rows of sharp, jagged teeth, kept opening and closing, as it thrashed around violently. Everything was happening so quickly, but to Wehi, it seemed like everything was occurring in slow motion.

What am I going to do? I am too scared to move. Dad can't help me…The shark would kill him if he swam out here! I can't do anything! What will happen to my family if I don't make it? Wehi struggled to keep her balance and stay away from the tiger shark, but its massive weight continued to push the surfboard down under the water as it inched its way further up toward her. *Oh no! The shark is getting closer! My legs, my legs!* Suddenly, out of the blue, Wehi caught sight of a big torpedo-like shape cutting through an oncoming wave. In a split second, the tiger shark that had placed its gigantic head onto Kahoku's surfboard disappeared under the water. As the back end of the surfboard popped back up, Wehi spotted a huge red cloud of blood floating up toward the surface of the ocean. *No, no, no! More sharks will come!* Wehi wanted to yell out to Manu, but she did not want to put his life at risk. He had been preoccupied with picking up old drift nets and had not yet seen what trouble Wehi was in. The sets started to come in faster and before Wehi knew it, she lost her balance and fell into the blood-stained ocean.

As Wehi kept her head above water, she glanced over at the beach and saw Manu looking for her. *What should I do? Do I take a chance and swim back to the board or do I try to swim to shore? I don't know what to do! I can't move!* Fear continued its relentless grip on Wehi's entire body as she struggled to tread water, taunting her with the knowledge that a larger shark was swimming nearby.

Now aware that Wehi was not on Kahoku's surfboard, Manu tossed the drift nets that he had collected to the side and started running toward the water. "Wehi! Wehi!" he shouted, as he took off his shirt. He was just about to dive into the ocean when he saw Wehi being lifted out of the water by a massive great white shark. "No, not my little girl!" wailed Manu, as he waded into the ocean.

"Dad, don't worry about me!" shouted Wehi, who was now seated on the shark's muscular back, right behind its huge first dorsal fin. Wehi was in awe of her mother's 'aumakua, whose sheer size was intimidating. "Mom, thank you for saving me," said Wehi, as the great white shark swam over to Kahoku's surfboard. The fear that once had a hold over Wehi finally started to diminish and she soon started to feel a little more at ease. *Oops! I need to let dad know what's going on because he is probably shocked at what just happened.* Wehi stood up on the great white's back and waved her hands at her startled father to let him know that everything was all right.

"I want to stay out here for a little while longer!" yelled Wehi. "I am going to send Kahoku's surfboard over to you on the next wave. Don't worry, Dad. Mom is with me!" Wehi then pushed Kahoku's board toward the shore and waved at Manu again. *Okay, Mom. Let's go for a ride!* To Wehi's astonishment, the great white shark heard her thoughts and swam out farther, where the waves were bigger.

Riding the waves on the back of a shark was very different from riding a surfboard--especially when the shark could read your mind. All Wehi had to do was hold on and enjoy the ride! Her mom, Mālie, was, after all, a great surfer, so she knew exactly where to go and how to catch the perfect wave. Wehi felt like she was riding a super-charged, submerged jet ski. Cutting through the waves was effort-less for the great white, and Wehi could feel her mom's power with every move of the great white's muscular body. *I love being out here with you, Mom. I can't believe that I am surfing the waves on the back of a great white shark.* Wehi looked around to see if there were any other surfers in the water. *Mom, we are so lucky because aside from dad, no one else is here--we have the ocean and the waves all to ourselves.*

Despite feeling a bit uncomfortable with the situation, Manu could see how much fun Wehi was having with Mālie, so he just sat down on the sand next to Kahoku's surfboard. After a couple of hours had passed, the sun's light slowly started to fade. *Mom, I think Dad wants us to come in, but he doesn't want to spoil our fun by asking us. Maybe we should go and join him on the beach.* As Mālie and Wehi swam up closer to the shore, Manu stood up and walked into the ocean. He was still a little frightened of Mālie's ʻaumakua, but he was also a little curious. After watching the great white shark transform back into his wife, Manu reached into the water and pulled both Mālie and Wehi up, then quickly wrapped a towel around Mālie and gave Wehi her orange beach towel. As Mālie and Wehi started to dry themselves, Manu picked up Kahoku's surfboard and headed over to his truck.

"I am going to start packing up and then I will be waiting for the both of you in the truck," he said, as he glanced back and smiled at Mālie and Wehi.

"Okay Dad," replied Wehi as she put her slippers on and smiled back at Manu.

"I love seeing you smile, Wehi," said Mālie. "Here, let me help you pin your long hair up in a bun."

As soon as Mālie had secured Wehi's hair, Wehi turned around to face Mālie. *Mom, let's go eat saimin for dinner, okay?* But Mālie did not respond. She just looked at Wehi and smiled. *That's it!* thought Wehi. *We can only communicate through our thoughts when you are an 'aumakua.*

"Where do you want to go for dinner, Wehi? Should we pick up some food for both Grandpa Pono and Grandpa Ke Ali'i?" asked Mālie as she wiped off the sand from her feet.

"Let's go and get some saimin for dinner," answered Wehi. "We haven't gone to eat saimin for a long time and Grandpa Ke Ali'i is still here on Kaua'i. He and Grandpa Pono love saimin!"

"You don't have to try so hard to convince me, Wehi. I have been kinda jonesing for saimin for a while now. Let's go! Your dad is waiting for us!" shouted Mālie as she started running toward Manu's truck.

"Manu, Wehi suggested that we invite both grandfathers to join us for dinner at the saimin restaurant," mentioned Mālie as she jumped into the truck and gave Manu a kiss on his cheek.

"You know, saimin sounds pretty good right now. Wehi, why don't you call both of your grandfathers and let them know that we will meet them at the saimin restaurant," said Manu.

"Okay, Dad," replied Wehi, as she quickly reached over, grabbed Manu's cell phone, and got in touch with both Pono and Ke Aliʻi. After she had invited both of them to dinner, Wehi couldn't keep the day's events to herself, so she blurted everything out to Pono and Ke Aliʻi. As Wehi continued talking, Manu felt compelled to speak with Mālie about the tiger shark incident.

"I didn't see anyone on the beach while we were there, but I wonder if an ʻaumakua was there and saw what you did to that tiger shark? What if that tiger shark was an ʻaumakua!" Manu rolled down his car window and then quickly glanced over at Mālie. "Mālie, I can't get my mind around what has happened to our family this past year. Look at what just happened a couple of hours ago. If you had not been there today, we would have lost Wehi. At this point, I don't know whether I should be grateful for the ʻaumākua, or if I should hate them for taking our son away from us."

"Don't worry so much, Manu," answered Mālie. "We can talk about it later tonight when both of our dads join us for dinner."

Having finished speaking to both of her grandfathers, Wehi just sat quietly, looking over at her parents. Mālie turned on the truck's old radio and then leaned back in her seat. "I wish that I could give you an answer, Manu, but I can't. I am still trying to figure this whole ʻaumakua thing out," said Mālie as she smiled at Manu.

"We will find the answers we need together, Mālie, I promise. I am just at a loss here because unlike yourself, I do not know what it feels like to be an ʻaumakua," responded Manu.

Mālie looked over at Wehi. "Wehi, please try to keep your voice down when we are at dinner with your two grandfathers tonight. We don't want other people to hear about what you and I did today--okay?"

"All right, Mom. I will keep my voice down," promised Wehi.

"Thank you sweetheart," replied Mālie.

Minutes later, Manu pulled up alongside the saimin restaurant.

"Mom, Dad, I can see both Grandpa Pono and Grandpa Ke Ali'i! They saved us a table. Hurry, let's go in! I am starving!" shouted Wehi, as she ran out of the truck and into the saimin restaurant. "Yum! It smells so good in here! I love how the Japanese noodles smell as they simmer over the stove. I can't wait to eat!" Wehi's stomach started to rumble as she ran over to the table that both Pono and Ke Ali'i were saving for them.

Just as she had always done in the past when her family came to eat at the saimin restaurant, Wehi made sure to sit in the seat closest to the kitchen so that she could watch Mr. Satoshi ladle the warm, tasty broth into each bowl of noodles and then sprinkle diced green onions and luncheon meat over the top. This had been Kahoku's favorite place to eat and he would always beg Manu and Mālie to bring both he and Wehi here at least once a week. "Mom, Dad, re-member all the times that we would come here to eat with Kahoku?" asked Wehi as she looked over at her parents.

"Yes, Wehi, we remember all those good times," answered Manu, who reached over and gave her a hug and then put his arm over Mālie and pulled her close to him. "Wehi, can you help Grandpa Pono grab a few napkins and chopsticks for all of us?" asked Manu.

"Okay, Dad," answered Wehi, who along with Pono reached over the counter and grabbed a few napkins and chopsticks and then passed them around. "Dad, I think we should all order Kahoku's favorite dish, since this is the first time that we have come here since...." But Wehi still couldn't say those last words.

"Yes," interjected Mālie. "I think we should all order a large, half-cooked saimin with two chicken barbecue sticks on the side and a slice of lilikoi pie. I think Kahoku would appreciate that very much, Wehi."

"Thanks, Mom," whispered Wehi. "I still can't say that...."

"That your brother passed away? I know, sweetheart. We all know how hard it is to go on without him. But I know that he is still with us and that he loves you very much."

The waitress soon returned with five large bowls of saimin and ten pieces of savory chicken barbeque, and carefully placed it all on the table. "Be careful, Wehi. The bowls are very hot. Here, let me help you get started," said Ke Aliʻi, who placed the saimin bowl in front of Wehi and drizzled a little soy sauce and hot mustard over her noodles.

"Thank you, Grandpa Ke Aliʻi," mumbled Wehi, as she shoveled a heaping pile of noodles and broth into her mouth.

"Wehi, you have had quite a day!" said Ke Aliʻi.

"Yup. Kind of junk, at first, when I was at school, then kind of scary, when I was in the water." Wehi paused for a moment to gulp down more noodles and a big spoonful of soup; then took a sip of water and wiped her mouth with a napkin before continuing with her story. "Then Mom showed up and saved my life!"

"Shhhh. Keep your voice down, Wehi," whispered Mālie. "Remember what I asked you to do when we were in the truck?"

"Oh--yes, Mom. I'm sorry."

Manu finished his slice of lilikoi pie and then looked over at Pono. "I don't know what to make of all of this, Dad," he said.

"It is very hard to wrap your mind around, isn't it, Son?" replied Pono.

Ke Aliʻi helped Wehi break apart the last chicken barbeque, then wiped off the barbeque sauce around her mouth and on her hands. By this time, everyone but the five of them had left the saimin restaurant. It was nine o'clock in the evening and the waitress had already placed the closed sign over the front door.

"Don't rush out," said Mr. Satoshi, who was the owner and a very good friend of Ke Aliʻi. "Finish your lilikoi pies. Just bring the keys to my house when you finish. Leave your dishes in the dishwasher. No worries, tomodachi [friend]."

"Thank you, Satoshi-san. I will make sure everything is cleaned up and secured, and then I will bring the keys over to your house later this evening," replied Ke Aliʻi, as he immediately stood up, bowed down in front of Mr. Satoshi, and then waited until Mr. Satoshi left the restaurant before sitting back down.

Once Mr. Satoshi had driven away, Pono stood up and walked around the restaurant to make sure that they were all alone. "It is okay to speak about what has happened today. No one is here," he said, as soon as he returned to the table.

Ke Aliʻi looked over at Wehi and smiled. "So Wehi, you mentioned earlier over the phone that someone at school bummed you out today. Tell me about that."

"Yup. Keanu Keomaka started teasing me again about how I am not a 'real' Hawaiian because of my looks."

"Well, the next time you see Mr. Keomaka, kindly inform him that being Hawaiian is more than just skin or hair color. It is about respect for the Hawaiian culture and everyone who embraces it."

"I did, Grandpa Ke Aliʻi. Keanu didn't say much after I mentioned it, but that could have been because Miss Pua started scolding him."

"Well, I am glad to hear that your teacher corrected Mr. Keomaka. You have said many good things about Miss Pua. I hope to meet her someday so that I may thank her for being such a great person in your life. What about your day at the beach? How did you feel about surfing with Kahoku's board?" asked Ke Aliʻi.

"It was awesome, Grandpa Ke Aliʻi! Kahoku's board is really big and so I had an easier time paddling out and I loved the way it felt on the water."

"What happened when you were waiting for your perfect wave?" asked Ke Aliʻi.

"Well, I felt a very strong tug on the end of Kahoku's surfboard, and when I turned around, I saw this HUGE tiger shark placing its HUGE head onto the back end of Kahoku's surfboard. Its teeth were so big and jagged, and its eyes were jet-black, and when it opened its mouth, it looked like a huge dark cave filled with water and teeth. I thought that it was going to swallow me and Kahoku's surfboard! I couldn't move, Grandpa Ke Aliʻi! I felt so small and weak compared to that tiger shark! I was really, really scared and my heart was beating so fast and hard that it felt like it was going to burst out of my chest! I thought that I was going to die, Grandpa Ke Aliʻi!"

"Wehi, I know the tiger shark scared you, and so I want you to focus on what happened after. Can you tell us what happened next?" asked Ke Aliʻi.

Wehi paused for a moment to pull herself together and as she remembered how her mom had saved her, she started to perk up. "All of a sudden the tiger shark got pulled under the water and the back end of Kahoku's surfboard popped back up. Then, a red cloud of blood rose up from under the water and surrounded Kahoku's surfboard! There was so much blood in the water, Grandpa Ke Aliʻi! I was so afraid more sharks would come that I lost my balance and fell right into the bloody water. Then, a bigger shark swam up toward me. At first glance, I thought that the shark was going to eat me but when it came closer to me, I knew it was Mom. She let me get onto her back, and we rode some big waves! It was awesome!" exclaimed Wehi as she looked up at Ke Aliʻi.

"That's what I want you to remember," said Ke Aliʻi, "just remember how much fun you and your mom had while riding the waves today!"

"Yes, sweetheart, just remember how you, my little heʻe nalu girl, rode all those big waves with your mom today," reiterated Manu. Wehi gave Manu a big hug before snuggling up against Mālie's shoulder. After a few minutes had passed, Wehi drifted off to sleep.

"Dad, now that Wehi is asleep, I have to get something off of my chest," said Manu. "I am confused about the code of the ʻaumākua.

Mālie just killed a tiger shark. Who knows if it was an ʻaumakua? What will happen in this case? I mean, until recently, all this stuff was just a fairy tale to me."

"I know that it is very hard to comprehend all of this at once," said Pono, but before Pono could finish answering Manu's question, Ke Aliʻi interjected.

"Why do you say such things? What is so confusing about the code of the ʻaumākua?"

"I am sorry Ke Aliʻi, I did not mean any disrespect with my comment. I just want to know what will happen to Mālie if she killed another ʻaumakua?"

"Dad, I was just protecting my child," interrupted Mālie. "Why should I be penalized for killing the tiger shark if the tiger shark was an ʻaumakua?" Ke Aliʻi did not respond to his daughter's question. He saw that Manu was getting restless in his chair and he knew that Manu needed to express more of his concerns, so Ke Aliʻi thought it best to wait until Manu had said everything he needed to.

Manu looked over at Ke Aliʻi then stood up and walked to the front door of the saimin restaurant. "I loved growing up on this beautiful island, with its many pristine beaches and green valleys. Yet, the most endearing part about growing up on Kauaʻi was the special bond that my friends and I had with our kupuna [elders]. These older gentlemen taught all of us many things--like spearfishing and woodworking, but they also entertained us with their stories about the menehunes and the night marchers. I remember one camping trip where several of my friends brought their grandfathers with them. These guys could tell tales that would make all the hair on your back stand up--you know, the real scary kind that makes all the girls scream and run back into their tents. Now, as I reflect on what has happened to our family, I am reminded of one specific story that my friend's grandfather told us. The story was about a powerful king who united the Big Island, Maui and Oʻahu by force. But because the supernatural power surrounding Kauaʻi was so strong, the king was never able to conquer Kauaʻi by force.

"My friend's grandfather said that when the king's warriors attempted to paddle their canoes from Oʻahu to Kauaʻi, an army of sharks intervened and the king's warriors never got the chance to land their canoes on Kauaʻi's shores." Manu shook his head and chuckled. "Of course my friend's grandfather embellished to a great degree, adding in gory details of how the sharks capsized some of the warriors' canoes, then eventually feasted on them. I actually believed that this was the reason that the king never took our island by force until I started intermediate school. In history class, we were taught that the channel between Oʻahu and Kauaʻi was unusually rough, and that it was quite a challenge for the king's army to cross; many of his men fell ill trying to make the journey and never made it to Kauaʻi.

"Now, after learning that the ʻaumākua do exist, I am starting to think that the story I had heard from my friend's grandfather was not all fiction. What if Kauaʻi circumvented the king's attacks because of ʻaumākua involvement--specifically Kauaʻi's manō ʻaumākua? If Kauaʻi's manō ʻaumākua did intervene, then they would have no other choice but to kill the king's warriors. I mean, think about it. If the king's warriors survived, they would just continue on their course to conquer Kauaʻi."

Manu was visibly upset, but because he did not want to raise his voice and wake Wehi, he paused for a moment to collect his thoughts, then continued. "What I am trying to say is that in this case, Kauaʻi's manō ʻaumākua were fighting to protect their family, just as the king's warriors were fighting for their king. Neither of these two groups of warriors were fighting because they wanted to just blatantly kill each other. What does the code of the ʻaumākua say with regard to lives that are taken during times of war? What about times like this, when a mother uses her ʻaumakua to protect her child?" Manu walked back to the table and sat down next to Mālie.

"There was much turmoil during that great war," started Pono. "Many lines were crossed, as far as the ʻaumākua were concerned. Back then, however, ʻaumākua were not as they are today. The bodies of wild manō and pueo were used as vessels for the chosen souls of our ancestors. When a patriarch or son died, a family member would immediately take his body to a sea cave or mountain cave, depending on what ʻaumakua protected their family. If the ancestors deemed that these patriarchs or sons should stay and protect their family, their souls united with the wild manō or pueo. This was an accepted way of life for many years, until these gifts were manipulated by a few people during this great war.

"Many husbands, fathers, and brothers, whose family had the gift of the manō ʻaumākua, were forcefully sought out by a few kāhuna ʻanāʻanā, who traveled to every village on the islands of Oʻahu, Maui, and the Big Island of Hawaiʻi. These kāhuna ʻanāʻanā informed all of the men in the village that if they did not sacrifice themselves, their entire family would be killed if the king's army did not prevail. All men with the gift of the manō ʻaumākua had no other option but to end their lives and dedicate their ʻaumākua to the king's cause. But all of this trickery did not occur under the direction of the great king. Rather, it was the kāhuna ʻanāʻanā who orchestrated this terrible event. Their only goal was to prove to the king that they were indispensable, so the kāhuna ʻanāʻanā needed to get the job done--no matter what the cost and no matter what lies they had to tell. The kāhuna ʻanāʻanā did not care who they had to sacrifice to attain their goal.

"Back then, the ocean played a very big role in our survival. Because of this, there were more manō ʻaumākua then there were pueo ʻaumākua due to the fact that island fishermen needed protection, and royal messengers that paddled their canoes between the islands needed assistance in navigating the channels. The pueo ʻaumākua, on the other hand, were not directly associated with war--they were instead tasked with guarding their family's genealogy and secrets. Most of Hawaiʻi's pueo ʻaumākua lived on Kauaʻi and Maui, where they kept watch over the gravesites of many powerful kāhuna. These ʻaumākua had impeccable memories and were revered, even by Kamohoaliʻi, the god of the manō.

"My uncle told me that during the Great War, the sudden flood of souls uniting the islands' manō angered Kamohoaliʻi, so he sought counsel from the oldest pueo ʻaumakua, who kept watch over the gravesite of a powerful kahuna. Kamohoaliʻi expressed his concern that the natural balance between wild manō and manō ʻaumākua had been thwarted by the souls of the men who had dedicated their ʻaumākua to the king's army. After meeting with the oldest pueo ʻaumakua, Kamohoaliʻi devised a plan that would restore the balance of the manō.

"After Kauaʻi's own army of manō ʻaumākua capsized many of the king's canoes, Kamohoaliʻi brutally killed the swimming warriors, causing the ocean to seethe blood and flesh. The souls of the men who had been coaxed into killing themselves and dedicating their shark ʻaumākua to the king's cause could not control the animal nature of the manō, and as a result could not stop themselves from going into a feeding frenzy. They had now broken the code of the ʻaumākua--which meant that their souls could no longer inhabit the bodies of the manō.

"It was at this point that Kamohoaliʻi captured all the souls of these brave men. With help from a pueo ʻaumakua, Kamohoaliʻi had found a way to use the code of the ʻaumākua to his advantage. After all the souls of the king's warriors were forced out from the bodies of the manō, Kamohoaliʻi captured and hid them far away from the other gods. According to my uncle, all of those brave warriors will never have peace and will never be reunited with their families as long as their souls are held by Kamohoali'i," said Pono.

Everyone sat silent for a few minutes, pondering over the fact that all of those brave warriors would never be reunited with their loved ones. "In response to this terrible act," continued Pono, "Ke Akua [God] changed the entire practice of the 'aumākua. Since that time, the souls of the departed are now free to ascend into heaven instead of being required to stay with and protect their family. The responsibility of the 'aumākua is now given to the living--both men and women. The code of the 'aumākua that we follow today em-phasizes greater responsibility while in the 'aumākua form. If we kill an innocent person, we lose our gift of the 'aumakua as do our descendants.

"To this day, neither I nor any other elder in the pueo council has heard of any more pilikia [trouble] like that which occurred during the great war. Still, there is something that troubles me," said Pono.

"What is it, Dad?" asked Manu.

"Yes. Please tell us," said Ke Ali'i.

Pono sat quietly for a moment and looked over at Wehi, who was still sound asleep. "Mālie, do you remember learning about molehu at our ho'oponopono session?" asked Pono.

"Yes, Pono. I remember discussing molehu. That is the moment when your 'aumakua form and human form talk to one another to make sure you did not hurt someone."

"Did you experience molehu right before leaving the beach with Manu and Wehi?" asked Pono.

"I can't remember. Everything just happened so quickly," said Mālie, who started to look a little bit worried.

"Don't worry, Mālie. You protected your child. If a manō 'aumakua attacked her, then you would not be responsible for what took place today. Do you remember eating the tiger shark after kill-ing it?" asked Pono.

Mālie looked at Wehi sleeping peacefully in her arms, and

then looked at Pono. "Pono, I cannot remember most of my actions. I was swimming around mindlessly until I felt Wehi's fear. What happened next is a blur. Only bits and pieces slowly come to mind. I remember the intense feeling of anger and rage that I had for the shark that was attacking Wehi. I grabbed it with my teeth and pulled it down, really fast. There was blood everywhere, but then my memory fades. The next thing I remember was Manu giving me a towel."

"You don't remember surfing all those waves with Wehi?" asked Manu.

"No. I just remember taking the towel from you, then I remember Wehi telling me about the waves that we surfed together and all the fun we had," replied Mālie, who had a puzzled look on her face.

"Did Wehi discuss any details about the tiger shark with you-- like any black markings on the tiger shark's dorsal fin?" asked Ke Aliʻi.

"No, Dad. Wehi did not mention anything to me about the tiger shark when we were drying off and leaving the beach," answered Mālie.

Ke Aliʻi took the dishes into the kitchen and grabbed a pitcher of ice water on his way back. "Don't worry, Mālie, we will figure this out," said Ke Aliʻi, as he handed Mālie a glass of water.

"Thank you for the water, Dad," said Mālie.

"Pono, you look like you have aged five years since we started this discussion," remarked Ke Aliʻi, as he poured some water into Pono's empty glass. "You have yet to tell us what it is that troubles you."

"Like I previously mentioned, many years have passed since any of the elders have heard of a man losing his gift of the ʻaumakua. But it is not like such information is put on to the police blotter in the newspaper or on the local news channels. If such an incident occurred, the elders would be informed only through the kāhuna in the community," said Pono.

"So there is no need to worry if you have not heard anything. Mālie probably just encountered a wild tiger shark--not an 'aumakua. Am I right, Dad?" asked a puzzled Manu.

"Well, this incident just happened, Son," answered Pono. "If this was a wild tiger shark that attacked Wehi, then you would be right in your assumption, but what if the reason for this brazen behavior is more sinister in nature?"

"Okay, Pono," said Ke Ali'i, "please just come out and tell us what is going on."

"Only a select, anonymous group of kāhuna possess such power to take away the gift of the 'aumākua. They are able to walk between our world and the spirit world and can take away the gift of the 'aumākua and deliver it back to our ancestors in heaven. So great is this responsibility that these kāhuna seldom divulge what they can do. They live amongst us, constantly watching for any hint of impropriety by any 'aumakua who breaks the code, and inform the council only through a trusted source if that happens," said Pono.

Pono stood up and walked over to the louvered windows at the front of the saimin restaurant. "It is odd that in my many years of being in the council, I have never heard of any man or woman losing their 'aumakua." Pono closed the windows, then walked back to the table. "What if these kāhuna are no longer with us? What if someone discovered who they were and killed them all?"

"What are you saying, Dad? Are you telling us that 'aumākua are now able to do as they please because there is no one who can punish them if they break the code? So they can kill my son and go after my daughter? I may not possess these gifts, but there is no way that I will let any man or 'aumākua take Wehi away from me," stated Manu as he tried to keep his voice down so as not to wake Wehi.

"I will not let that happen either," said Mālie, who then held

Wehi closer to her.

"We will all protect Wehi," interjected Ke Aliʻi. "But we also need to figure out who is behind all of these attacks on our entire family. Look at what happened long ago with Aukele and your father, Pono. Then Kahoku was taken from us and if Mālie had not been there to protect Wehi today, we would have lost the youngest member of our family," asserted Ke Aliʻi, as he looked over at Wehi and sighed. "I cannot watch my family disappear right in front of me. I have tried to gather as much information from my sources, but so far, none of them are aware of any organizations that would want to harm our family. I can think of only one other person that I can turn to, but I have not spoken with him since I was a young man."

"Ke Aliʻi, are you talking about your Uncle Makoa?" asked Pono.

Mālie's eyes widened as she turned to face Ke Aliʻi. "Dad, from what you have told me, your uncle would sooner see you dead than help you."

"I am prepared for whatever my uncle may try to do to me, and I am not intimidated by him anymore," responded Ke Aliʻi. "If Makoa knows anything that could help keep all of you alive, then I must face my fear of him and seek his counsel."

Chapter 11:

WHISPERS IN THE WIND

The next morning brought the fresh scent of rain and the perfume of Mālie's ginger plants into the house. The cool breeze that came down from the mountains enticed everyone to sleep in for just a little longer--everyone except Manu, who had just gotten off the phone with Martin and was rushing to get ready for work.

"Manu, it is Saturday, and it is a beautiful, comfortable morning. I thought we were going to sleep in and then spend the rest of the day together," whispered Mālie as she gave Manu a big hug.

"Martin just called. We got some information on who the murdered boy was."

"You mean the boy that you found up in Kalalau Valley?"

"Yes, Mālie. Martin thinks that the boy's family is living in Hāna, on the island of Maui, so he arranged for us to depart on the next flight. I am sorry to leave you and Wehi, but if this means that we can find the answers we need to close this case, then I must go."

"Of course, Manu, I understand. Please be safe," said Mālie, as she gave Manu a big hug and kiss, then walked with him to his truck.

After saying goodbye to Manu, Mālie tiptoed into Wehi's room to see if Wehi was awake and ready to eat breakfast. As she opened Wehi's door, Mālie couldn't help but chuckle to herself. "Oh, my beautiful daughter. You always pull the quilt over every part of your body except your feet," whispered Mālie as she closed Wehi's window curtains. "I'll let you sleep in, Little One. Enjoy the cool, fragrant breezes that this morning brings." Mālie pulled the quilt over Wehi's feet and then shut Wehi's bedroom door and went into the kitchen. She had just sat down at the table and was about to enjoy a freshly picked papaya when she felt a surge of confidence rush over her. Since annihilating the tiger shark, Mālie's belief in her ability to control her manō ʻaumakua was growing, as was her desire to find the ʻaumakua that killed her son.

After finishing her papaya and reading the newspaper, Mālie felt the ocean beckoning to her. It was calling her back to the place where she felt the strongest, the place she needed to return to. Mālie quickly walked over to her bag on the kitchen counter, took out her cell phone, and called Pono. "Hello, Pono. Do you think that you would be able to come over after you finish work and watch Wehi while I go down to the beach for a little while?"

"Was Manu called in to work today?" asked Pono.

"Yes. He and Martin are on their way to Hāna to see if they can find information on the young man who passed away in Kalalau valley," answered Mālie.

"Sure Mālie. I will come over and spend the day with Wehi. I will see you in a couple of hours," answered Pono.

By the time Pono had gotten to the house, it was already noon. The temperature had risen and the plumeria had become more fragrant with the increasing heat. Mālie had opened all the windows to let in the cooling trade winds before Pono arrived so that the house would remain comfortable. "Pono, Wehi is still asleep, so feel free to watch some television or just relax," said Mālie, as she headed over to the door.

"Don't worry about me, Mālie. I brought over lots of medical journals to read. Wehi and I will be fine," replied Pono as he gave Mālie a hug before closing the door. After checking on Wehi, Pono went into the kitchen, grabbed a banana, and then walked out onto the covered porch to read a few of his medical journals. He had just come from an overnight shift at the emergency room and was a little tired. After he finished reading his first journal and began reading his second journal, Pono found himself struggling to keep his maka (eyes) from closing, especially since his surroundings were so comfortable and fragrant. Soon after putting down his second journal, Pono drifted off to sleep.

"Grandpa Pono, time to get up," implored Wehi, as she gently tickled Pono's nose with a mint leaf that she had picked from Mālie's herb garden. "It is now after four o'clock in the afternoon and I have been up for several hours watching over you." Pono slowly opened his eyes and saw Wehi staring at him, so he smiled back at her. As he started to get up from the weathered old Adirondack chair, his cell phone started beeping.

"Sometimes, I prefer old telephones to these newer phones."

"Why, Grandpa? Our cell phones let us go everywhere and allow us to keep in touch with our family," responded Wehi.

"Because older phones hang on the wall, away from people who are trying to get some sleep," chuckled Pono.

"Do you have to go back to the hospital, Grandpa?" asked Wehi. Pono then looked down at the text message he had gotten but didn't answer Wehi's question, so she asked again. "Grandpa Pono, do you have to go back to the hospital?"

"I'm sorry, Wehi. No. I do not need to go back to the hospital. Are you hungry? How about I make you a peanut butter and guava jelly sandwich with a glass of milk?"

"We ran out of guava jelly, but we do have bananas," responded Wehi.

"Okay, then it is settled. We will have peanut butter and banana sandwiches for dinner," said Pono.

"Yippeee!" yelled Wehi. "Mom never lets me eat that for dinner!"

"Well, tonight is an exception. Let's go into the kitchen and you can help me cut the bananas," said Pono.

Pono and Wehi quickly made their way into the kitchen and made their peanut butter and banana sandwiches, then returned to the Adirondack chairs on the porch. After finishing her second sandwich, Wehi curled up beside her grandfather and watched the sun disappear over Mount Waiʻaleʻale.

"I love this time of day, Wehi. The songs of the birds, the distant crash of the waves against the cliff and the lilac and mango colors of the sky as the sun sets behind our great mountain," said Pono as he pulled Wehi closer to him and gave her a big squeeze. The once-comfortable trade winds had now become a little chilly as the sun completely disappeared from the sky, so Pono reached over and took out a little throw blanket from under the bench seat and placed it over Wehi, who despite sleeping in for most of the day, was starting to doze off.

"I think someone is falling asleep," whispered Pono, as he picked Wehi up, walked into the house, and placed her onto her bed, then turned around and quietly started to walk out of her room. Pono was about to step into the hallway when Wehi jumped onto his back and covered his eyes with her hands.

"Grandpa Pono, I know that you are going to leave soon. Please take me with you."

"Wehi, I was only going to step out for a little while. Don't worry. I was about to call Miss Pua to come over and stay with you until I return."

"Grandpa Pono, you can't call Miss Pua because she is away visiting with family on a different island," answered Wehi.

"Auwē [oh my]! I didn't know that." Pono walked over to Wehi's little koa chair that she had used for tea parties with Kahoku, and sat down. "Wehi, I cannot take you where I am going, and I cannot leave you alone. Your mom needs time to assimilate with her 'aumakua, and your dad is on Maui trying to solve a case. What am I going to do?" Pono brushed back his salt and pepper colored hair with both hands and then looked back over at Wehi, who could tell that her grandfather was pressed for time as he kept looking down at his watch and checking the text message that he had received earlier when they were both outside on the porch.

"Why can't you take me with you, Grandpa Pono?" asked Wehi.

"Remember when we had our family ho'oponopono and we talked about staying safe?"

"Yes, Grandpa Pono, I remember. That is exactly why you need to take me with you. You will keep me safe and I will keep you safe!"

Pono smiled at Wehi, then stood up from the koa chair and walked over to sit beside her. "In a strange way, what you have just said makes a little sense; but I am concerned that you will not be able to tolerate the journey to this meeting that I have to attend because it will be very cold and I will have to fly higher so that the other pueo 'aumākua do not see you. Plus, I don't know how the other elders will react once they see that I have brought you to our secret meeting place on O'ahu."

"Grandpa Pono," said Wehi, as she clutched her boar's tooth, "you have no other option. I will be safe if I am with you--I know that you will protect me."

Pono stood up and took a deep breath. "You are right, Kawehi Nahele. I have no other option. I will just have to be more vigilant and hope that the other elders understand our situation." Pono looked down at the text message again, then looked at Wehi. "Well, we better get going. Please go put on a sweater and jeans, and the jacket I gave you when we visited Haleākalā last year."

"Okay, Grandpa Pono," said Wehi, as she grabbed a pair of jeans and a sweater, then looked in her closet for the jacket that Pono had given her. After she had set aside the clothes that she was going to wear, Wehi ran into the bathroom, found a rubberband, and tied her long hair up in a tight bun. She didn't want to fuss with it if it got in her face; otherwise, she could lose her grip on Pono during their journey over to the island of Oʻahu.

"Oʻahu means 'the gathering place' and I assumed that it was a gathering place for only people, but now I know that it is also a gathering place for the ʻaumākua elders," mumbled Wehi, as she put on her jeans, turtleneck sweater, and jacket, then ran to join Pono, who was waiting for her in the family room.

"I know that you are going to go over the rules and tell me over and over again about how important it is for me to stay alert and to not fall asleep--especially because the cool temperature and the high altitude might make me feel tired, and how I need to hold on tightly and follow the rules," said Wehi, as she bolted into the family room and jumped up on the couch. Pono looked at his granddaughter for several minutes. Before he could utter his first word, Wehi blurted out, "Yes, Grandpa, I understand that once you become the pueo ʻaumakua, you will not be able to speak with me like how I am speaking to you right now." Pono shook his head from side to side, as if he had water in both of his ears. In the meantime, Wehi reached over and grabbed both of Pono's hands and then looked straight into his eyes. *Your hearing is fine, Grandpa Pono. Don't worry. I can hear your mind speaking to me. Can you hear me speaking to you without using my voice?* Pono's eyes widened. *I am able to communicate with Mom in the same way, but only when she is in her manō ʻaumakua form. Now I know that I can communicate telepathically with you while you are in your human form. Let us find out if we can communicate through our thoughts when you are in your pueo ʻaumakua form*, thought Wehi, as she and Pono walked outside the house and stood on the porch. But before Pono transformed, Wehi quickly turned away from him and covered her eyes so that he could remove his clothes and place them into his satchel before transforming into the pueo 'aumakua.

Okay, Wehi, you can turn around now, thought Pono, as he quickly preened his feathers before they started on their journey over to O'ahu. When Wehi turned around, the first thing that she noticed was her grandfather's huge gold-colored eyes that illuminated the light-brown feathers around his face. Wehi knew that she would have to get used to his appearance, but she still could not believe that this huge owl was also her grandfather with whom she had just held hands with moments before.

As Wehi continued to stare at Pono, he nonchalantly clicked his powerful beak and moved his head from side to side. Wehi couldn't help but chuckle a little, because Pono made gestures that she had only seen in television documentaries of owls; but this owl was her grandfather. *Okay, Wehi. We should get started. It will take us a couple of hours to get there, depending upon the wind speed. Please grab hold of my neck and try to get close to the down of my feathers, where it is warm. Do not fall asleep, Wehi. If the winds are strong, I fear that I will not be able to tell if you lose your grip and fall.* Wehi then placed Pono's satchel over his neck, climbed onto his back, and attached herself to him like a flea attaches to a cat's hair. She knew that she had to be responsible for her own safety, since Pono did not have the time to fashion a rope that would secure her to him without impeding the airflow to his great lungs. If Wehi was not careful, both she and Pono might not make it back.

Pono slowly stretched out both of his powerful wings and flexed them high above the middle of his back, where Wehi had situated herself. As Wehi looked up and admired her grandfather's great wings, which had completely blocked her view of the moon and stars, Pono rotated his head around and stared straight at her.

His big, glowing eyes were mesmerizing to Wehi, but Wehi suddenly realized that to any other person or 'aumakua, the same eyes that made her feel safe, would most definitely impart a feeling of insecurity and fear. After staring at Wehi for a while, Pono tilted his head to the right and gazed at his tail while he moved it back and forth. Wehi couldn't help but giggle. *I know, I know,* thought Pono. *It looks like I am performing a strange dance move, but I am carrying very precious cargo. I need to make sure everything is in top shape! Hold on!* Pono then hopped off the porch and started running toward the edge of the cliff. Wehi's heart started pounding uncontrollably! Prior to this night, she had always flown with a seat belt, securely attached to a seat inside an airplane, and now there was no seat belt, no seat and no airplane! All Wehi had was her Grandpa Pono--he was her only protection from the sky above and the ocean below.

In one quick motion, Pono jumped off the edge of the cliff and free-fell toward the ocean below. Then, in just a few seconds, Pono stretched out his wings and immediately stopped his downward acceleration. This quick change in their momentum made Wehi's stomach feel like it was now in her mouth, but as Pono started to gain altitude, Wehi started to feel invigorated and strong. They were now soaring through the sea mist, and below them, the waning crescent moon's pale light gave rise to a thin, glimmering trail on the ocean's surface.

Pono continued flying low, close to the ocean, for the first thirty minutes of their journey, until they could no longer catch a glimpse of Kaua'i's mountain range. He was tredpidatious about starting his ascent because there would be no sea mist to hide in and other pueo 'aumākua might see them and follow them to the meeting place. Although these meetings for the elders were supposed to be held in secrecy, anyone who made it their full-time job to follow any of the elders could find their secret meeting place. Therefore, all the elders, including Pono, had to be several steps in front of any potential threat. Very strict rules were in place, for this very reason, and Pono was breaking several of them by bringing Wehi along.

I know that bringing you is kapu [forbidden], but I do not have a choice. Leaving you with anyone who does not know our family's situation can leave you vulnerable, Wehi. But I cannot turn my back on this meeting either, as it is my responsibility as an elder to be there. I hope that the other pueo elders understand this decision I have made. Hold on tighter, as I am going to take us high above the clouds for the remainder of our journey.

Wehi tightened her grip and inhaled as much of the warm salt air as she could. She had always loved the smell of the ocean, and therefore had enjoyed the first segment of their journey. Soaring above the calm ocean, in the faint light of the waning crescent moon, catching glimpses of the flying fish jumping out of the water, was soothing to Wehi's soul. The only thing missing was the fishing pole that Manu had given to Wehi on her birthday. It was a perfect night for trolling.

As Pono started his ascent into the clouds above, Wehi couldn't help but wonder if her mother, Mālie, was swimming nearby. Wehi did not have any visions about Mālie being in trouble, so she was hoping that Mālie was safe and making the right decisions. While Wehi continued to worry about her mom, the rhythmic beating of her grandfather's wings, coupled with the warmth of his down feathers, started lulling her to sleep, but Wehi needed to keep her eyes open. After all, Wehi had made a promise to Pono and to herself--a promise to stay awake during their journey to Oʻahu.

Grandpa Pono, I am trying really hard to stay awake, but it is becoming more difficult to keep my eyes open. Do you think that you could fly higher? I know that the colder temperature will make me feel more awake--like how I feel when I splash cold water onto my face in the morning.

I am sorry, Wehi. I fear that if I fly too high, you may lose consciousness, thought Pono.

Oh come on, Grandpa! I am not afraid! Let's go higher!

No, Wehi. This is not a game. We don't have the luxury of time to challenge your body's limits. We will continue on this course for the remainder of our journey, until we arrive at the meeting place of the elders. Please just try to stay awake, chided Pono.

As Pono continued flying toward Oʻahu, he started remembering the night that he and Kahoku had first flown together and how Kahoku behaved just like Wehi--begging and pleading with him to fly higher and higher. It was also a dark evening, with limited moonlight to light the way. Pono was taking Kahoku to the Big Island to show him how magnificent the orange lava looked as it shot out from the Kīlauea volcano into the darkness of the night.

When they arrived at Kīlauea, both Pono and Kahoku became so overwhelmed by the beauty and awesome power of Pele, the goddess of fire, that neither of them paid much attention to their surroundings. As they inadvertently flew over the volcano, the rising hot air caused Pono to ascend quicker and higher than any human would have tolerated, but instead of losing consciousness, Kahoku just started shouting for more! At that moment, Pono knew that Kahoku's destiny was to ride the winds, just as he did. *I miss him too, Grandpa. I miss him too,* thought Wehi, as she continued to share Pono's memory of her brother.

Suddenly, the cloud cover became dense, so Pono placed the wonderful memory of Kahoku back into the most protected area of his mind and focused on the journey he was now sharing with his granddaughter. An hour and a half had passed since they had left Kauaʻi, and both Wehi and Pono were looking forward to being on land. As Pono instinctively started his descent from above the clouds, Wehi could hear how worried he was. *Don't worry, Grandpa*

Pono. We can do this together! thought Wehi, as she tried to calm her grandfather's fears.

When they had finally descended below the clouds, Wehi found herself captivated by what she saw. *Look at that!* thought Wehi, as her eyes focused on a trail of lights that looked like a large snake slithering up to the top of a very steep mountain.

Wehi, the light-snake you are looking at is the H-3 highway, which runs up and through the Koʻolau mountain range. We are flying over the Kāneʻohe side and will soon arrive at the meeting area which is on the opposite side, or the Hālawa side, of the Koʻolau mountain range, thought Pono as he started flying toward the highest point of the intimidating Koʻolau mountains.

A few minutes later, Pono landed on the branch of a large ʻōhiʻa tree that grew above the H-3 highway's tunnel. *Wehi, we are lucky that the winds are gentle and that we can take a little time to enjoy the soothing sounds of the waterfalls and the distant swishing sounds of cars coming into and going out of the H-3 tunnel below,* thought Pono.

I love the sound of the waterfalls and the fresh scent of the rainforest, thought Wehi, as Pono started to stretch out his wings, but just as they were about to take off and fly toward a little flat clearing on the Hālawa side of the H-3, the boar's tooth on Wehi's necklace started to feel uncomfortably warm and Wehi's heart started to beat faster.

Wehi, I hear the other elders coming, but I also hear the beating of wings that are unfamiliar to me. They are not flying in the same direction as the elders, but I cannot discern whether or not they are just innocently passing by or if their intentions are to find our meeting place.

How can you tell who they are without seeing them first, Grandpa Pono? thought Wehi.

Every owl makes a distinct sound when it beats its wings. It is almost like a human voice. I know who that voice--or in this case, that wingbeat--belongs to. The pueo 'aumākua refer to the sound that an owl makes when it beats its wings as 'whispers.' There are whispers in the wind that I am unfamiliar with. We must be vigilant, Wehi.

Wehi's mind was racing and she was scared, but she refused to succumb to her fear. Wehi held on tightly to her grandfather as he glided over to the pueo 'aumākua meeting place on the Hālawa side of the Koʻolau mountain range.

Wehi, are you all right? I know that you are scared, but hopefully this will be over soon.

Don't worry about me, Grandpa Pono. I am okay. I will be quiet and I will listen to whatever you ask me to do.

Pono soon landed at the edge of the clearing and Wehi jumped off of his back then walked over to a nearby rock and sat down. The boar's tooth had stopped feeling uncomfortable and her heart was not racing anymore, so Wehi started to relax a little. After she had sat down on the rock, her fingers soon discovered a pattern of grooves that formed an outline of an owl.

Grandpa Pono, is this a petroglyph?

Yes, Wehi. The rock that you are sitting on has not moved since the first meeting of the pueo elders. There are many other rocks in this area that bare the pueo petroglyph. You would be able to see more of them if there was a full moon above. Prior to the construction of the H-3 highway, when this area was remote and inaccessible, the pueo elders were able to meet under the full moon. Now, because of the many motorists that utilize the H-3, we must conduct our meetings under a waning crescent moon to avoid being seen.

Wehi could tell that her Grandpa Pono was eagerly awaiting the arrival of the other elders, so she just sat quietly and continued to run her fingers over the petroglyph. *I hope they don't get mad at you for bringing me, Grandpa,* thought Wehi, as she looked over at him. But Pono was no longer listening to her. He was listening to whispers in the wind that he was familiar with.

The other elders are almost here, Wehi. Stay alert!

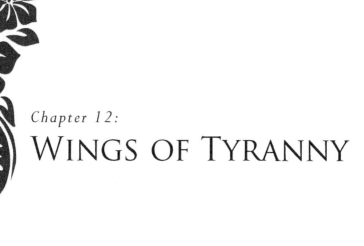

Chapter 12:

WINGS OF TYRANNY

That same evening, on the island of Maui, Manu had just parked the rental car alongside a dilapidated house located deep within the rainforest of Hāna. The day had brought nothing but confusion and frustration for Martin and Manu. In the course of twelve hours, neither of them had come up with any new information on the boy who had been murdered in Kalalau Valley.

"This might be another dead end, Manu," whispered Martin as he put on his jacket. Martin was tired and very disappointed that they had not found the boy's relatives. It was now almost nine o'clock in the evening. There were no lights on the isolated road and no lights in the house. It would have been completely pitch black had it not been for the low glow emanating from the lights of their rental car. "Why did we come up here at such a late hour?" asked Martin.

"Well, I thought that there was a better chance that someone would be home at this time of day. I mean, think about all the doors that we have already knocked on and got no answer because people were probably at work or running errands," responded Manu.

"Well, we are here, so let's at least take a look around," said Martin, as he opened the trunk lid of the rental car and took two flashlights out of his duffel bag, then handed one to Manu.

"Thanks for the flashlight," said Manu, as he carefully and quietly shut the trunk lid for Martin.

"This gives me the chills," whispered Martin as they crept slowly toward the eerie house. "It feels like no one has lived here for many years. Whose place is this, anyway?"

Manu turned his flashlight on and started to walk toward the front door of the old house. "The last guy I talked to said that it belonged to an old Hawaiian man named Kona. The guy said that Kona lived like a hermit--never really showed his face around town, not even for his children's funeral services; but he also said that this old man, Kona, might know the name of the young man who was murdered, because he is supposed to be a kahuna of some sort," said Manu.

"What a piece of work. What father doesn't attend their children's funeral services?" asked Martin, as he and Manu both stepped onto the porch. Manu then knocked on the door, but the only thing there to greet the two of them was the humming sound of the mosquitoes circling over the stagnant pools of water scattered throughout the rotting porch and the gurgling of a small stream that ran through the back of the property. "Does anyone live here anymore?" asked Martin. "This place gives me the heebie-jeebies. Maybe we should just come back in the morning."

"We are here already, Marty," said Manu. "I don't really want to come back if we don't have to. Plus, the sooner we get this over with, the sooner I can return home to my family. I tried calling my dad's cell phone several times, but my calls immediately went to his voice mail. My father always answers his calls--unless he is working in the emergency room, or something bad happened."

"Your dad is probably busy in the emergency room, Manu. Don't worry. Mālie and Wehi are probably safe at home wondering about how we're doing. I am sure that all of them are okay."

"That's the part that is worrying me, Marty. Mālie has not answered her cell phone either. All my calls have gone to voice mail."

As they both started to leave the porch, Martin suddenly fell to the ground. Manu immediately turned around and saw a deranged old man squatting alongside Martin and holding a large piece of koa wood stained with Martin's blood. The old man quickly pulled off Martin's jacket, grabbed Martin's flashlight, and crushed Martin's cell phone with his calloused feet. He was just about to toss Martin's jacket aside when he noticed the embroidered name above the right pocket. His voice cracked as he read the name aloud: "Detective Martin Kainoa Johnson."

The old man paused for a while, which made Manu wonder if perhaps the old man was remorseful for his outburst toward Martin. But before Manu could utter one word, the old man let out a loud, deep scream and kneeled down alongside Martin's unconscious body. Raising the piece of koa wood above his head, the old man was just about to deliver a fatal blow to Martin's skull when Manu tackled him to the ground, consequently breaking the old termite-eaten porch floor. Fearing that the frail old man might have succumbed after being tackled, Manu immediately got up and walked slowly over toward the old man's body lying prone on the ground. But to Manu's amazement and horror, the old man pulled himself up, spat out the blood in his mouth, and smiled eerily at him.

Manu quickly drew his side arm and moved Martin away from the porch with his free hand. "We don't want any pilikia with you, old man. Just want to ask you some questions, that's all. We are trying to find more information on a young teenage boy that was killed on Kaua'i. I have a picture here. I can show it to…" Manu immediately stopped talking. The old man had started grunting and posturing, all the while seemingly unaware of the blood oozing from his right palm, which had been lacerated by one of the old rotted boards that made up the porch. "Old man, your palm is bleeding. Let me bandage it for you!" But the old man pretended that he couldn't hear Manu. He continued to smirk at Manu as he quickly untied a bag that he had around his waist and then placed his bleeding hand into it. "What have you got there?" asked Manu, as he shined his flashlight onto the bag. He was relieved when he saw that the bag was too small to hold a weapon, but he was still cautious as to what the contents could be. "Hey, old man, you must be cold. All you have on is a malo [loincloth]. Why don't you slowly pull your hand out from the bag and I will get you a jacket."

The old man looked up at Manu, licked his bloody lip, and started walking toward him. Manu cocked his gun and aimed it directly at the old man. "Does my bag appear large enough to hide a weapon, Detective?" asked the old man, sarcastically.

"I asked you to slowly take your hand out of your bag. I am not going to play a guessing game with you!" said Manu, firmly.

The old man backed up a little. He needed to time things perfectly for his plan to work. He could feel his power growing, but he needed to finish one more vital step to solidify his transformation. As he slowly raised his hands, the old man shouted back to Manu, "You can see for yourself that I do not have a gun or any other weapon in my hand, just dirt!"

Even though Manu had a flashlight, it was still very dark. All Manu could see was that the old man was not holding a weapon. "I don't know what you are up to, old man, but I want you to slowly lie down on the porch with your face on the ground and your hands behind your head."

"No problem, Detective. I will be happy to oblige your request," snickered the old man. As he slowly started to kneel down, the old man pretended to lose his balance and fell head first toward the ground. The commotion allowed the old man to conceal the fact that he had shoved the black dirt from his bag into his mouth and swallowed it. Manu quickly returned his gun to its holster and ran over to where the old man was laid out on the ground, straddled him, and grabbed the old man's hands and cuffed both of them behind the old man's back. As Manu pulled the old man up and walked him over to the car, Manu noticed that the old man had ingested a black substance, which had coated his lips, fingers, and palm.

"What did you eat, Old Man? This isn't dirt!" shouted Manu, as he looked down at his fingers and then rubbed his hands on his jeans to try and remove the black substance which had been transferred to him when he had subdued the old man.

The old man started to squirm and stomp his feet. "My name is Kona, and soon I will not be trapped in this weak old body anymore!" Manu had witnessed this before, but he didn't recognize what was occurring until it was happening right in front of him again. The once frail, decrepit old man started filling out--muscles that had atrophied were now well-defined, and his posture was straighter than it had been in years. As he continued to grow more muscular, Kona soon broke free of the handcuffs that Manu had placed over his wrists. But before Kona could fully stand in front of Manu as a man, his metamorphosis into his pueo ʻaumakua form shifted into high gear. Manu fell to his knees in fear as Kona now stood before him completely transformed into an enormous owl. In his ʻaumakua form, Kona was bigger and more intimidating than Manu's father, Pono.

Kona shook his muscular neck and fluffed up his feathers before focusing his big orange-colored eyes on Manu, who in shock remained still, looking up at Kona. In a split second, Kona lashed out at Manu and lacerated his chin with his beak. Meanwhile, Martin finally regained consciousness. As Martin's vision slowly started to improve, he could not believe what was standing just ten feet in front of him. But Martin did not have time to try and sort the details out. Without further hesitation, Martin scooped Manu up, pushed him into the back seat of the car, closed the car door, then leaped up into the front seat, started the car, and slammed his right foot down on the gas pedal. Kona then let out a blood-curdling screech, as he stretched out his enormous black-tipped wings and ascended into the night sky.

Martin's mind was racing as he and Manu made their escape, and he struggled to catch his breath after bringing the car to a complete stop under a thick canopy of ironwood trees. He had seen Kona fly away through the rearview mirror, so he planned to hide under the cover of the trees until he knew that Kona was not waiting for them to emerge on the other side. After a few seconds had passed, Martin turned around to face Manu, who seemed much calmer than Martin had expected him to be. But Manu didn't say anything to Martin. Instead, Manu just casually opened the back door of the car, stepped outside, and checked his gun and its holster. After a few minutes had passed, Manu shut the back door of the car, then opened the front passenger's side door, sat down next to Martin, and then closed the car door as if nothing had happened.

"Man oh man. Manu, what the heck just happened?!" exclaimed Martin. But Manu said nothing as he ripped off a piece of his shirt and firmly held it over his chin to try and stop the bleeding. After the bleeding had subsided, Manu reached for his cell phone and started to call Mālie.

"Brother, I am not moving from this spot till we, or you, make some sense out of what just happened back there!" shouted Martin, as Manu continued dialing. But Manu didn't say anything to Martin as he waited for Mālie to pick up her cell phone. Just as Manu was about to hang up, Mālie answered her phone. It was now nine forty-five in the evening. There were no planes available to take Martin and Manu back home to Kaua'i. They would just have to wait until the morning.

Manu put his index finger over his lips so as to shush Martin while he was speaking with Mālie. "Mālie, I was so worried about everyone at home," started Manu.

"Manu," interrupted Mālie, "do you know where Pono and Wehi are? I came home about thirty minutes ago, and I have left several messages on Pono's voice mail. Did he call and let you know where they were going?"

"I have not heard from Pono or Wehi. Maybe they left a note for you in the kitchen," answered Manu.

"I found a butter knife in the sink and someone forgot to throw away a banana peel, so I think that Wehi must have made a peanut butter and banana sandwich, but aside from that, there is no note, Manu. I also checked with the hospital, and Pono was not there," Mālie said anxiously. Her voice started to crack and Manu could tell that she had been crying. "Manu, something is not right. I cannot reach my father either. I have tried calling him at home and I have called all of the people on the contact list he gave us before he left to go see his uncle, Makoa. I even went out and looked for him in my manō ʻaumakua form, but I was unable to locate him. Manu, I am afraid!" Mālie started to cry, and Manu, feeling as though he were powerless and unable to protect his family, let the phone fall onto his knees.

Martin quickly picked up the phone and waved it in front of Manu's face, hoping Manu would come to his senses and speak to his wife. Manu grabbed the phone from Martin and continued his conversation with Mālie. "Sweetheart, please lock all the doors, shut off the lights, and run into the woodshop and wait for me there." After ending his call, Manu placed his phone in his lap and shook his head. "What am I going to do?" sighed Manu, as he looked over at Martin.

"Don't you check out on me now, Brother!" shouted Martin. "I am not stupid. I know that you are hiding something from me. So first, you are going to tell me what you already know about all of this supernatural stuff. Second, you are going to tell me how all of this involves your family and finally, after you have come clean about everything, we are going to sort out all of this trouble and kick some ʻōkole! [butt].”

Manu sat motionless in his seat for a while as he stared at Martin, who was looking over at him. “Manu,” started Martin, “there is nowhere that we can go. It is too late to catch a plane and way too early to head out to the airport. To complicate matters, we don't know where this old man Kona is. For all we know, Kona could be circling over us, hidden under the cover of darkness, waiting until we come out from under this tunnel of trees to continue his assault on both of us. You need to tell me what you know,” pleaded Martin.

“Okay, I will tell you everything that I know, Marty, but I am still trying to figure it out,” said Manu, as he looked into the rearview mirror and stared at the wound on his chin.

“Brother, I wish I had some popcorn right now, because I know that the story you are going to tell me is gonna be EPIC!” exclaimed Martin. Although Martin's intention was to make Manu feel a little more at ease, all Manu felt was a strange sense of discomfort. His skin felt extremely itchy--like it had tiny mites crawling under it, and he was starting to perspire profusely. Everything around him was spinning. His temperature shot up, and his breathing rate increased rapidly. “Manu, brother, are you okay?” asked Martin, but Manu could not hear him. His head started to ache and his eyes felt like worms were crawling through them. Seconds later, Manu opened the passenger's door and vomited up stomach acid onto the side of the road.

Back in Hālawa, all the pueo elders had finally arrived. After they had changed back into their human forms, Pono took his rightful position within the circle of elders then motioned for Wehi to come stand in front of him. "Before we start this meeting, I would like to introduce all of you to my granddaughter, Wehi."

"We all feel for you and your family's struggles, Pono, but I don't understand how you could violate one of our rules by bringing an outsider to our meeting," said Kamaka, who was second in command under Pono.

"Then you do not really empathize with my family's situation, Kamaka. Listen, I understand the importance of fulfilling my responsibility to the pueo council, and so I am here tonight. My family and I are still trying to pick up the pieces, so please allow me this one pardon," retorted Pono, as he pulled Wehi closer to him.

Wehi, I hope that in the midst of all the verbal exchange and posturing, you will be able to read the minds of all the elders who are here, because I am skeptical of the company that I keep--I no longer know where the allegiances of the elders lie, thought Pono, as he glanced over at all of the elders that continued to stare at Wehi. *There is one thing that I am sure of--one of the elders here tonight knows more than he is letting on. Life has taught me that sometimes people who simply inherit leadership positions are the very ones who are easily swayed into betraying those whom they should protect.*

Kamaka cleared his throat, then addressed Pono. "Pono, may I speak with you in private?" As Kamaka and Pono walked off together, Wehi grabbed her boar's tooth necklace, which had again become very warm. All of a sudden, Wehi felt dizzy and very nauseous.

Grandpa Pono, thought Wehi, *something is very wrong with my dad. He is in pain! He is hurting!* At this point, the nausea was so overpowering that Wehi fell to the ground and started dry heaving.

"What is wrong with her?" asked Kamaka's oldest son Kaleo, who immediately started to distance himself from Wehi.

Grandpa Pono, continued Wehi, *I can see through my dad's eyes. He is scared! A very old man on Maui changed into a pueo--a very big and very dangerous pueo! His name is Kona!*

Pono's gaze settled back on Kamaka. "Kamaka, do you know of an old man named Kona who lives on Maui?" he asked sternly.

"Your father served with Kona in the war, Pono. Didn't he tell you about Kona?" asked Kamaka.

"No, my father never told me about Kona," replied Pono, who then walked closer to Kamaka. "If this involved the ʻaumākua then perhaps my father had his reasons for not telling me."

"Perhaps, Pono. After all, when you first became an elder, you did admit to the council that you shunned your family's ʻaumakua legacy when you were a younger man. Therefore, it does not surprise me that your father, who was a respected kahuna, did not tell you about his relationship with Kona," quipped Kamaka, as he stared at Pono for a while before continuing on. "The council elders, who passed away before you were asked to join, did mention the great rift between Kona and your father, Pono. After the war ended, your father severed all ties with Kona. But it wasn't until some time had passed and both men had gotten on with their lives that the reason for their falling out came to the surface. Most of the information came from Kona himself, who spent many nights ranting while locked up in a holding cell after being arrested for drunken brawls. Thus, many ʻaumākua viewed whatever he said as conjecture. But some of the pueo ʻaumākua elders believed that it was your father who was instrumental in taking away Kona's ʻaumakua--though none of them knew if your father did it himself, or if he knew the kahuna that possessed such power. The only fact that was undisputable was that Kona broke the ʻaumākua code. Pono, why are you now inquiring about Kona?" asked a puzzled Kamaka.

Pono's mind started racing. He was trying to put all the pieces of this puzzle together, but he could feel Wehi's concern for her dad growing. Just as Pono was about to address the other elders and end the meeting, Kaleo reached over and grabbed Pono by the shoulder.

"I heard rumors that this guy named Kona was trying to find some-one's iwi [bones], but that was some time ago," admitted Kaleo.

"I must get Wehi home so I can tend to her medically," said Pono as he motioned to the other elders to come together in a circle, so that he could end the meeting. Pono knew that Kamaka and the other elders would not ask for more details from him if he needed to take care of Wehi.

"You will have much to explain at our next meeting, Pono," said Kamaka, who then took a few steps back, transformed into his pueo ʻaumakua, then flew away from the meeting place, followed by his son, Kaleo.

Don't worry, Grandpa. I feel strong enough to fly with you. I can no longer see what is happening to my dad. The last thing I saw was him vomiting outside of a car, thought Wehi.

I am sorry, Wehi. I cannot take you to find your dad. I fear that I will not be able to protect you from Kona. If what I have heard is true, and Kona has found a way to regain his pueo ʻaumakua, then I will be hard-pressed to keep you safe while trying to subdue him. Your dad would agree with me. Let me take you home. Your mom is probably very worried about you.

Pono then found an old rope lying on the ground by the meet-ing area, and asked another elder to tether Wehi to him after he had changed into his pueo ʻaumakua--just in case Wehi fell asleep or had more visions of her father.

After Pono and Wehi had flown away from the meeting area, Wehi fell asleep and Pono finally felt a sense of relief wash over him. *Wehi, I am hoping that you are able to sleep because your fa-ther and Martin are safe. I promise you that I will find the solution to our family's plight. I just need a little more time.* Yet, no matter what he told himself, Pono knew that he could not save his family on his own.

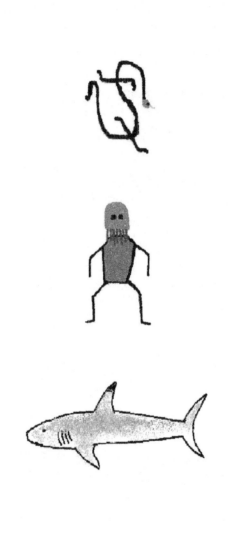

Chapter 13:

DARK WATER

K e Aliʻi was barely conscious when a big ominous shadow walked into the damp, cold, partially submerged cave. "You are smaller than I remember, Ke Aliʻi, and you are still a big disappointment to our manō ʻaumākua," taunted a deep voice.

As the shadow came closer, Ke Aliʻi finally saw the face of his captor, who then grabbed him by the neck and lifted him high above the floor of the damp cave, causing Ke Aliʻi's feet to dangle in the air. "Uncle, I thought that after all these years you and I would exchange words instead of blows," said Ke Aliʻi, calmly.

"Nothing has changed between us, except that you are weaker and look older than when I last saw you," said Makoa as he motioned for one of his followers to come closer. "You have lost your edge in the water, Ke Aliʻi. I thought that it would be more difficult to subdue you, but it was just like catching a seal pup," said Makoa as he shook his head in disgust, then threw Ke Aliʻi onto the wet floor of the cave. "Instead of getting stronger as you age, you grow weaker. You are still not embracing the legacy that you were given. Not only are you manō, but you are a direct descendant of the first warrior who was bestowed the gift of the manō ʻaumākua," roared

Makoa, as he started breaking apart pieces of animal flesh and eating it right in front of Ke Aliʻi.

"The gift of the manō ʻaumākua was given to protect our people during times of hardship. It was not given to intimidate or control them," replied Ke Aliʻi sternly.

Makoa threw the remaining animal carcass onto the floor of the wet cave, walked up to Ke Aliʻi, and then struck him across the mouth. He did not care that Ke Aliʻi was his nephew. All Makoa cared about was manō hegemony, and he would not hesitate to beat others into submission. Ke Aliʻi spit out the blood from his mouth and looked up at his uncle. Both of Ke Aliʻi's hands and feet were in chains so he could not fight back.

"You are pathetic, Nephew! If I had been captured and placed in chains, I would immediately harness the strength of the manō and break them. Unlike you, I embrace my manō nature in its entirety. I roam the sea as manō, feed as manō, and relish the fact that I am the top predator, as I was born to be. But you, Nephew, choose to ignore this side of yourself instead of embracing it as I do. You cower at the thought of losing your human side and that is your weakness. Perhaps you fear the consequences of breaking one of the ʻaumākua codes, which dictates that if you feed while in your ʻaumakua form, you will eventually lose your ability to change back to your human form. Look at me! I have fed while in my manō form, yet I stand in front of you as a man. But then again, I am stronger than you, Ke Aliʻi," scoffed Makoa, as he placed his large hand on Ke Aliʻi's head and pushed Ke Aliʻi down until he was on his knees.

"By the way, Nephew, it did not take much to capture you and bring you here. All I had to do was quickly swim up behind you, while in my manō form, stretch out my human arms and grab your tail fin, and hold you still until you became unconscious. My men then pulled you out of the ocean, placed you into a zodiac, and brought you here. I doubt that you have mastered this ability to use both human and ʻaumakua traits at the same time. Only the strongest can perform such a feat and you, my nephew, will never ascend to my level." Ke Aliʻi did not say anything as his uncle turned and walked away from him. "Funny how the descendants of such formidable opponents have all fallen at my feet: a father taken from his son, a mother taken from her son, a son taken before his time, and a grandfather taken from his precious little granddaughter," said Makoa as he exited the damp cave.

At that very moment, Ke Aliʻi's greatest fear had materialized. Makoa was the manō that Ke Aliʻi had spotted in the picture that was in Kahoku's room. Makoa's treachery and murderous acts were all starting to come to light. But what was his end game? What was he after? What could he possibly attain from killing Ke Aliʻi and his family? Although he was tired and beaten, Ke Aliʻi's mind continued to race as he tried to figure out what Makoa was after. Despite all the questions that were now swirling around in his head, Ke Aliʻi had found the answer to the most heart-wrenching one: his uncle, Makoa, was responsible for the death of Pono's father, Pono's wife Aukele, and Ke Aliʻi's beloved grandson, Kahoku.

As Ke Aliʻi inspected his chains for weak links, his anger and rage continued to escalate while his physical strength diminished. He was so emotionally overcome with feelings of loss and embarrassment. His own uncle had not only broken all of the codes of the ʻaumākua, but he was also responsible for killing Ke Aliʻi's family.

"There has to be others who are part of this insidious plan," whispered Ke Aliʻi as he got up and paced back and forth within the length of his chains. Visions of sinister, callous, evil acts played out in his mind, challenging the very backbone of his character, torturing him throughout the evening. With every thunderous sound of the waves crashing against the walls of his prison, Ke Aliʻi was reminded that he was a beaten man. He was weak! He was a man who had failed to keep his family safe! There was nothing he could do.

All the hope that he had drifted out into the open ocean. The tide was changing, and with it, the fate of the ʻaumākua. After contemplating his situation, Ke Aliʻi put his back against the wall of the damp cave, buried his face in his hands, and wept.

"I am going to leave him in there until his spirit is completely broken and his body is all but a skeleton of his once-great stature," said Makoa to one of his followers who stood outside Ke Aliʻi's prison. "He will succumb to the elements. His sorrow is preventing him from gathering the strength he needs to transform into his manō ʻaumakua. When the time is right, I will present him with an opportunity to get the revenge he desires. Then I will kill him, and when he is dead, I will take his power from him--just like that wretched old man Kona harvested the power from the remains of Kekipi, the most powerful kahuna ʻanāʻanā. In the end, after I have acquired Ke Aliʻi's strength, I will make the pueo ʻaumākua realize that manō are intelligent, mighty ʻaumākua that should be feared and worshipped!"

Chapter 14:

RETURN OF THE 'IO 'ĀHINAHINA (SILVER HAWK)

The chill in the Maui night air provided a welcome respite for Martin, who had just gotten comfortable in the driver's seat. The wound that Martin had sustained from Kona's blow to his head had finally stopped bleeding, and Manu had fallen asleep in the passenger's seat. But much to Martin's dismay, Manu's body temperature continued to escalate, despite the cool breeze that Martin had let in. Martin looked over at his sleeping friend and sighed. "What am I going to do, Brother? Your wound is probably infected and that is why you are so warm. I want to start this car and take you straight to the hospital, but what if that freak of nature gets to us before we get off this treacherous road?" Martin gingerly opened his door a little wider to let more cool air into the car.

It had been two hours since the attack. The only sounds Martin could hear were the chirping of the crickets and the gurgling of the mountain stream that ran alongside the road. The fragrance of the fern and the white ginger, surrounding the area where Martin had parked the rental car, comforted him by bringing back memories of stringing leis for parades and other special events with Senator Braga's family, who had adopted him after his mother had died in Kōkeʻe. Martin was just about to start the car when he noticed a big pair of orange-colored eyes staring right at him through the windshield.

Before Martin could close his door, Kona used his powerful beak to grab hold of the door, and rip it out. In the few hours since their last encounter, Kona had become bigger and stronger. He had broken another code of the ʻaumākua to do so, which was evidenced by the piece of pig flesh hanging from the tip of his beak. Martin kicked Kona's body as hard as he could, but to no avail.

Once Kona pulled Martin out of the car, Kona unleashed his rage without any hesitation, and Martin knew his life was about to end. In his final moments, Martin looked over at Manu, who had opened his eyes but sat frozen in a catatonic state in the passenger's seat. "Goodbye, my friend; goodbye, my brother," said Martin. Then in one quick motion, Kona punctured Martin's heart with his talons, took hold of Martin's legs, and carried Martin's lifeless body off into the night sky.

At the opposite end of the Hawaiian island chain, somewhere between the islands of Oʻahu and Kauaʻi, Pono was a third of the way home when he felt the tension of the rope, which tethered Wehi to his body, loosen. His heart dropped as he felt the rope slip from his body and fall away. As Pono changed his position quickly and started to dive down to look for Wehi, his fear suddenly turned to amazement.

Hi, Pops. It is good to fly with you again. Pono's heart started to race, and for a very brief moment, Pono almost forgot how to fly.

Careful, Pops. Remember all the lectures you gave me about keeping my composure, especially while flying?

How is this possible? thought Pono. *There is only one person who called me that, but he is gone. Where is Wehi?*

Don't worry, Grandpa Pono. I am here with Kahoku, thought Wehi.

Both confused and stunned by what he had just heard, Pono looked down and saw a majestic 'io powering through the air currents beneath him. *I can't believe it! Is this real? Wehi, what happened?*

Kahoku is back with us, Grandpa! thought Wehi.

Wait a minute. A few seconds ago, the rope broke and I thought that I had lost you, Wehi. How is it that you are now a hawk, flying beneath me, and Kahoku is with you?

Sorry, Pops. If we did not break the rope, we would have injured you during our transformation. I apologize for worrying you, thought Kahoku.

Grandpa Pono, stop worrying. Kahoku is back. My big brother is back! Uku is back with us!

Wehi, depending on how you spell it, the word uku can mean "flea." You are the only one I know of that calls your brother "flea"--more specifically, "head lice," thought Pono, as he and Kahoku started chuckling together within their thoughts.

Hmmm....head lice. That is what the school nurse is checking for when she looks through everyone's hair with a wooden chopstick. Yikes. I didn't know that the word "uku" referred to head lice. Oh well, I like the way it sounds, and Kahoku doesn't mind, thought Wehi.

We are on this journey together, Pops. It is through Wehi that I am able to be here physically. Together, Wehi and I form the 'io 'āhinahina [silver hawk]. I wish we had more time to catch up, Pops, but we must find my dad and stop Kona.

Agreed. Let us find Manu and Kona together, thought Pono, as he and the ʻio ʻāhinahina adjusted their course and flew off toward the island of Maui.

Meanwhile, back on Maui, Manu's body temperature continued to rise, along with his need to get out of the car and stretch his arms, which caused him to awaken from the trance-like sleep he had fallen into for a couple of hours. As he stretched out and felt the cool air, Manu caught a glimpse of himself in the reflection of the car window. He might have been a disbeliever, even up to the moment he witnessed Kona's transformation, but now he could not deny his heritage. Manu was a pueo, mighty and stately. All of his senses were heightened, and the strength he felt as he inhaled the night air into his great lungs made him want to test his newfound abilities.

But just as his amazement had peaked, so too did his memory of Martin's last moments. Manu's incubation period allowed his body's cells to perform his metamorphosis while sparing his mind from the events that had occurred around him. But slowly, Manu's memory of what had happened started to return. He needed to find Martin at any cost. He needed to master his abilities now, not later. He needed to bring his friend home. As Manu tried to figure out how to fly, both Pono and the ʻio ʻāhinahina descended from the sky and landed right beside him.

Manu, we are glad that we found you, thought Pono and the ʻio ʻāhinahina. Manu was, at first, taken by surprise. But soon after being reunited with his father and children, all the questions that flooded Manu's mind were quickly answered, as no words needed to be said. Reading each other's thoughts provided a much faster and purer form of communication, and within seconds, Manu knew everything he needed to know. As Pono started to put all the puzzle pieces together in his mind, so too did Manu and the ʻio ʻāhinahina.

Of course they could choose not to share certain thoughts; however, that would take more practice. This was a new experience for everyone except Wehi, who was a little more polished, having used this skill before on Mālie and Pono.

Now united, under the waning crescent moon, Wehi and Pono quieted their thoughts and allowed only Kahoku to communicate with Manu. Since reuniting with Manu, both Wehi and Pono could feel the special bond that existed between Manu and Kahoku and how it transcended everything else. *Dad,* thought Kahoku, *do you remember the first time you taught me to spear fish? Do you remember the parrot fish and gigantic eel that I caught for you when we went camping on my eighth birthday?*

Manu was overcome with joy and emotion. He knew that his son had returned the minute that the 'io 'āhinahina stood alongside him, but this was the first time that he could hear only Kahoku's thoughts and feel how much his son missed and loved him. *Yes, my son, I remember everything I taught you and everything we did together.*

Dad, thought Kahoku, *let me now teach you how to fly so that we may go on this journey together.* Manu wanted so badly to return to his human form and hold Kahoku close to him, but he knew that he needed to find Martin and stop Kona from harming anyone else. He listened to Kahoku's thoughts and then ascended slowly into the sky with Pono and the 'io 'āhinahina.

The stars blanketed the heaven above, and the white caps of the waves beneath them slowly started coming into view as the dawn of a new day was upon them. After practicing with the 'io 'āhinahina for a little while, Manu felt ready to start the journey, and all of them headed out after Kona.

Even with their great eyes and speed, Pono, Manu and the 'io 'āhinahina could not cover such a large distance if they stayed together, so they decided to split up and concentrate on the area surrounding the island of Maui and the Big Island. They knew that

Kona had to be in that particular region because Pono and the ʻio ʻāhinahina had recently flown in from Oʻahu and had not encountered Kona on the way over to Maui. *Grandpa Pono, you and Dad circle over Maui. Wehi and I will fly toward the island of Hawaiʻi,* thought Kahoku.

Agreed, thought both Pono and Manu, who then flew off in different directions--over the island of Maui--to find Martin and Kona.

Now alone, for the first time, Wehi finally had the opportunity to speak with her brother without anyone else listening in. Wehi was a conduit for Kahoku; she allowed him to telepathically communicate with their father and grandfather and to have the physical form that he needed to accomplish his destiny. In turn, Wehi was able to experience the incredible abilities of the ʻio ʻaumakua. But neither Wehi nor Kahoku gave much thought to the power of the ʻio ʻāhinahina that they formed together; the only thing that meant the most to the both of them was that they were together again!

I missed you, Uku.

I know, Wehi. But I was always there watching you. I am so very proud of how you have handled all of this.

How does this work, Uku? Do you get to stay with us like before?

ʻAʻole [no], Wehi. I must leave when my work here is done.

Where do you go when you are not here with us, Uku? Do you return to Heaven?

What do you think of when you wonder about Heaven, Wehi?

Well, I think both of our grandmothers are there, along with all of our loved ones who no longer live on Earth with us. Oh, I also think that Heaven is beautiful--with blue, clear oceans and green valleys and lots of fragrant flowers. Do you stay with our family members, Uku? Did it hurt to die? Were you afraid?

It hurt, just for a moment, but then I felt like I had returned to a place that was familiar to me. I felt like I had returned home. This will be hard for you to understand, Wehi, but I feel closer now to everyone I love than I have ever felt before. It is like when Grandpa Pono, Dad, and both of us are together and we feel connected through our thoughts. That is how I feel--totally connected with everything and everyone. When I drowned, I looked back at my body and immediately felt an overwhelming sense of appreciation for the experience it allowed me to have while I lived here with all of you. Then, I realized that I was returning to the place where I had existed before my life here started--I was going home.

Can I go with you when you return to Heaven, Uku?

My dearest sister, you are going to influence so many people and help them realize that their lives mean so much. Therefore, I cannot take you with me. Heaven is not yet ready to receive such a precious soul like yours. Do you understand this, Wehi?

Wehi was saddened by Kahoku's response, so she blocked him from hearing her thoughts. She detested the idea of having to say goodbye to him again. Although Wehi understood what Kahoku was telling her, she hated the thought of having to live without him.

Wehi, please don't shut me out, thought Kahoku, but Wehi remained silent. *Wehi, I will always be proud of you, and I will always love you. When you have accomplished everything you need to do and have helped all the people you need to help, and when Heaven is ready for your arrival, then I will come to take you home.* But despite Kahoku's attempts to reach out to her, Wehi continued to keep her thoughts to herself. Kahoku knew that his little sister was struggling with the answer he had given her, and he again felt a deep-seated negativity festering within Wehi's soul--the same negativity he had first felt when they started their journey with Pono. He knew that Wehi was trying very hard to hide a dark side from him; a side that fed off of her pain and her need for vengeance against those who had taken him away from her.

Back on Maui, Manu was just about to fly over the Hāna forest reserve and head toward Haleakalā when he caught sight of Kona, perched above the ocean on the rocky cliffs of Honokalani Beach. Kona turned his head toward Manu's position and immediately released his hold on Martin's lifeless body, which plummeted into the ocean below. Manu despaired at witnessing such blatant disregard for life--especially when the victim had grown up with him and was his best friend.

As Manu flew in closer toward Kona, he could see Martin's broken body below. The water surrounding Martin changed to a dark shade of red, and the once-formidable crashing, thunderous waves now appeared to gently caress Martin's body, like a mother wrapping her baby in a blanket. Then, in a matter of minutes, the ocean moved Martin's body from its surface down into its deepest recesses, far away from everyone that had loved him.

As Manu circled over the site one more time, he witnessed something that would haunt his thoughts for the rest of his life: a big manō appeared in the same spot that previously cradled Martin's lifeless body. Manu's heart sank as thoughts of what the manō was doing to Martin's remains made him sick to his stomach. How could he ever accept the fact that his father-in-law and his wife were manō 'aumākua after witnessing this? Both rage and grief overcame Manu while his mind struggled to differentiate between wild manō and manō 'aumākua. Manu had now completely lost his focus, and if he could not clear his mind, he would become Kona's next victim.

Notwithstanding his inner conflict regarding the manō 'aumākua, Manu's mind also started reflecting on the special bond he shared with Martin, who had always been there for him since they were toddlers. After losing their mothers, both Manu and Martin found solace in each other's company. As they grew into adults, both men came to depend on the other for advice and support. But unlike Manu, who was very soft spoken, Martin was not afraid to say what was on his mind; therefore, Manu always knew where he stood with Martin and he grew to appreciate Martin's honesty and forthrightness.

You saw me through the most difficult times in my life, and I let you down, Brother. I let you down, thought Manu, as his earlier resolve to catch Kona without harming him slowly started to slip away. A vengeful Manu now homed in on Kona, who after releasing Martin's body into the ocean, never once moved from his perch. As Manu circled around Kona, Manu surmised that Kona was trying to intimidate and frighten him by not moving from his perch at the edge of the rocky cliffs. But regardless of how intimidating Kona was, Manu was not about to back down. In light of what Manu had witnessed since he had encountered Kona at Honokalani beach, Manu willingly set aside his previous resolve to not harm Kona. A greater, more visceral need had surfaced within Manu--one that mandated Kona's obliteration.

One way or another, I will bring you down for what you have done to my brother, old man. If I were you, I would pray that my father Pono and the ‘io ‘āhinahina get to you first, because I am not going to show you any mercy for what you have done, thought Manu, as he made his final approach toward Kona.

Several miles south of Manu and Kona's location, Wehi became despondent. She had seen what Kona had done to her uncle Martin, through the connection she shared with Manu, and she could feel Manu's anguish as he watched a giant shark swim over to where Martin's body had last been seen. To make matters worse, Wehi could also feel that Manu's initial resolve to only capture Kona had changed. Manu was now intending to kill him.

We need to hurry, Uku. Dad needs us. He is planning to kill Kona, thought Wehi, who along with Kahoku, immediately changed their direction and headed over to Manu's location. Pono, however, did not yet know of Manu's dire situation: he was still too far away for Wehi to alert him to Manu's plight, since Wehi had to physically see Pono in order to telepathically communicate with him.

Chapter 15:

DESTINY AWAITS

The tide began to change and the morning sun started to stretch out its warm rays across the Hawaiian Islands. For Wehi and her family, Ka Lā (the Sun) was a force that perpetuated throughout time, unyielding and ever-vigilant, always remaining a beacon of hope for all who believed that they could find and fulfill their destiny.

Our family loves this time of day. Grandpa Pono refers to it as Ka lā hiki ola [the dawning of a new day]. I hope that on this new day, we are not too late to prevent our father from making a huge mistake, thought Wehi.

Don't worry, Wehi, thought Kahoku. *You and our family will enjoy many more of these moments together.*

As Wehi and Kahoku flew in closer to Manu, Wehi caught a glimpse of her grandfather Pono, and three others that were pursuing him. *They have been following me for some time. I don't think they are after me. Otherwise, they would have made a move already,* thought Pono.

All of a sudden, Wehi overheard the thoughts of Pono's pursuers. *Grandpa Pono,* thought Wehi, *the bigger pueo is called Kalei, and her rider is her mother, Kawahine. The pueo that is flying alongside Kalei is Kawika, the youngest son of the pueo elder Kamaka. You were right, Grandpa Pono! They are not after you, they are after Kona. He has desecrated Kawahine's family's burial place and has stolen the bones of Kawahine's mother, Kekipi.*

So that is how Kona regained his 'aumakua, thought Pono.

That is why I am here, Grandpa Pono, responded Kahoku.

Wehi was very troubled. Somehow, Manu's uncontrollable anger had blocked out her attempt to telepathically communicate with him. All Wehi could feel was Manu's intense hatred for Kona and his unwavering resolve to kill him. Wehi feared that if she and Kahoku did not reach Manu in time, Manu would attempt to kill Kona, or he would become Kona's next victim. On the other hand, if Wehi and Kahoku did not help Pono, Kawahine and her two followers would harm him, then dispatch Kona, and seriously injure Manu. *What should we do, Kahoku? How can we help them both? Should we continue on our course to help Dad or should we change direction and help Grandpa Pono? How do we make such a choice? How can we choose between our father and our grandfather?*

I do not know, Wehi. I too cannot choose between our dad and our grandfather, thought Kahoku.

Time was running out for all of them. A decision needed to be made! As Wehi and Kahoku approached the point where they needed to either change direction and fly toward Pono or continue flying toward Manu, a gust of wind came out of nowhere and blew them off course. Suddenly, Kahoku could no longer feel his sister's presence or hear her thoughts anymore. The only thoughts Kahoku had were his own. Somehow, their collective spirit had been severed, but how? As Kahoku took complete control of the 'io 'aumakua and got back on course, he slowly started to hear Wehi's thoughts again, but he could not make sense of what she was feeling or thinking.

Initially, Kahoku thought that Wehi was arguing with him, but as he continued to concentrate on Wehi's emotions, Kahoku realized that his little sister was, in fact, quarreling with Kalei. In a matter of seconds, Kalei let out a gut-wrenching shriek as she started to lose altitude. Kawahine dug her heels into Kalei's body and grabbed on to Kalei's neck feathers with both hands. "Stay the course, girl!" screamed Kawahine, as Kalei struggled in vain to control her actions and stay in the air.

With Kalei struggling to maintain her position in the sky, Kahoku knew what he needed to do. There would be no second-guessing on his part--he would help Manu sequester Kona. As he flew over to help Manu, Kahoku finally realized what had just happened to his little sister. Even though Wehi still empowered Kahoku physically to maintain the form of the 'io, like the waves that carry a surfer toward the shore, the wind had carried Wehi's soul away from him.

His little sister's destiny was truly intertwined with his mission. Besides being able to communicate through thoughts, Wehi also had the ability to seek out and join with another soul. Wehi was a soul surfer! She was the most integral part of the 'io 'āhinahina. This was the reason that she could feel Kahoku's presence after his death! This was the reason that Kahoku's soul could connect with her, and this was the reason that Wehi could access the souls of others!

As Kahoku approached Manu and Kona, Kahoku's mastery over the 'io's body weakened, alerting him to the fact that he could not engage in physical combat. Though he really wanted to help Manu, Kahoku had just been given a stern reminder: his destiny was to remove a troubled soul from its vessel and return it to the heavens for judgment--nothing more. *I hope that you can forgive me, Dad,* thought Kahoku, as he changed his direction and flew high above the rocky cliffs of Honokalani Beach.

Kahoku's departure from the lofty battleground did not interrupt Wehi's intense resolve to help Pono; all it did was make Wehi more aware that she needed to force Kalei and Kawahine from the sky. But, in spite of the mental torture that Wehi inflicted upon Kalei, Kawahine was not all that concerned over Kalei's situation; she knew that Kawika feared her, so she counted on the fact that Kawika would continue to pursue Pono even if Kalei was not able to. Kawika, though not as powerful and fast as Kalei, could still be a formidable opponent for Pono.

Wehi was now at a loss. She had thwarted Kalei's efforts to reach Pono, but could not, at the same time, stop Kawika from pursuing Pono. Searching through Kalei's memories, Wehi quickly extracted information on how to force Kawika from the sky. Because she now had control over Kalei, all Wehi needed to do was have Kalei remove several of Kawika's tail feathers, and he would not be able to stay in the air. *Hopefully*, thought Wehi, *once Kawika is gone, Grandpa Pono will be able to reach Dad and prevent him from confronting Kona.*

Watching from his high vantage point in the sky above, Kahoku could see Kalei vehemently pursuing Kawika. He knew that Wehi was using Kalei to force Kawika out of the sky, but it was what Kahoku did not know that troubled him the most. *I hope that you don't become emotionally scarred from all of this, Wehi,* thought Kahoku, as he continued to worry about his little sister.

Midday was now upon them, and the sun--with its powerful rays--had positioned itself directly above, causing the ambient temperature to rise. The cool morning trade winds had all disappeared and the humidity had become unbearable. *We need to hurry and capture Kona before we exhaust all the power of our ʻaumākua,* thought Kahoku.

Pono was finally closing in on Manu's location, but to his dismay, he and Manu were unable to communicate telepathically because Wehi, who was their conduit, was too preoccupied with Kalei and Kawika. All Pono could do was hope that Manu would stand down and let him confront Kona. To make matters worse, Pono also had to deal with the evil chants of Kawahine, which reverberated in his mind like a horrible song that kept playing over and over again. Pono knew that Kawahine was focused on killing Kona and that she would seriously injure everyone else who got in her way.

Meanwhile, Wehi continued to force Kalei to chase after Kawika. Kalei's body struggled to get behind Kawika as Kawahine continued to kick and prod Kalei in an attempt to rid her of Wehi's influence. But after half an hour of uncomfortable positioning and constant changing of direction, Wehi finally got Kalei into position right behind Kawika and extended Kalei's talons, then pulled out Kawika's tail feathers from his tailbone. The solid-bodied pueo screeched in pain. Despite his fear of Kawahine, Kawika was no longer able to chase Pono, let alone stay in the air. Instead, Kawika now had to focus on finding air currents that would get him to the ground quickly and safely.

With Kawika out of the picture, Kawahine had no other option but to stop focusing on Pono and instead, turned her dark chants and spells on Wehi. *So you are the granddaughter of Pono*, thought Kawahine. *I have not seen someone with your abilities for a very long time, Wehi Nahele. The only other person that has come close to having your power was your grandmother, Aukele. Tell me, little girl, did you delve deep enough inside my daughter Kalei's memories to find out what happened to your grandmother Aukele so many years ago? That's right, you naive little girl! I took her far away from your grandfather, Pono.*

Wehi had to quickly shut off her thought connection with Kawahine because she did not want Kawahine to find out how much information she had discovered, and she definitely did not want Kawahine to know what she was planning to do. As Wehi kept her thoughts to herself, Kawahine continued her tirade and abusive assaults. *I orchestrated the death of your grandfather Pono's dad, and Kalei put an end to your Uncle Martin's mother. Tell me, Wehi*

Nahele, granddaughter of Pono, how do you feel now? But Wehi did not answer, despite all of the anger and hatred that was building up inside of her. *I don't care if you don't answer me, Wehi Nahele. The longer you choose to linger in the dark soul of my daughter Kalei, the harder it will be for you to return to your life unscathed. Maybe I should just capture your precious little soul and keep it there, in Kalei, forever.*

Kahoku could feel Wehi's soul ache to be free of her prison inside Kalei's body, and he felt her anger and hatred toward Kawahine growing. Wehi was trying to be as brave and courageous as she could, but to Kahoku, Wehi was still his little sister who needed his help in order to get away from a bully. Despite the non-aggressive role that was bestowed on him, Kahoku could not let Wehi be further exposed to Kawahine's verbal abuse and threats. He could no longer remain a passive spectator while his little sister was fighting for her soul. The bond that he and Wehi shared meant more to him than fulfilling his destiny, which would not come at the cost of his little sister's well-being.

Kahoku had practiced the "death dive" many times with Pono. Many pueo ʻaumākua would not even attempt such a feat, because it was difficult to gauge the exact point at which the pueo ʻaumākua needed to project their wings out in order to stop their sudden descent. This ability came naturally for wild ʻio and pueo, but not for the ʻaumākua, who had to practice such a scary feat over and over again just to get it right.

With his resolve to rescue his sister from Kawahine firm, Kahoku straightened the ʻio's body and neck and tucked its wings tightly into its sides. *I hope that Heaven can look the other way for just a couple of minutes*, thought Kahoku. Faster and faster the ʻio descended. Its inexperienced body struggled to not give way to the stinging air currents that ran over its arrow-like shape, but Kahoku would not stop its descent. He knew that he had to do this in order to save Wehi's soul from Kawahine. There was no other way. Just as the 'io reached its body's limit, Kahoku stretched out its wings. He had arrived at his target--Kawahine!

At that moment, just as he had experienced before, Kahoku felt a familiar puff of wind blow toward him as Wehi re-entered the 'io's body. *Uku, I missed you*, thought Wehi. But before Kahoku could return a thought to her, Wehi extended the 'io 'aumakua's talons, which hovered above Kawahine, and pierced the old kahuna 'anā'anā's shoulders. Kawahine shrieked in pain as Wehi dug the 'io's talons in deeper. *You caused my grandfather Pono so much pain, you evil witch. How does this feel?!* Wehi then tightened her grip on Kawahine and lifted Kawahine off of Kalei.

Wehi, please do not seek revenge. It may feel good and justified in this moment, but believe me, you will live the rest of your life with deep regret, and your soul will never recover from the action you take now. Let her go, thought Kahoku lovingly.

Despite her anger, Wehi listened to her big brother Kahoku and released Kawahine from her grip, only to realize that she had sent the old witch hurtling down to her death below. *Oh no, Uku, I forgot that she could not fly! We have to go and get her!* panicked Wehi. But just as the 'io 'āhinahina was about to dive down after Kawahine, Kalei swooped in and gently caught her mother in her giant talons and flew off in the opposite direction.

Meanwhile, Manu had become distracted by the 'io 'āhinahina's struggles and consequently had gotten his wing clipped by Kona's sharp beak. Although Manu was still able to ride the warm air currents, he no longer had the power to push through opposing currents of air and ascend into the sky. Though he did not want to leave Pono alone with Kona, Manu knew that Pono would stand a better chance against Kona without him there.

After Manu had left the battle, Pono was able to focus all of his attention on Kona. Both pueo 'aumākua had climbed high into the sky, above the peaks of Haleakalā--each of them trying to outlast the other by going to the very limit of what their great lungs and wings could handle. Then, like two mountain rams locking horns without any fear of falling off of their mountain battleground, Pono and Kona were now locked to each other, talon to talon; neither one of them offering up any sign of fear whatsoever.

Now flying alongside Manu, who was soaring below Pono and Kona, the ʻio ʻāhinahina finally caught a glimpse of Pono, and Wehi was able to re-establish the telepathic connection between her family. *Grandpa Pono, Kahoku and I are here with Dad, and are flying below you,* thought Wehi. But Pono did not respond. His focus was clear and his resolve iron-clad. He knew that he needed to hold on to Kona, regardless of how tired and dehydrated he was. This same fortitude had always helped Pono throughout his education and practice as a medical doctor. He would not give up until his task was complete--period!

As the hot air continued to bear down on all of them, Pono and Kona continued their aerial duel. They were now falling quickly from the sky, still joined together by their talons and sharp beaks, both of them trying to gouge out the other's eyes. But just before they reached Manu and the ʻio ʻāhinahina, Pono and Kona released their grip on each other. Then, as if they could not get enough of the scary rollercoaster ride they had just taken, Pono and Kona once again flew higher and higher; each trying to secure a position above the other so that the flyer above could descend upon the one below with such a great force that it would strike the lower flyer unconscious. But Kona did not want to stop there; he wanted to rip Pono's heart out from his chest!

As Pono continued his quest to outfly Kona, Pono finally tuned in to the thoughts of his family and was made aware that the purpose of the ʻio ʻāhinahina was not to fight, but to collect souls. Powerful as he was, Kahoku was discouraged from fighting. *Don't worry about me, Kahoku. I have a plan*, thought Pono, as he continued pushing himself to fly higher. *However, if my plan doesn't work and I cannot subdue Kona, I fear that Kona will go after all of you!* thought Pono.

Meanwhile, as the 'io 'āhinahina continued flying alongside Manu, Wehi made sure to keep her emotions and thoughts to herself. Wehi had learned much about Kalei, and the many secrets she and Kawahine tried to hide from everyone else. *How could they have done so many horrible things to all those innocent people--especially to my grandmother Aukele?* Wehi knew that if she were to bring these dark secrets to Manu and Pono's attention, it would surely cause them to lose their focus; and this alone would be detrimental to all of them. *I will not tell my family what I have discovered until we are all back on Kaua'i*, promised Wehi.

As the 'io 'āhinahina and Manu continued flying below Pono and Kona, Kahoku could feel Wehi's demeanor start to change. Her innocence and sweetness seemed to slip away with every beat of her wings. Because Wehi was a soul surfer, she alone had the power to keep the secrets of souls buried far from the collective thoughts of Manu, Pono, and even Kahoku. However, the bond she shared physically and mentally with her big brother was also very powerful; consequently, Kahoku knew that Wehi was struggling with what she had learned while she was connected to Kalei's soul. *Stay with me, my sweet little sister. Do not find solace in hatred and despair*, Kahoku warned. But to his dismay, Kahoku could no longer feel a gentleness in Wehi's spirit.

Instead, a dark need for vengeance festered deep within Wehi's soul. As Wehi tried to keep Kalei and Kawahine's repulsive and immoral actions out of her mind, her hatred of people like them--people who manipulate and kill others for their own gain--grew exponentially. Finally, when she could no longer bear the horrible visions of what Kalei and Kawahine had done, Wehi made a choice to no longer remain a passive bystander. Before Manu, or even Kahoku, knew what was going on, Wehi started her ascent into the clouds above. She was coming up on Kona just as a great white shark comes up from the deep to catch its ignorant prey at the surface of the water. This was the attack maneuver that Wehi's mother, Mālie, had used to save Wehi from the rogue tiger shark that attacked her while she was surfing. As Wehi ascended faster and faster, her power increased tremendously. *I am going to bring the immense strength of the ocean's manō to this battle between the wind riders in the sky,* thought Wehi.

Wehi, let's give Grandpa Pono a chance to sequester Kona. Please don't do this, little sister! thought Kahoku, but despite his strong objections, Kahoku could not control his sister's raw, intense resolve to save their grandfather. Though he and Wehi were both integral parts of the 'io 'āhinahina, Wehi was not held to the same standard that Kahoku was. Since their last encounter with Kawahine, Wehi had taken all responsibility onto herself, absolving her brother Kahoku from any ensuing consequences. All Kahoku could do was hope that his little sister would not soil her innocence by taking Kona's life. Wehi was now on her own. She was on a collision course straight for Kona, and there was nothing Kahoku or his father, Manu, could do to stop her.

Grandpa Pono, thought Wehi, *I need you to dive down straight toward Kona! Do it now, Grandpa--right now!* Pono had been holding a position above Kona for a while, but his stamina was slipping away from him. Flying several feet below Pono, Kona could sense that Pono was starting to tire from the many vertical miles they had traveled in the sky, and Kona reveled in the thought that he was stronger than Pono.

Though Kona could not hear the thoughts of Pono and his family, Kona knew that Pono was worried about his companions below. *Soon,* thought Kona, *I will kill you, Pono. Then I will kill your companions.* But just as Kona started to close the gap between Pono and himself, Pono suddenly repositioned his body and started his descent straight for Kona. Pono did not know how it was going to end; all he knew was that he needed to trust his little granddaughter, Wehi.

Pono's sudden descent did not raise any concern with the ego-centric Kona, who felt invulnerable. *I will let you get close enough to me, and then I will rotate my body so that my talons will be there to pierce your heart and end your life, son of the backstabber Nahele*, thought Kona. But what Kona didn't count on, or altogether dismissed, was a strategic attack on him from below, orchestrated by a young girl fighting for no other reason but to save a life--the life of her grandfather.

As Pono finally came within striking distance, Kona quickly turned his giant body and positioned his huge talons directly at Pono--expecting to impale him. But just after Kona got into position, a great force hit him from below, propelling Kona's body forward and pushing his talons away from their striking position, allowing Pono to deliver a powerful blow that knocked Kona unconscious. As Kona began to fall from the sky, Pono grabbed onto Kona's wings, and both wind riders rode the warm air currents to the ground.

Their journey downward had taken them back to the very place that Manu and Martin had first encountered Kona. The rental car was still there, as were the memories of the last moments that Manu and Martin had shared together. *I am sorry, Manu*, thought Pono, as he tightened his talons around Kona's neck and pinned him to the ground.

I will miss him, Dad, thought Manu. But before Manu and Pono could continue their telepathic dialogue, a Police Jeep drove up and a tall Hawaiian man jumped out. Immediately, Pono, Manu, and the 'io 'āhinahina, sensed that this policeman was different from other people; this policeman was not alarmed by their formidable appearances and was also able to read their thoughts.

Hello, Pono, thought the policeman. *I got a call from another officer in the Maui Police Department who had spoken with your daughter-in-law, Mālie, this morning. She told the officer that she was having trouble getting in touch with your son, Manu. The officer knew that Manu was in this valley because one of the local guys who lives in this area had mentioned to the officer that Manu had been asking lots of questions about old man Kona's deceased apprentice. I figured that I would drive up here and try to find some sort of clue as to Manu's whereabouts.*

Hello, Makana, thought Pono. *Sorry to put you through all that worry, but as you can see, we have gotten what we came for.*

Makana glanced down at Kona then looked up at Pono. *I know him, Pono. He is my second cousin. It is unfortunate that I have to arrest my own flesh and blood*, thought Makana, as he walked up closer to Kona and shook his head back and forth in disdain. Kona just stared up at Makana; he was not able to telepathically communicate with Pono, Manu and the 'io 'āhinahina, so Kona had no clue as to what they were planning to do with him. Makana looked over at Pono. *Kona's mother was my grandfather's sister, but, unlike Kona's mother, my grandfather encouraged all of his children to learn about their Hawaiian heritage and told us about our ancestors who practiced the sacred arts of the kahuna. It was my grandfather who noticed how much I loved to bird-watch in my spare time, so he sent me to stay with a kahuna who taught me how to search for messages from our ancestors; messages which were all around me, placed in the stars above or displayed in the different behavior of birds. This is how I am able to communicate with all of you when you are in your pueo or 'io 'aumākua form*, thought Makana. Pono loosened his grip around Kona's neck. Makana's presence was enough to make Pono feel a little more at ease.

"You've been causing a lot of trouble, Cousin," said Makana, firmly, as he glared down at Kona. "It is time to pay for all your crimes."

Makana, I must ask a favor of you, thought Pono.

You may ask as many favors as you need from me, Pono, thought Makana. *My family and I are forever in your debt for saving Martin's life so many years ago. Before my father passed away, he told me that a month before my older cousin Kēhau moved to Kaua'i, she had confided in him that Kona hated her son, Martin, and that she feared that if any harm came to her, Kona would in turn harm Martin. After Kēhau suddenly passed away, my father said that he had traveled to Kaua'i to ask you if you could find a good home for Martin because our family was poor and could not afford to care for him. My father also admitted to me that when he asked you for help with Martin, he intentionally omitted the fact that Martin was Kona's grandson because he feared that you would not want to help the grandson of a man that loathed your father, Mr. Nahele.*

Makana, how did your father know about the relationship between Kona and my father? thought Pono.

My father used to work in a little bar in Maui long ago. After my cousin, Kona, returned from the war, he made it a point to go to my father's bar every night and get ridiculously drunk. Besides running up a huge tab, my father told me that Kona also ran his mouth off about your dad, Mr. Nahele, thought Makana.

My father never told me about his relationship with Kona, thought Pono. *However, after speaking with Kamaka, and after hearing your thoughts, Makana, my family and I are now aware of the tempestuous relationship between Martin and Kona and also my father and Kona.*

Pono glanced over at the 'io 'āhinahina. *It is time to focus on the present matter at hand. It is now up to you, Wehi, to find out if Kona knows anything about the other 'aumākua who wish to do our family harm. Makana,* thought Pono, as he continued to hold Kona down, *the 'io 'āhinahina has seen the soul of Kekipi, the most pow-erful kahuna 'anā'anā, being held prisoner in your cousin Kona's body. This is how Kona was able to regain his pueo 'aumakua. It is Kekipi's power that propels Kona's strength!*

But as soon as Pono had announced Kekipi's presence, Pono had to stop and collect his thoughts. He still could not wrap his mind around all the horrible things that Kona had done. *Grandpa Pono*, thought Kahoku, *we don't have a lot of time. We need to hurry and get the answers you need from Kona.*

Makana looked at the 'io 'āhinahina, then looked over at Pono. *I will give you time to do this. I understand the mission of the 'io 'āhinahina.* Then Makana turned to face Manu. *Manu, I feel the love you have for my cousin, Martin. It permeates through your thoughts. Mahalo for showing Martin so much love while he lived.*

As soon as Makana started to walk back to his Police Jeep to get his recorder, Pono tightened his grip around Kona's neck, flapped his giant wings and lifted Kona's massive pueo body up--suspend-ing him right in front of the 'io 'āhinahina. *Wehi*, thought Kahoku, *we have only a few minutes to do this. You must get into Kona's soul and retrieve all the information that you can. Once I call forth and capture Kekipi's spirit, you will only have a few minutes before Kona becomes human again, and in the course of his transformation back to his human form, your power might be taken from you. We have seen you enter only the soul of an 'aumakua, not a person. You could end up trapped inside Kona's body if you do not hurry. Can we count on you once more to do this, Little Sister?*

Yes, Uku, I will do this for all of you--including Uncle Martin and Kona's young apprentice, whom Dad found in Kalalau Valley, replied Wehi. But unbeknownst to Kahoku, Wehi already had infor-mation regarding Kawahine and Kalei's involvement in the murder of her great grandfather Nahele and the disappearance of her grand-mother Aukele. The only remaining pieces of information that Wehi needed to find were the names of the other 'aumākua who had killed Kona's apprentice, taken Kahoku from her, and were now after her family. *Okay, Uku, I am ready,* thought Wehi.

Kahoku then gazed into the insidious orange-colored eyes of Kona. As Kahoku forced out a big breath, he could feel Wehi's anxiety growing. Both brother and sister could sense how strong Kekipi's dark magic was, so it was imperative that Kahoku draw out and retrieve Kekipi's spirit first, otherwise Wehi would not be able to enter Kona's soul.

E hele mai [come here], Kekipi. E hele mai i kēia manawa [come here, right now]! ordered Kahoku, who then took a deep breath in and started the process of drawing Kekipi's spirit out of Kona's body. No soul could resist his call, not even one as defiant as Kekipi. After all, the 'io 'āhinahina was the vessel by which the gods collected all wayward spirits.

As soon as Kekipi's soul started to exit Kona, Wehi found her way in. The darkness that enveloped Kona made Wehi feel as though she were trapped in a never-ending dark tunnel. There was no sense of humanity within him--only an overwhelming sense of hatred existed. At his core, Kona desired nothing but vengeance against Kawahine, Martin, and Pono's father, Mr. Nahele.

As Wehi continued to dig deeper into Kona's memories, Kona let out an agonizing scream. His blood pressure shot up and his entire body started shaking. *You have done so many heartless things!* thought Wehi, as she meticulously peeled away and inspected the many decades of intolerable acts that Kona had inflicted on those around him. During this process, Wehi had shown Kona how monstrous and abhorrent he truly was. But in her heart, Wehi felt sorry for Kona. His lifelong pursuit of power ultimately cost him everything! Kona was alone, afraid, and more aware than ever before that he would soon be forgotten. After Wehi had finally completed her search, the darkness that had enveloped Kona for most of his life finally gave way, and he was now left with a deep sense of regret and shame.

Not wasting any more time, Wehi exited Kona's body and rejoined Kahoku. All that was left of the once cruel and violent Kona was a frail, pathetic old man, who was no longer boasting or carrying on about his desire to execute vengeance upon the descendants of Mr. Nahele, whom he believed had ruined him so long ago. Shortly after returning to his human form, Kona tucked his body into a fetal position and placed his arms over his head so that no one could see the tears streaming down his face. "I will admit to all my horrible acts if you don't look at me," whimpered Kona.

"What are you rambling on about, old man?" asked Manu, who had just transformed back into his human form and had put on the spare clothes that he had packed in his duffel bag, which was in the trunk of the rental car.

"Your daughter, the soul surfer, made me see and feel everything I had done in my past--it was like watching a picture show of my life. I don't want to feel that horrible and grotesque again! I don't want to see all the horrible things I did to the people around me!" Kona started wailing. "I killed my grandson, Martin, and sent my gentle daughter Kēhau to her death so very long ago! I also sent the teenage boy--my apprentice--to Kaua'i to find the gravesite of Pono's father. But I did not know that my apprentice was murdered. I just assumed that he wanted nothing to do with me because the last time he called and spoke with me, he mentioned that he was done spying on your family. I never heard from him again. You have to believe me. I did not kill my apprentice!"

Makana stopped the recorder on his phone. He had gotten all the information he needed to put his cousin away for the rest of his life. He would edit out any mention of Wehi's involvement. "Manu, I have enough information to take Kona in. I will take care of the reports, and I will contact you when my cousin is sentenced and placed in jail. Can I take you and your family to the airport?"

Manu had already placed Kona in handcuffs and covered him with a blanket, but Pono and Wehi had not yet assumed their human forms. "That's okay, Makana. I think we will be able to get home on our own," answered Manu, who then handed Kona over to Makana. As soon as Makana placed Kona into his Police Jeep and started driving down the road, Manu walked over to rejoin his father Pono and both of his children. He knew that Kahoku's time with them was slowly coming to an end.

Since Kahoku had taken in Kekipi's soul, the 'io 'āhinahina had become covered in an ethereal, silver luminescence. *My time here is over. I must return Kekipi's soul to the heavens where it belongs,* thought Kahoku.

Uku, thought Wehi, *will I speak with you again? Will I fly with you again?* Kahoku could feel his little sister's body start to grow weaker now that he had captured Kekipi's soul. He knew that he needed to free Wehi from their connection quickly. But Kahoku was still worried about how Wehi would cope with everything that she had been through, without his physical presence there to comfort her.

I only know that I will always be with you, Wehi, wherever you are. Remember that I love you very much, my precious little sister. Suddenly, before Wehi could send out another thought to Kahoku, she found herself standing on her own two legs. As Manu ran to her side and covered her with Martin's spare police jacket, Pono quickly transformed, put on his clothes, then joined Manu and Wehi. Both men could feel Wehi's heart break as her connection with Kahoku had come to an end. Wehi now looked older than when they had first started their journey, and her countenance showed just how sad she had become since saying goodbye to her brother again.

Pono and Manu felt helpless. Neither of them knew how to console Wehi. They missed Kahoku too, but they rejoiced in knowing that he was only a breath away from them and that they would be with him again. As Pono looked over at Manu for suggestions to ease Wehi's pain, a familiar smile found its way back onto Pono's face and his heart no longer carried a heavy burden. "Look at the sky above, Wehi!" shouted Pono. There, in the afternoon sun, Kahoku had found a way to ease his little sister's pain: shimmering strands of silver lit up a path from their location into the heavens above.

"Tūtū kāne [Grandfather], Makua kāne [Father], it looks like diamonds leading to heaven! Do you think they are real?!" exclaimed Wehi.

Both Pono and Manu hugged Wehi tightly, then lifted her high above their shoulders so that she could try to catch the shimmering strands of silver that sparkled in the warm Maui sunshine.

LOOKING AHEAD TO THE NEXT STORY....

Upon returning home to Kaua'i, Pono, Manu, and Wehi find Mālie worrying about her father Ke Ali'i, whom she has not been able to find since he left them after dinner at Satoshi's saimin restaurant. Pono becomes worried about Mālie because she tells him, in confidence, that she lost her strength while she was in her manō (shark) 'aumakua form earlier that day. Alliances with other pueo (owl) 'aumākua are questioned--especially after witnessing Kawika's allegiance to Kawahine and Kalei. After soul surfing between Kalei and Kona, Wehi struggles with her anger at all the people who had a hand in hurting her family. Since returning to Kaua'i, Wehi's resolve to tell her family what she had learned from Kalei and Kawahine, slips away as time passes. In the midst of dealing with her deep-seated hatred, and still indecisive about sharing the information that she retrieved from Kalei and Kawahine, Wehi decides to embark on a journey without her father, mother, and grandfather Pono. Wehi's determination to find her grandfather Ke Ali'i puts her in grave danger, and without the help of her family, Wehi must now rely on the courage of a new friend and the waning strength of a frail, elderly woman. As Wehi's family continues to grapple with the actions of the ancient Hawaiian guardians, a lost loved one from the past reappears and must choose between family and birthright.

DEDICATION

This book is dedicated to my baby brother, Kahoku. We were blessed to have him join our 'ohana (family) when I was eleven years old. Since that time, I had the honor of being his "big sis" for eighteen years of his life. I would not change any second of it--except to have followed that soft inner voice that urged me to call Kahoku and ask him to forgo any plans he had with his friends. Call it what you will, but I should have never ignored the "soft voice" that kept whispering to me, throughout that entire day, to call my baby brother.

At nine-thirty, on that fateful evening in February, my cousin and her husband came to my apartment to tell me that Kahoku had been involved in a skateboarding accident. My heart stopped beating and I fell to the floor, all the while yelling, "NO, NO...NOT MY HOKU, NOT MY HOKU!" My frantic mind flashed back to earlier that day, reminding me of the horrible mistake that I had made. Why didn't I just pick up the phone and call Kahoku? What was so hard about doing that one simple thing? Why didn't I listen to that soft, persistent whisper?

My kaikunāne (brother), Kahoku, was the youngest member of our family, and he was also the most thoughtful. One evening, while Kahoku and my parents were at home watching television, my brother randomly mentioned to them that he wanted to be an organ donor. Unbeknownst to Kahoku and to my parents, Kahoku's altruistic wish would be carried out a week later.

On the evening of Kahoku's passing, my dad and mom, with tears streaming down their faces, carried out their youngest son's wishes and signed the release form to donate Kahoku's organs. It was at this heartbreaking moment that our family realized that our Hoku--our star--would never open his beautiful eyes again. The painful process of living without Kahoku had begun, and although it was difficult to watch the nurses wheel him out of his hospital room and take him to surgery where the doctors would remove his organs, our family was, at the same time, humbled by Kahoku's last wish. In that moment, as our family struggled to come to terms with what had just happened, we somehow came to realize that Kahoku's destiny far exceeded our own. Our Hoku would ultimately save another family's father, mother, brother, or sister.

Today, our family is still learning how to live without Kahoku, and as time continues to move all of us forward, we often find ourselves glancing backward--if only to be able to relive all the precious moments that we shared with the youngest and most kindhearted of us all.

A Letter of Love

Dear Kahoku,

Since your return to heaven, fourteen years ago, life has gone on, but with "less color," if you will. Time does not heal a wound such as this: it just places "Band-Aids" over the gaping hole in my pu'uwai (heart) and pushes me to learn, day after day, how to cope without you. But if this is the price of loving you, then I am willing to pay for it, baby brother. You are worth every single tear that rolls down my cheek with every memory of rocking you to sleep in my arms while singing about cows jumping over the moon and Little Boy Blue.

Hopefully, I have not embarrassed you too much, as I just want to share your special spirit with those who will never have the opportunity to know you.

I will love you beyond my last breath, little brother. I will love you forever.

Nani

MAIN CHARACTERS (PRONUNCIATION AND TRANSLATION OF NAMES)

Aukele	*Ow kay lay*	Hawaiian form of Audrey
Kahoku	*Kuh ho coo*	The star
Kalei	*Kuh lay*	The child or floral wreath
Kaleo	*Kuh lay oh*	The voice
Kamaka	*Kuh muh kuh*	The eye
Kawahine	*Kuh vah hee nay*	The woman
Kawehi	*Kuh vay hee*	The song
Kawika	*Kuh vee kuh*	Hawaiian form of David
Keala	*Kay Ahh La*	The pathway
Ke Ali'i	*Kay ahh lee ee*	The chief
Keanu	*Kay ahh noo*	The coolness
Kēhau	*Kay how*	Gentle land breeze
Kekipi	*Kay key pee*	Rebel
Makana	*Muh kuh nuh*	A gift
Makoa	*Mah ko ahh*	A Bold Man
Mālie	*Muh lee ay*	Calm
Manu	*Muh new*	Bird
Pono	*Poh no*	Righteous
Pua	*Pooh ahh*	Flower

Hawaiian vocabulary and meaning

ʻAina	*eye nuh*	Land
ʻAnakala	*ahh nuh kuh luh*	Uncle
ʻAumākua	*ow muh coo uh*	Family protectors, guardian spirits
ʻAʻole	*ah oh lay*	No
Aikane	*Eye kuh nay*	Good friend
Aloha	*Ahh low huh*	Greeting, salutation, love
ʻEle ʻele	*eh lay eh lay*	Black
Hale	*Huh lay*	House
Hanai	*ha nigh*	To adopt, take in as family
Haumana	*how muh nuh*	Students
Heʻenalu	*hey eh nuh loo*	To ride waves (surf)
Hoʻoponopono	*ho oh po no po no*	To correct
ʻIo	*ee oh*	Hawaiian hawk
ʻIo ʻāhinahina	*ee oh ah hee nuh hee nuh*	Silver hawk
Iwi	*ee vee*	Bones
Kahuna	*kuh who nuh*	Guardian of secrets, teacher, sorcerer
Kaikamahine	*ka+eye kuh muh hee nay*	Daughter; girl
Kaikuahine	*ka+eye coo uh hee nay*	Sister
Kaikunāne	*ka+eye coo nuh nay*	Brother

Kanaka	*kuh nah kuh*	Hawaiian person
Kāne	*Kuh nay*	God of creation; Man
Kaukau	*cow cow*	Slang word for food; to eat
Keiki	*kay key*	Child
Keiki kāne	*kay key kuh nay*	Son
Ki'i pohaku	*key ee po huh coo*	Petroglyphs
Kuleana	*coo lay ahh nuh*	Right, responsibility
Kupuna	*coo poo nuh*	Elder, ancestor
Ku'uipo	*coo oo(=like oops) ee po*	Sweetheart
Lā	*Lah*	Sun
Maile	*my lay*	Fragrant vine used in lei
Maka	*muh kuh*	Eyes
Makua kāne	*Muh coo ahh kuh nay*	Father
Makuahine	*Muh coo ahh hee nay*	Mother
Malo	*Mah low*	Loincloth
Mana	*muh nuh*	Spiritual power
Manō	*muh no*	Shark
Menehune	*meh nay who nay*	Skilled little Hawaiian craftsmen
Moana	*mow ahh nuh*	The ocean
Mō'ī	*mow ee*	King
Mo'opuna	*mo oh pooh nuh*	Grandchild
Mokihana	*mo key huh nuh*	Fragrant berry
Molehu	*mo lay who*	Half-light, Twilight, dusk

Noho	*no ho*	Canoe seat
ʻOhana	*Oh huh nuh*	Family
ʻŌkole	*oh ko lay*	Buttock
ʻŌkolehao	*oh ko lay how*	Hawaiian moonshine
ʻOno	*oh no*	Delicious
ʻŌpala	*oh puh luh*	Trash
ʻOpihi	*oh pee hee*	Saltwater rock snails
Pilikia	*pee lee key uh*	Trouble
Poʻo	*po oh*	Head
Puʻuwai	*pooh oo va+eye*	Heart
Pueo	*pooh eh oh*	Owl
Pupule	*pooh pooh lay*	Crazy
Tūtū kāne	*too too kuh nay*	Grandfather
Tūtū wāhine	*too too vuh hee nay*	Grandmother
ʻUku	*oo (=like oops) coo*	Head lice; flea
Waha	*wah hah*	Mouth
Wahine	*vuh hee nay*	Woman
Waiwai	*va+eye va+eye*	Vast amount of property or land

Pau (The End)

CPSIA information can be obtained at www.ICGtesting.com
Printed in the USA
BVOW08s1412070815

411952BV00003B/159/P

9 781478 759249